Published: R.S. Grey 2023
authorrsgrey@gmail.com
Editing: Editing by C. Marie
Proofreading: Red Leaf Proofing, Julia Griffis
Cover Design: R.S. Grey

THREE STRIKES *and* YOU'RE MINE

a single dad romantic comedy

USA TODAY BESTSELLING AUTHOR

R.S. GREY

ONE

CHLOE

I THINK I'm about to have to be a hero.

Let me set the scene for you: it's late. The fancy restaurant where I work is dark and deserted. I shouldn't even be here. I left thirty minutes ago, dead on my feet. My boyfriend stayed behind at his desk.

"Can't you come home with me?" I pleaded.

He sounded annoyed when he replied, "I have some work to catch up on. Call an Uber if you're worried about walking home alone."

"It's 1:00 AM, Miles. Can't it wait until the morning?"

He leveled me with a pointed glare, so I got the hint and left. According to Miles, a head chef's job is never done. A head chef is the captain of the ship. Without him, we'd all sink. Oh my *god*, how many times have I had to listen to that spiel?

I left without saying goodbye and was mere inches from my doorstep when I realized I'd forgotten my keys back at the restaurant. I clenched my teeth in suppressed annoyance. It wouldn't have been a problem had Miles just come home with me. We could have just used his apartment key and picked mine up in the morning.

Instead, I begrudgingly turned around and trudged back through the desolate city streets, reflecting on my frustration as I went, just me and all the other weirdos out and about at this time of night.

Unfortunately, all wasn't right when I arrived back at the restaurant. Immediately, I noticed the back door was slightly ajar, but there was no Miles inside. His desk chair was empty, doing an ominous slow spin. Papers were strewn about on his usually immaculate desk.

Now, from the kitchen, I hear guttural groans. Muffled crying. Flesh hitting flesh. *Oh god*, Miles has gotten himself into trouble.

I have to lean over and clutch my knees. I feel sick.

What has he done?

Who is it? Loan sharks, the mob, drug dealers? Miles doesn't seem the type to mess with anyone, but you never know!

My mind starts racing, matching the terrible sounds to my imagination's worst-case scenarios. The deadened thuds are loan sharks breaking his kneecaps with a baseball bat. The clanking on the metallic table must be from the shiny instruments the mobsters are using to pry off his fingernails. I pull out my phone, ready to dial 911 as I creep closer to the kitchen, but I realize I have no time to wait for backup when I hear the thud of the refrigerator door. Is he dead? Are they stuffing his body into the cooler?

I have to act if I want to save Miles.

A weapon—obviously, I need one, and the bigger the better. In the movies, there is always a perfectly blunt lamp to slam down on a henchman's head; we're fresh out of those. Instead, I find a reasonably durable umbrella by the back door, and to my been-at-work-for-twelve-hours brain, it seems ingenious. I'll whip it open, blind the bad guys, and— voila!—save the day.

I inch closer to the swinging door that leads to the kitchen and wince when I hear another sharp cry of pain. For a split second, I think, *You know what? Miles is scrappy. He can take care of himself.* But no. I can do this. I can—

I push the door open and am about to slash and jab with the umbrella, but instead, I freeze in place.

There are no mobsters in this kitchen and there is no murder taking place. There are two lovers intertwined against the industrial-sized refrigerator. Butt cheeks press right up against the cool stainless steel. And through all the hazy confusion and panic, I still think, *Gross, that's really unsanitary.* The city inspector would have a field day with that. Miles would *flip.* He's a crazy person when it comes to maintaining the cleanliness of his kitchen.

Only I suppose he's made an exception to that rule because he's one of the two lovers. I see that now. It's his dimpled butt I'm staring at. But who is he with? I squint to make out the other person in the shadows.

Oh, it's Angie. That makes sense. Angie is my good friend here at the restaurant, the friend to whom I've been pouring my heart out the last few weeks about all my problems with Miles. Cool.

As seconds pass, I realize they didn't hear me come in. They still don't realize I'm here watching them. I've missed my big opportunity to announce myself, to make this a real soap opera production. Or have I? There's a pan to my left I could chuck at them, but that's Ernesto's pan and I'd hate to put a dent in it. Also, I'm surprised to find I don't have all that much fury in me. I guess working a 12-hour shift, walking a few miles, then psyching yourself up for a battle royale with a room full of mafiosos tends to diminish one's ability to generate large feelings for anything.

I clear my throat, but they don't hear me.

I sigh and decide to just go for it.

"Hi, sorry, don't mind me," I say lightly, like I'm trying to cut past someone in a cramped supermarket aisle.

"Chloe!" Miles gasps.

Angie screams.

They break apart, and there is entirely too much naked flesh in this kitchen. I'll never be able to look at that refrigerator the same way. Nor the colander Angie picks up to cover her chest.

"Sorry, guys." I hold up my hands while my face contorts into a tight apologetic grimace. "*Truly* pretend I'm not here. I just need to grab my keys…"

I step into the kitchen, drop my now-unnecessary weapon, and let the swinging door swish closed behind me. My keys are exactly where I thought they would be on the counter, except now they're partially concealed beneath delicate blue lace.

"Whoopsies, they're right under your bra, Angie. *Oh*, that's soft. Where'd you buy this set?"

Angie groans. "Chloe, I am so sorry."

Miles turns around and steps forward, his penis just *out there* for the world to see. "Chloe—babe. This is not what… This is *nothing*. I don't even have feelings for her."

Angie shoves him hard in the back so that he stumbles forward. "What the hell, asshole. You were just going on and on about how much you love me like ten minutes ago."

Love?

Wow.

My voice is only slightly wobbly as I reply, "That's…great. I'm happy for you guys."

I can think of a thousand other things I want to say, but I can't conjure the mean, vile words. I've never been able to. I'm just not that person. All I've heard my entire life is, *Oh Chloe, she's so nice.* Need someone to cover your shift? Go ask Chloe. Forgot to take out the trash? Chloe's on it. Babysitter? House sitter? Pet sitter? She's your girl. No lunch? No worries. Take half of Chloe's.

While I've recognized my role as a consummate pushover,

I haven't lamented the trait until this moment. It would feel so satisfying to make a scene, to shout and curse and call them all the things they already know they are. Slut would roll off my tongue nicely all drawn out and slow, emphasis on the S, maybe even taking the artistic liberty of a deep Southern drawl while saying it. Only it doesn't seem right to lay the blame solely at Angie's feet. Maybe I should pluralize it to "you sluts"? I could double-barrel it with 'you slut' and 'that whore', but see...now I'm already past it.

So, I take the high road, grab my keys, turn on my heels, and shove over a nice big bag of flour on my way out of the kitchen. A cloud of white powder erupts into the air as if I fired it from a cannon. It coats every surface in sight. It'll take them hours to clean it up. Enough time for me to grab my things from Miles' apartment and find a hotel for the night. Enough time for me to come to terms with the fact that my life as I currently know it is over.

TWO

CHLOE

I'VE BEEN WANTING change for a while, but like so many other people in my shoes, it felt impossible to actually achieve it before now. I went straight from high school to culinary school, culinary school to assistant chocolatier at Fleur de Sel. I continued my patisserie training there for three years. After, I spent a year learning at Spiced Pear before landing a coveted position working for *the* Miles Wilson at Fig & Olive. It was my dream setup, or so I thought. My white uniform was embroidered especially for me: *Chloe Ricci, Head Pastry Chef*. I even had an employee working under me—Angie. Well, now I guess she's working under Miles.

I'd laugh if I had the energy.

I've been job-hunting nonstop. There's not a restauranteur in the city who hasn't had the pleasure of receiving a slightly desperate phone call from me over the last few days. I've applied for the few prestigious positions currently open in the area, interviewed for some, even, but none have come to fruition. It's a tricky thing working your way up in the restaurant world. I can't backslide now. I don't want to leave an establishment as illustrious as Fig & Olive only to lick my wounds in the back of the Whole Foods bakery department.

Though to be clear, that store sure knows how to make a mean cake. That berry Chantilly? Di-*vine*.

So you see, I'm no snob. Good food is good food, but there's money involved here. Culinary school was expensive. My parents couldn't afford to help me out, and I only *just* finished paying off my loans. I have no nest egg to speak of, and now, there's also the little fact that I have to find a new place to live. The night I found Miles spooning Angie in the kitchen (*wink*), I packed up all my things from his apartment and left. I haven't gone back there or to the restaurant since. I haven't returned his phone calls either. I texted him once, to give him my parents' address so he could mail my last check. That's it.

As my mom would say, "Once a cheater, always a cheater." And the thing about Miles is, he wasn't even a great boyfriend *outside* of the cheating. He's a major workaholic with such a big head I'm surprised his neck can still hold it up. He's also way older than me, which seemed fine, even cool, when I first started working for him last year.

Chloe, let me show you around the kitchen.

Chloe, stay back after work. I want to walk you through how to perfect that tahini chocolate mousse.

Chloe, hey, it's just a kiss. We'll take it slow.

Now, I realize I was naive. We should never have been dating. He was my direct superior. I've learned my lesson the hard way. No boyfriend, no job, no apartment—all in one fell swoop.

Cue defeated sigh.

Quite frankly, now that I'm reaching the end of the road in terms of potential head pastry chef positions in town, I'm having a hard time ignoring a niggling feeling in the back of my mind. It's a desperate, blaring warning that I shouldn't continue down this road. There's no other way to slice it: restaurant work is absolutely grueling. I knew that getting into the profession, but somehow enduring it is another thing entirely. Fig & Olive is a 32-seat Mediterranean restaurant serving six- and nine-course tasting menus Monday through Saturday. Miles describes his seasonal menus as love letters to the Mediterranean islands. He's vying for a Michelin star (or three), and the entire staff has cosigned that goal too. To him, we're toy soldiers. Even though our first seating for the evening isn't until 6:00 PM, we're expected to arrive at the kitchen no later than 9:00 AM. Most of the time, we don't finish cleanup for the day until well past midnight. This last year has taken a toll on me. I used to enjoy running; I don't have time for it anymore. I used to dabble in the kitchen on the side, cooking not just pastries and desserts but all sorts of savory delights. Now, if I see so much as a spatula on my day off, I want to scream. The job has very nearly sucked the joy right out of me, but where do I go from here?

I mean figuratively. *Literally*, I'm going to my parents' place because it's Sunday and every Sunday we have a big family dinner with all my aunts and uncles and cousins. I didn't go last Sunday because I wanted to spiral into a pit of despair in private, but all week my family has been hounding me about it.

From my brother: *You sick, Chlo?*

From my father: *Why'd you miss family dinner? You upset your mother.*

From one of my overbearing aunts (of which I have three): *Family is family, you don't turn your back on family.*

If I missed again, they'd likely file a missing person report with the police. *Yes, she's about this tall, brunette, freckles, always smiling.*

As you might have guessed, my big Italian family is a little *loco*. Oh, and yes, as a rebellious act, I took Spanish in high school instead of Italian. You can imagine how that went over.

I wince as I adjust my heavy duffle bag over my shoulder. I walked here in the boiling heat. I'm sweating, panting, lamenting every single life choice I've ever made as I walk up the stoop to my parents' apartment building. They've lived in the same slightly run-down building in Little Italy off Baxter Street for thirty years. In fact, they took over the lease from my grandparents.

In a six-story walkup, they're fortunate to be on the first floor, and though the lobby is worse for wear, they take pride in keeping their apartment clean and welcoming. My dad is handy; he's worked as an appliance repairman since I was a kid. Meanwhile, my mom's been a maid at the Plaza her entire adult life. She used to take me to work sometimes when I was off from school or out for summer break. She'd give me clear instructions: make yourself scarce, be respectful, don't get in anyone's way.

I would never dare to disobey her because I knew she was serious. If I messed up or made her job difficult, she wouldn't take me back, and I *loved* going to the Plaza for one specific reason: the kitchen.

I'd sneak behind the swinging metal doors like one of those little bushy-tailed rats from *Ratatouille*. The manager was too busy to care, and some of the cooks hated it, but most thought I was cute enough to let it slide. All that really mattered, though, was that the pastry chef, Ms. Paulette, as I was instructed to call her, absolutely loved me.

She was a diminutive gray-haired woman from Paris, alone here in the States. She barely spoke English; it didn't matter. She put me to work.

"Tablier," she'd snap with a twinkle in her eye.

I came to learn that meant apron, and I'd don mine quickly. It was comically large, and she had to tie it up so I wouldn't trip over it. Some days she'd teach me the proper way to wash dishes (yes, there is an art to it), other days she'd show me how to make the laminated dough required for croissants. It's an intensely complicated process, and to this day I still don't come close to mastering it the way she did.

Ms. Paulette inspired me to go to culinary school, and she was the first person I ran to with my acceptance letter. She's retired now, and her successor has no open positions. I know; I asked just yesterday.

I hear the ruckus from inside my parents' apartment even before I arrive outside their door, and I drop my duffle on the welcome mat with a sigh of relief. I have a duffle bag because for the last two weeks, I've been couch hopping and hotel hopping, but tonight, desperate to save my friends' goodwill and what little of my dwindling savings I have left, I'm staying with my parents.

I'm only there on the mat a second, not even two, before the door is flung open and my brother Gio greets me with a big smile.

"She's here!" Then he shouts over his shoulder. "Ma, hang up with the police." He grabs the bottle of Campari—my contribution for the evening—from my hands. "Aw, you shouldn't have, sis."

Then his big meaty arm is around me and he's dragging me inside. I get passed from one relative to the next like a rag doll. My cheeks are squished and kissed. My hair is brushed from my face. My chin is tilted this way and that. They ask when I last ate, why I look so pale, why it took me so long to arrive, how come I didn't bring one of my fancy desserts.

"Let her breathe!" my mom insists, clutching my hand and dragging me out of the throng of concerned aunts and uncles.

Like me, she's small. Our family is a study in contrasts. My brother Gio is as tall as a house and built like a bull, as is my dad. By comparison, my mom is so fragile I genuinely worry she'll blow away in a heavy gust of wind.

There's a lot of personality crammed in that pint-sized body though, and her hair adds to her height too. She teases it every morning. It stands inches taller than the top of her head, and she used to do the same thing to me for special

occasions. Every framed family photo in this apartment probably required two to three bottles of hairspray to execute. To
this day, if I scrub hard enough, I'm sure I could find some
remnants of Dollar Tree hair gel still lingering on my scalp.

She leads me into the relative quiet of the kitchen, acting
as my shield. Then, when she has me to herself in a corner,
she turns and grabs my chin, tilting it this way and that just
like all the others.

"Now, tell me, why do you look so pale and what took
you so long to arrive?"

I roll my eyes.

She throws her hands up. "What? Can't a mama worry
about her baby? You've had a hard few weeks. That Miles…
scum of the earth." This quickly devolves into a string of
Italian cursing.

"*Ma.*"

"I'd spit on his grave!" she insists with flushed cheeks.
Then she does spit.

"It's not that big of a deal."

"Not a big deal?" she erupts. "He broke my baby's heart.
Who does he think he is? You want me to have Gio go down
and rough him up?" Her eyes grow wide with an idea. "*Or
your uncle Antonio might know somebody.*"

She waggles her eyebrows to be sure I'm catching her
meaning. I truly think she wants me to put out a hit on my
former boss and ex-boyfriend.

"Have you and Dad been watching reruns of *The Sopranos*
again?"

She looks offended. "I don't see why that matters."

"I told you! You two can't—"

"When's dinner?" Gio shouts from the living room. "I
could eat a horse!"

My father shouts back at him about respect and not
yelling in this house, which is absurd because there is one
default setting in this family: loud.

Just then my little cousins come flying through the kitchen, playing chase. My mom grabs a dish towel and whips it at them, telling them to mind their manners. They squeal like feral pigs and keep right on running and laughing.

Over the next hour, I help my mom and aunts in the kitchen, finishing up the last of the food. There's an aperitivo spread of olives, cheese, and nuts; bruschetta al pomodoro; sausage-stuffed mushrooms; zuppa toscana; and shrimp and lobster. For dessert, I make tiramisu, and after it sets, we'll eat it along with sipping strong espresso, despite the late hour.

By the time we have it all laid out, it's quite an array— probably *too* much if I'm honest—but everyone chips in for the costs. We might all be working class, but scaling back Sunday family dinners isn't an option. Tradition is tradition.

By the time Nonna blesses the meal, there are twenty of us crammed in at the dinner table and the card tables flanking either side to help accommodate everyone. Checkered table-cloths are overlaid on top of one another, stretching over the length of all three tables. Lit candlesticks act as centerpieces, and my little cousin shoves the end of his buttered bread into the flame, trying to get it to light until his mom, my aunt Amara, smacks him in the back of the head. *Lo stupido.*

A cacophony of chatter fills the room, and there are no less than ten conversations going on at once, encompassing an array of topics, everything from baseball to politics to the new bunion on my uncle's foot. It will only devolve more with each drop of alcohol consumed.

I have plenty of food on my plate, but with my mom on one side of me and Aunt Amara on the other, for every bite I take, another gets piled on.

My arguments fall on deaf ears.

"You're too skinny," my aunt says. "Men want curves. Maybe that's why your man—"

My mom curses at my aunt, telling her to hush.

She does, for two minutes, and then she feels compelled to

ask me if I was servicing my man enough in the bedroom. Just, you know, your average dinner conversation.

My brother Gio gags as if he's about to throw up, but this does not dissuade Amara.

"Men, they're dim creatures," she continues, to which even the men at the table all nod in agreement.

You'd think this would be borderline traumatizing, all of it, but it's oddly comforting. My life might be imploding before my eyes, but Sundays at my parents' house will always remain the same, overbearing relatives and all.

Later, after the meal, we're spread around the apartment, fending off our food comas. Well, not all of us... Uncle Nico is already passed out in one of the recliners, snoring so loud it's a wonder we haven't received a noise complaint from the city. My aunts gossip together in the kitchen as they clean and do dishes. My cousins fight over control of the old Nintendo console that only works half the time. I sit, alone on the couch, trying to stay in the moment rather than worrying about my plan for the future.

My mom comes over to collect my empty espresso cup, and then she nudges my arm with her elbow. "I know you said you would only be here for a day or two, but you could always move in for a while, share the back room with Nonna."

Nonna gives me a wide dentured grin from her spot across the couch.

Tempting...

"I'll land on my feet," I insist.

She pats my hand and walks away. I have no doubt she'll present her offer no less than a dozen more times.

I watch my cousins playing their video game for a few minutes, laughing at their whispered curse words. None of them want to get their mouth washed out with soap. Then Uncle Antonio comes over and takes the seat beside me.

Compared to most of my family, Uncle Antonio is

nearly mute. He's content to sit back and listen, merely existing in the chaos rather than helping to create it. We're similar in that way. He's big like my dad, their faces similar too, but my uncle is losing his hair much faster than his older brother. It makes his face look rounder. His cheeks are ruddy, his eyes a kind, dark brown and a match for mine.

Antonio always wears black suits, even to family dinners. It's part of his job. I asked him about it once, and he told me it's important to present yourself the way you want to be perceived.

"You doing okay, kiddo?" he asks me now.

I nod and smile.

"No more fancy restaurant?"

"No more fancy restaurant," I confirm.

"No more uppity boyfriend?"

"Hey, you liked him, I thought."

I brought Miles to Sunday family dinner once. He loved it, of course. We're good cooks in this family, and he was lucky to have been invited. It gives me great pleasure to know he'll never get to enjoy Nonna's pasta sauce ever again. Now that's a real punishment.

"He was…" He shimmies his hand back and forth as if his mind isn't made up. "Eh, I liked his food."

Miles and I treated some of my family to dinner at Fig & Olive once a few months back. I remember him making such a stink about it. He was put out to have to give up a few seats for them. I had to talk him into it for *weeks*, and then afterward, he still hung it over my head like he'd done me this huge favor.

I sigh. "Yes, unfortunately, I can't fault him there."

"So what'll you do now?"

My gaze drifts back to Nonna. It could be her and me, every night, tucked in together like the grandparents in *Charlie and the Chocolate Factory*.

"I'm not sure, but I want a change of pace. Something different."

Do I?

Truly?

The answer just spilled forth before I'd fully registered it. Up until this moment, I was still fairly sure I was going to continue job-hunting in the city, keep moseying down the same path I've been on for the last few years.

I nudge his shoulder, half-teasing, half-serious as I ask, "You need someone else behind the wheel?"

My uncle's been a driver for the last thirty years. He's got an in with all the right people, very discreet and respectful, completely by the book. He's always shuttling around these glamorous people. "Big tippers, real nice folks" is how he describes them. I know for a fact there are some celebrities in the mix. We beg him for the inside scoop, but he always keeps his lips zipped, never one to drive and tell.

"Let me put some feelers out. See what I can do."

Next Sunday dinner, Uncle Antonio shows up late and walks through my parents' door with a proud grin. He heads straight to where I'm playing cards with Nonna and shoves a bent-up business card my way.

"I asked around. One of my guys, Pat—you met him at your cousin's wedding, real tall, skinny—he says he might have a position open that you could fill. Easy, property management type thing. Only catch is you'd have to go and live out there, but I told him maybe that'd be okay since you said you were lookin' for a change. Maybe it'd be nice to get away from the city for a while."

I study the business card. Patrick Alessi is the man's name.

"What exactly is the position?"

"It's like I said, you'd be the caretaker for the house."

Oh…

I start to pass the business card back to him. "I'm not that handy, not like my dad and Gio."

He shakes his head adamantly, holding up his hand to block me from giving it back. "No, no. It's not that sort of thing. No fixin' nothin'."

My brows crinkle in confusion. "So I'd just live there and they'd...pay me?"

He laughs. "It's the way these rich people are. Too much money, too many problems. They want one less thing to worry about. Hamptons house ain't worth the trouble. Anyway, Pat's number is on that card if you wanna call him. Just see what it's about. It might be right up your alley."

THREE

LUKE

I'VE NEVER BEEN CONFRONTED with a challenge quite like this.

Pitching in game seven of the World Series—*difficult*. Recovering from shoulder surgery three years ago—*excruciating*. Traveling to city after city, game after game, season after season—*daunting*.

But this…it's something else entirely.

"DAD! You're pulling too hard!"

I wince. "I'm trying, kid. Rewind that video a few seconds."

"We've watched it through eight times!"

Hair braiding isn't for pansies, let me tell you. I wouldn't even be attempting it, but it's International Day or Heritage Day or some kind of other hellacious dress-up day at my daughter's school, and it's my job to make sure she looks the part.

She came into the kitchen two nights ago as I was burning dinner and boldly stated, "I need you to give me milkmaid braids to go with my outfit."

"Milk *whats*?"

She rolled her eyes like I was an absolute idiot and then said again, more slowly, "Milllllkkkmaaaiiid brrraaidddss."

"Got it, smartass. Now set the table for dinner."

"Oh! Add a dollar to the swear jar!" she joked. There is no swear jar. If there were, I'd probably be out a million dollars by now.

So here I am, a 6'4" dad with veritable bear paws for hands, hunched over his daughter trying to somehow piece together dainty hair so it creates a braided crown on top of her head. I'm failing, miserably, and Harper sees that. She's really trying to keep her composure. She's like that, wise beyond her years. Some kids would already be throwing a fit, but Harper sits stoically, letting me claw at her hair even though we both know by now that this ain't happening. There's a better chance of hell freezing over.

I sigh and let her hair fall. We're right back at square one.

"Okay, how about this? I drive you to school early and we see if Mrs. Treadwell can help you out. I bet she's good with hair."

Harper's teacher knows the deal. We talked about it at the start of the year. Harper's mom passed away when Harper was two. It's just me, single dad and certified bad braider. Mrs. Treadwell has stepped in just as I hoped she would, giving me feedback and advice on the sly whenever needed.

We strive to handle conflict with respectful dialogue. Telling Harper to, and I quote, "Rub Corey's face in the dirt" after he pushed her on the playground isn't quite in line with our policies here at Trinity Prep.

If a lunch is not packed, it is better to load cafeteria funds into her online account rather than paper-clipping a crumpled fifty to her empty lunchbox. And though well-meaning, ballpark peanuts don't provide all the necessary nutrients we hope for our children to receive at lunch time.

Additionally, the swearing must be reined in. Six weeks into the year and she's inadvertently taught the whole class the big 5: S, C, D, A, and F.

As she should be, Harper is very excited and proud of your team's performance in the postseason, but it's against school dress code for her to wear one of your jerseys beneath her uniform.

We've changed some things, gotten the hang of others. Swearing is now relegated to home *only*. I loaded her online lunch account with the max amount so I'd never have to remember to reload it, and the thing with Corey...well, if he pushes my daughter again, he'll have a lot more to worry about than a little dirt up his nose.

We've just about survived first grade together. If only we can get over this braid hurdle, we'll be scot-free. Come next Friday, school will break for summer, and I'll have a short reprieve from failing miserably day in and day out.

"Can we go to Aunt Tate instead? I know she can do it."

"Sure, kiddo. Let me call and see if she's home."

My younger sister has been my saving grace one too many times this year. She's the only family I have close by; everyone else is back in Texas. If she ever got a wild hair to leave the city, I'd somehow convince her to stay.

You want a better apartment? Two apartments? You want a driver? An account at Barney's?

I reach for my phone to call Tate, but it starts vibrating with an incoming call from David, my agent.

I roll my eyes and answer. "Not now."

"*Luke Allen!* Just the man I was hoping to reach."

"I told you I'd give you a call back."

"*Yes*, but that was last week," he points out. "I'm worried you don't understand the meaning of 'call back' so I thought I'd reach out. You see, proper etiquette states—"

I hang up.

"That was mean," Harper says, crossing her arms.

"It was a spam call," I lie.

David persists.

DAVID: We need to talk. They're willing to throw even more money your way. Retirement can wait!

I can't think about baseball right now. I have to get Harper to school.

And after I get her to school? Well…I need to go to the grocery store. We're out of those tiny red-wrapped cheese snacks she loves so much. And lunch meat. And bananas. And…

Fifteen minutes later, I'm banging on my sister's apartment door.

Tate doesn't open it; one of her roommates does. I don't know which one it is, Sophia or Daphne. They're sisters, and I have a hell of a time telling them apart.

This one has a big smile and curly red hair…but they both have red hair, so that doesn't help me. "Luke! Oh my gosh, had I realized you were coming over, I would have changed…"

She draws a hand down the front of her black nighty, then proceeds to arch her back and lean forward so I'd have an easier time getting an eyeful of her cleavage if only I wanted it. I very nearly toss a hand over Harper's eyes.

This one must be Daphne. Sophia is dating one of my old teammates, so I doubt she'd be showing up to the front door dressed like this. Or…let's hope not. Josh would lose it if he knew his girlfriend's breasts were about two inches from my face.

Harper tugs on my hand and rises up on her toes so she can loudly whisper to me, "Why is she blinking like that? Like over and over so fast. Does she have an eye disease?"

Tate bursts out laughing as she walks out of her room dressed in an oversized New York Pinstripes shirt with my old jersey number on it paired with baggy gray sweatpants. Her brown hair is wet from a shower, and I wouldn't be surprised if she's already gone on a run this morning. Instead of walking toward us, she bolts straight for the coffeepot on the counter.

"Daphne, you're hopeless. Get away from my brother."

Daphne throws up her hands. "*What?* Can't a girl try to lock it down with Luke Allen!? I believe in taking every opportunity the universe presents me."

"Excuse me," Harper says.

Daphne looks down at her as if only now realizing she's there.

"Your dress is very short," Harper states. "I think I can see your butt and maybe even your va—"

I tug my child to me and slap a hand over her mouth before she can continue.

Tate, who by now is taking her first sip of coffee, sputters and chokes on it as she tries not to die from laughter.

Daphne rolls her eyes and steps back. "What a precocious little girl you are."

Harper swats my hand away and puffs up her chest. "I'm not little. I'm six, and *only* for two more months!"

Daphne smiles and bends down to boop Harper on the nose. Harper frowns with annoyance.

"Of course. Silly me. Now, tell me, does your daddy—"

Tate runs over and wrenches Daphne away from the door, shoving her back toward her room. "No more hitting on my brother."

"It's not my fault he's so hot!"

Tate continues the challenging task of getting Daphne back in her room, acting like a lion tamer at the circus. Meanwhile, Harper asks me to bend down so she can press her palm flat to my forehead.

She looks utterly confused when she pulls it away. "What is she talking about? You're not hot."

Tate finally makes it back to us and leans down to scoop Harper up into her arms.

"Oh my gosh, you're getting so big. I'm not sure how much longer I'll be able to carry you like this."

"Really?" Harper asks excitedly. "So it's working then. Dad says even if I don't like what he cooks, I have to eat my dinner every night, and I do. I eat the food even when it's really bad. Don't tell him, but Dad is the worst cook ever."

"Is he?"

"*I can hear you,*" I tease Harper.

She ignores me. "Yes. Very bad. But you know why I eat it anyway? Because I'm going to be a baseball player even though girls don't play baseball."

"Hey, that's not true!" Tate tells her. "Girls can play baseball, just ask Grumpa." Tate winks back at me. "He forced me to play Little League with all the boys."

It's true. There was no getting out of it in the Allen household. My grandfather was in the majors, and my dad played a few seasons too before he went on to coach at the University of Texas. Everyone played ball in our house. Tate and I each had a glove on our hand by the time we could toddle around. Had there been a league for dogs, I'm sure ol' Sunshine would have had to run the bases too.

Private lessons, travel teams, weekend-long tournaments —it was the way of life as we knew it, and Harper thinks that's her destiny too. No matter that most days she'd rather color than go outside and throw the ball.

"Here," I say, holding out the bag of supplies I brought from the house. It's everything the YouTube video said we would need to create the braid. "I can pull up the video I was watching if you want to see. They said you need to start by—"

Tate levels me with an *I got this* glare. "This isn't my first rodeo."

She's spunky, my sister. She gets that from my mom.

To survive in our house, you had to be able to stand up for yourself. There were a lot of personalities to contend with.

My mom was a small-town Texas beauty queen who went on to compete in Miss Texas and Miss USA. Tate might have been out playing with the boys in Little League, but she was always wearing a big ol' hair bow while catching fly balls in the outfield. I wonder how she managed it, straddling two worlds like that. I had it easy compared to her.

Tate positions Harper on a stool at the kitchen counter and gets to work on her hair.

"Are you still planning to get out of the city this summer?" she asks me.

I'm busy watching her hands, amazed at how easily she braids. No fumbling on her part. Already, it's starting to take shape just like it's supposed to. *Jesus.* I used to be impressed by what a guy could bench-press, the speed achieved by his fast ball, his batting average. Times have changed, I guess.

"Once Harper's on summer break, yeah, we'll head to Colorado."

"Dad says we need to *bond*. It's going to be just him and me all summer. No nannies!" She shimmies her shoulders with excitement.

Tate arches her brows at me. "Oh really? No Maria?"

"She's taking a few months off to help her daughter with her new baby."

"I'm going to miss her. She's so nice. You'll still come visit me in Colorado for my birthday, though, right, Aunt Tate?"

"Of course. Are you kidding? We'll have so much fun. Now tell me, what do you want for your present?"

Oh boy. Harper has an exhaustive list of gifts she wants for her seventh birthday, and by now, I could recite it by heart. It includes everything from a Barbie Dreamhouse to front-row concert tickets to see some singer named JoJo.

While she rattles items off for her aunt, I tug my phone out of my pocket so I can shoot an email to my property manager. Tate's question reminded me that I need to check in with him. We've been corresponding back and forth about my upcoming stay at the Colorado house for the summer, ensuring everything is ready to go for Harper and me. Last month there was a small leak in one of the guest bathrooms, and Pat assured me his team would get it patched up in no time.

Later, as I'm browsing the cheese aisle at the grocery store, my phone buzzes with a new email from Pat. The subject line reads: COLORADO - MAJOR LEAK.

FOUR

CHLOE

THIS HOUSE IS INSANE. Beyoncé levels of insane. I mean, this *could* be Beyoncé's house; it's certainly big enough. I'm standing in the foyer with my bag at my feet, scared to move lest I accidentally break something and have to sell an organ on the black market to be able to afford to replace it.

So yeah, I called Pat and I got the job.

Clearly, my uncle put in a good word for me because all it took was a short phone interview. I didn't shy away from the fact that I've never had a job like this before and I wasn't sure what all it involved, but Pat said it's a no-brainer. Above all else, he just needed someone trustworthy. He promised he'd send me over a list of household duties and tasks I needed to do once I arrived on the property, and he made good on that promise.

I read through the list as I was on my way down here on the Jitney. It isn't all that much work, day to day. Broadly, I'm supposed to supervise daily operations, identify repair needs, maintain property value, commission repair work, and coordinate maintenance workers. I also need to maintain a base level of cleanliness within the house, clean up after myself, dust and vacuum as needed. If time allows, I can help tend the garden, though there is a groundskeeper who's supposed to be in charge of the outdoor spaces, sport courts, and pool.

To maintain privacy, Pat didn't give me any information on who I'm working for. I guess it's not exactly relevant. Pat is my boss. I'll be reporting to him, and he'll be the one signing my paychecks. I doubt I'll ever even see the owners of this house. They're probably off galivanting in Saint-Tropez. Vacationing with the Kardashians. Laughing maniacally as they swim in a bathtub filled with cash.

Something rubs against my leg, and I jump a mile in the air.

Holy shit. My heart feels like it's come untethered, dangling precariously by a string. I look down and see an orange tabby cat dancing between my legs.

"Jesus, you scared me!" I say with a laugh.

The cat ignores me, twining around me a few more times before deciding my legs are boring. Then it proceeds to prance confidently into the foyer. Pat made no mention of any pets, but then again, I could have just missed it somewhere along the way. These last few days have been a whirlwind.

Preparing to leave the city wasn't all that complicated, but explaining to my parents that I was merely going to the Hamptons and not *off to literal war* was something else entirely. When I told my mom about the job, she wouldn't talk to me for two days.

"You've broken your mother's heart," my dad said. "Why can't you just live here? Haven't the last few days been fun? Well, besides…listen, Nonna didn't mean to walk in on you while you were pooping."

"DAD."

They eventually came around to it though. Demands were agreed upon. I am to visit at least once a month, and I am to attend Sunday family dinner every weekend via FaceTime, no exceptions.

To further soothe hard feelings, I take my phone out of my

back pocket and snap a photo to send to my big family group text.

CHLOE: I've arrived! Look at this place!

In a minute, the replies will start flooding in. My cousins will all *ooh* and *ahh*. My mom will ask if I've locked all the doors. My dad will want to know if they have Sub-Zero or Wolf appliances.

I decide first I should give myself a tour. In all, it takes me fifteen minutes to traverse the whole house. I passed six bedrooms, or was it *seven* bedrooms? A home office, media room, library, game room, living room...room...room...room. You get it. It's absolutely absurd that anyone would need this much space. My entire extended family could fit into this house four times over. Sunday dinners in this dining room would be an absolute pleasure, no one cramped next to another.

I know nothing about design, but I know this place is nice, the sort of house you'd see on the cover of one of those architecture magazines you flip through in the waiting room at the dentist's office while you prepare your lie about how often you floss. *Easy, after every meal. Doesn't everyone, doc?*

The house is situated on a bunch of land and faces a private pond. From one of the bedroom windows, I even saw a slightly neglected garden out back I can't wait to explore.

My favorite space so far: the kitchen.

It's a chef's dream. It has an open layout for cooking and entertaining, cabinets stretching all the way to the ceiling, marble countertops, and a separate butler's pantry for prep work. The two sets of double ovens and the industrial-sized fridge hidden behind sleek white paneling would have my dad salivating. I'm more into the pot and pan selection and the knives; they're exactly what I would buy if money were no issue.

Standing in the kitchen, I decide this will be a cushy job. I'll maintain this house no problem.

It's at this precise moment that I hear a knock on the glass door that leads from the kitchen out onto the sprawling back porch. I turn to see a masked madman standing there with a scythe in his hand, and I let loose a bloodcurdling scream.

Slowly, he slides the porch door open, and I act quickly, reaching for a knife from the butcher block on the counter.

Threats tumble out of my mouth as I wield it wildly, swinging it out in front of me in great big slashing motions. "Don't come any closer. This bad boy is so sharp it'll slice through flesh like butter! And...and I'm not afraid to use it!"

He curses and tugs down the fabric he had covering the bottom half of his face then pushes back his wide-brimmed sun hat.

"What's wrong with you, girl?"

The pieces start to fall into place. This is a man well into his 70s, dressed in overalls with muddy boots, standing innocently before me. In his hand is not a scythe, but a rake. The fabric mask he was wearing? Probably to keep allergens from getting in his nose while he was doing yardwork.

Feeling like a complete idiot, I drop the knife onto the counter then clutch my chest while I release a relieved laugh.

"I'm...I'm sorry. I thought—"

I'm smart enough to let the last half of my sentence dangle. No need to make this situation worse by insulting the man. *Yes hi, oh that whole slashing knife thing? I thought you were a terrifying murderer.*

I know who this man is. Pat explained that there would be another employee working with me at the house: Ned, the groundskeeper.

I step toward him and hold out my hand. "I'm Chloe. Sorry about all *that*." My gaze slides to the massive butcher knife I was just threatening him with. It looms larger than necessary on the counter. Okay, c'mon, did it just grow like three sizes when I wasn't looking? "You just took me by surprise."

He stares at my hand like he'd rather swat it away than shake it. Unsurprisingly, he doesn't come closer, but he does uphold his end of the introduction. Barely.

"Name's Ned."

I smile wider than I've ever smiled in my life. I have a lot of ground to recover. "What a *great* name. Ned. I love that name. You don't hear that much anymore. Is it a family name?"

Yes, I'm going slightly overboard, but I'm trying to get us back on track.

Ned is uninterested in doing his part. Ignoring my question, he pinches his thumb and index finger together in front of his mouth and lets out a whistle. The orange tabby cat I let in earlier comes swaggering past me, back to its apparent owner.

"Cat's not supposed to be in the house," he says as he waves for me to follow him out onto the porch. Then he points at the backyard and the house, respectively. "That's my domain, this is yours," he states plainly. "Stay outta my way."

Oh how friendly!

"And what if I...ope!" I make a joke of barely putting one foot outside, thinking this will elicit a little chuckle from Ned, but he remains stoic in the face of comedic gold. "Okay, I see," I go on. "Very particular about your space. I can understand that. I grew up with a brother who was always getting in my stuff. I can't tell you how annoying it was."

Nothing. Ned's face doesn't inform me of anything beyond his general annoyance at having to deal with me. I see it now. I know this face. He's Filch from *Harry Potter*, only without the long hair and warm personality.

"What about the garden?" I ask. "I thought it could use some love."

He grumbles something unintelligible, and when I press

him on it, he only seems more annoyed. "That's fine. Just nothin' else."

"No raking the leaves, ha-ha! Got it!"

He's already walking away.

"I will not so much as *touch* a hammer. No nails either!"

He completely ignores me, instead bending down to pick up his cat.

Well I, for one, think this year's employee Christmas party is going to be a real *riot*.

FIVE

LUKE

"WHY DO we have to go *here* instead of Colorado?"

"I told you, Harper. Because of the leak. The whole first floor flooded, and they have to gut it."

"*Gut it?*" she asks.

"Tear it down so they can fix it," I amend quickly.

Some asshole in front of me swerves into my lane then slams on his brakes. I just about lose it. Laying on my horn doesn't feel good enough.

"I liked that house!" she wails suddenly.

My patience is hanging on by a thread. I'm channeling the Dalai Lama, Mother Teresa, and my kindergarten teacher, Ms. McDonald. That lady was a real saint. I think I once put glue in her coffee mug when she wasn't looking.

It's late and we're driving out to the Hamptons house to start our Fun-Filled, Memorable, Definitely-Not-A-Bad-Idea Summer Vacation. I wanted to get on the road earlier, but with our last-minute change of plans, Harper and I had to spend the day running around the city, grabbing everything we need for our *new* summer destination. No more jackets and hiking boots; bring on the sunscreen, bathing suits, and flip-flops. After we'd packed up the car, naturally, it was time for dinner. Harper insisted we have one last meal in the city, so we got takeout from our favorite Chinese food restaurant down the block. By the time we set off, it was close to 8:00 PM. Bumper-to-bumper traffic means we'll pull up to the house well past Harper's bedtime. Hell, past *my* bedtime too.

I reach back over the center console and give her knee a reassuring squeeze.

"*Hey*, the house will be just fine once they fix the water damage, and we'll still have a fun summer together. Just…at the beach instead of the mountains."

Harper sniffs and nods. I know she's just tired, so I turn up her favorite music to help get us through the last few miles of the drive. Today, it's Taylor Swift. Apparently, she's "over JoJo," so I guess I'll be reselling *those* concert tickets online.

We stay on the highway and pass Shinnecock Hills, Tuckahoe, Southampton, and Water Mill before we make it to Bridgehampton and turn right onto Ocean Drive.

The last time I was here was to celebrate my mom's 60th birthday with the family. We spent a week lying low, playing board games, swimming, and grilling. Then the weekend took a turn when Tate accidentally booked a stripper to entertain us during the actual party.

"*I thought I was hiring a magician!*"

"*Lady, just say the word, and I bet I can make those panties disappear.*"

My dad just about lost it.

My mom, not so much.

"*Well he's already here. Why don't we let the nice man do his show?*"

The memory makes me laugh. Trying to explain that one to Harper was a real trip.

That was two years ago, and I haven't had the time to make it back since, not with my MLB schedule.

The house hasn't changed though. In my absence, it's remained as impressive as always. It's a quintessential shingle-style mansion with large windows and an expansive porch sitting on five acres and boasting all the amenities anyone could ever want. It's just a golf cart ride away from the beach, and more important than that, it's nice and secluded from the surrounding neighbors. Hedgerows and trees make it feel like we're the only ones around for miles. I was never a big Hamptons guy, but I was talked into purchasing the property to help diversify my real estate portfolio, and I don't regret it. It's worth twice as much as I paid for it, and Harper loves it here. She'll remember that when she's not so tired.

She's out cold in the back seat, head tilted at a weird angle, drool dribbling down her cheek. I park and kill the engine; she doesn't stir one bit. I'll come back for the bags later. For now, I unbuckle her gently, lifting her up into my arms so I can carry her inside the house. It takes me a second at the door to fumble for my keys in my back pocket without jostling Harper too much, but it's easy enough. She's still light as a feather. Holding her like this reminds me of those baby and toddler days, the chance to get to be close to her whenever I wanted. She still likes to cuddle, especially if I'm reading to her, but every day she grows a bit more independent, a little less inclined to want daddy hugs. It kills me. I'm squeezing her tighter without realizing it, and she stirs in my arms.

Inside, I carry her down the hall toward her bedroom and get her all tucked in. Shoes off, blankets covering her up to her chin. I'll worry about pajamas tomorrow.

I turn on the white noise machine on her bedside table and make sure the blackout curtains are pulled closed. The desire to let myself plop down right beside her on the bed is almost overwhelming. Instead, I head back out to my SUV to unload. I'll regret it in the morning if I don't get all our crap inside. Harper brought four huge bags, and only one is filled with clothes. The other three are filled with "things she can't live without": an array of stuffed animals and Barbies, a whole bunch of art supplies, a seemingly random assortment of throw pillows from our living room. I realize now I probably should have supervised her packing a little more closely.

I drop her bags outside her door, listen for a moment to confirm she's still out cold, and then head for the room a ways down the hall. There's a palatial primary suite on the second story overlooking the grounds and the pond out back, but I don't like being that far away from Harper. I prefer sleeping in a room down here. It's just as nice as the primary suite, just smaller.

I open the door and flip on the light, and then something collides with my head.

What the hell?

The projectile clatters to the floor: a fuzzy purple slipper.

"DO NOT COME ANY CLOSER!"

I blink and look up to find a petite girl—no, *woman* propped up on her knees in my bed, wielding a second purple slipper.

I take another step into the room, and she holds it up like she's taking aim.

"What do you want?!"

Alright, my brain is admittedly not firing on all cylinders here. It's been a long day, it's late, and I'm slightly disoriented. My first thought, and I'm not proud of it, is that I might have somehow wandered into the wrong house. But then, obviously no. This is my fucking house.

"Who are you?" I ask, my voice thundering.

She throws the second slipper, and I catch it, easily.

"Could you chill out for a second?"

"Who are *you*?" she asks, throwing the question back at me.

"The owner of this goddamn house. *Who are you?*"

"Oh no."

The color drains from her face.

I realize it's the first time I really give her appearance a passing thought. She's not exactly dressed for company. Her spaghetti-strapped tank top is two sizes too small and slightly askew, and her pajama shorts are tugged too low. Her chestnut brown hair is a tangled mess, and her face is a mask of horror.

When she speaks, her voice is whisper quiet. "I'm your new employee. Chloe."

New employee.

New employee?

I rack my brain trying to corroborate that information. There's been a lot going on this week what with Harper's last few days of school, the leak in the Colorado house, and my agent calling me every five seconds. Did Pat hire someone to help take care of things at this house? I know we discussed it a few weeks back and I gave him the green light to start the interview process. I wouldn't be surprised if I have an email about it waiting unread in my overflowing inbox.

"Pat hired you?" I ask.

"Pat Alessi," she confirms with an enthusiastic nod. "Started today, actually."

Jesus Christ.

I drag a hand through my hair and curse under my breath.

She flinches. Apparently, it wasn't *quite* so under my breath.

"Well you're in my room."

Her eyebrows knit together. "Your room? The primary bedroom is upstairs."

"Yeah, well, I like being down the hall from my daughter."

Her warm brown eyes widen in horror, and then she scrambles off the bed, entirely too much of her tan cleavage on display. I avert my eyes.

"I can be out of here in just a minute."

I don't bother telling her to stay. I don't even know her; I don't want some stranger sleeping down the hall from

Harper. This girl can move upstairs for now. We'll deal with the rest of the bullshit in the morning.

She's running around gathering up her stuff as quickly as possible. Fuzzy socks, a dog-eared paperback, a scraggly polka dot blanket. In the bathroom, she just sweeps everything off the counter straight into her bag as if she can't get out of here fast enough.

I only realize I'm standing at the door like some menacing overlord after she's finished and about to rush past me. She stops at my side, looks up at me, and then up some more. She's a pipsqueak.

From this angle, her face is all eyes, like some princess sprung to life from one of Harper's Disney movies.

For a fleeting second, we assess each other. Her eyes rove over my face, and then she winces.

"Listen, I'm sorry about the slipper. And, okay, there was another incident earlier with a knife, but—"

My brain can't unscramble her words fast enough. Knife? "*What?*"

She shakes her head. "You know what? Never mind. Just —I'm sorry. I really am. I can just go if that's easier?"

"Go?"

"Leave," she says, frowning. "I bet the last Jitney hasn't left yet. Surely there's another one before midnight. Or if not, I can just…I don't know." She looks at my forehead with regret and maybe even a little bit of awe. "I'm sorry. I didn't think I had aim that good. I got you right above your eyebrow. It's all red."

I touch the skin where her slipper made contact with my face. It doesn't even hurt.

"I'm sorry," she says again, her voice soft with remorse.

For some reason it only makes me more annoyed. "Stop apologizing."

She startles and steps away from me. "I'm—*oh my gosh, I was about to do it again!* Okay. *Leave, Chloe.*"

The last part she mutters to herself. I realize I never invited her to stay here. For all I know she's about to walk right out the door. I might be incapable of most decency at the moment, but I'm not about to throw this girl out on the street in the middle of the night.

"Just go upstairs. We'll worry about everything else in the morning."

With a nod, she steps out into the hall, but then she pauses momentarily when she hears the low murmur of Harper's white noise machine through her door. "Do you think we woke up your daughter?"

I shake my head. "She's a heavy sleeper."

Her shoulders sag in relief and away she goes, down the hall.

Already, guilt is starting to set in. I could have handled that better.

I'll fix it in the morning. For now, I just want to go to sleep. I head into the bathroom with my suitcase and unpack just enough to find my toothbrush and toothpaste. I'm brushing my teeth at the counter when I look down and notice a silky pink thong Chloe forgot to pack in her haste to leave the room.

It's...cute.

Like she is.

That thought has absolutely no place in my mind, so I ignore it, finish up in the bathroom, and then leave the thong there to deal with in the morning. I tug off my shirt and pants and lie down on the bed in my boxer briefs. My last few waking moments of the day are accompanied by the scent of Chloe's shampoo on the pillow, the smell of her clinging to the sheets.

SIX
CHLOE

LAST NIGHT WAS SO silly and funny and everyone will be laughing about it this morning. *Ha ha ha.* See?! I'm *already* laughing and not at all freaking out about the fact that I've irrevocably embarrassed myself in front of my new employer.

Once I made it up to the primary suite last night, I could barely sleep. My heart wouldn't stop racing. Residual adrenaline coursed through my veins. Yesterday's events were cut straight from a horror movie, jump scare after jump scare. First the cat, then the amiable (ha) groundskeeper, then the hunky employer. You know what? How about no one sneaks up on me anymore?! It's really that simple!

After my encounter with Ned in the kitchen, I spent the rest of my day getting acclimated to the house, unpacking, and getting settled in. I took the bus to a nearby grocery store for some provisions and baking supplies, and then I made myself a quick dinner. When the yawning silence of the house grew too great (and too creepy), I hurried to my chosen bedroom, the one with the pretty view of the pond, and decided to turn in early.

I was dead asleep when I was jolted awake by the sound of footsteps in the hall, the taunting creak of a bedroom door opening and then closing. Then the footsteps started heading in *my* direction. And to be clear, it's not my fault I assumed the worst! It's strange being by myself in such a large house, and I'm not accustomed to utter silence. The city is *never* silent. I routinely go to sleep to a soothing cacophony of shouts, honks, and sirens. It's nice.

So yes, I threw a slipper at my employer, and it collided with his face.

It's surprisingly not my worst first impression.

I make a fool of myself rather regularly, and I've learned that nothing is so terrible that it can't be fixed with food, specifically breakfast. I'm not going small. I've been up for almost two hours already. I have cinnamon rolls proving, a quiche Lorraine in the oven, a fresh fruit platter arranged artfully, and a carafe of coffee steaming on the counter when my employer finally strolls into the kitchen.

I'm slightly taken aback by the sight of him.

He's not altogether...*ugly*.

But that's as much as I'm willing to admit.

It won't serve me at all to acknowledge his intimidating height, or his muscular biceps, or his distinctly handsome manly-man features. He could be a cowboy on the cover of one of Nonna's romance books—well, sans assless chaps.

"Good morning!" I chirp with a winning smile. "Are you hungry? I've laid out quite the spread, and if this isn't to your liking, I can also whip up just about anything, assuming I have the ingredients on hand. The quiche is still in the oven, but if you're not a quiche guy, I can do an omelet, or just scrambled eggs."

He surveys the food with a look of confusion but doesn't immediately answer.

I thunk my hand on my head and hurry toward him. "Duh, *sorry*. I guess we should actually do a proper introduction. I'm Chloe Ricci, slipper assailant and your new employee. Ha! Glad to see you've recovered well. Hope you weren't hoping for a mysterious tough-guy scar on your fore-head because you won't be getting one. You look good as new."

My hand has been outstretched between us through all my chattering, but he only accepts it once I pause. His hand is comically large, but nice, warm. I wonder what he thinks of mine. Does it feel like he's shaking hands with that Kristen Wiig character on *SNL* with the tiny hands?

"Luke Allen," he says, supplying his half of the arrangement.

"Luke Allen..." I mull his name over for a second as I shake my head. "That sounds...oh right! There's a famous baseball player with that name. That's so funny."

He tilts his head to study me, our hands still clasped together.

Three...two...one.

My eyes widen in shock. "OH MY GOD!"

His tough guy exterior finally cracks, just a bit. He very nearly smiles.

"I know you! You're famous!"

"Barely."

"Oh don't be modest! Come on—you're like a superstar! My dad is obsessed with you. My *brother* is obsessed with you! I'm...okay, I admit, I'm not a super big baseball fan— I've been a little busy—but I'm still really impressed."

"You don't have to keep shaking my hand."

"Oh!" I let go. "Well this changes things." Last night flashes through my mind for the thousandth time, only now it's somehow worse. My hand flies up to my mouth as I gasp. "I assaulted Luke Allen. My dad will never forgive me."

"No offense, but there wasn't that much of an assault."

"*Dear god!* What if I'd hit your hands! I bet they're insured for like a billion dollars each!"

"Not anymore," he says, sounding amused.

I frown, trying to figure out what he means by that, but he's already moving on.

"About last night...did you not realize I was coming? Is that why you were so surprised? Because Pat knew about the change of plans. I told him I was coming here for the summer rather than going to Colorado, and if he failed to inform you—"

Horrified, I grab his forearm with a reassuring grip. "No. The fault is entirely mine. Pat *did* send me a text message, but I didn't see it. The thing is, I have a *very* large family, and we have a group text. It can get out of hand sometimes, and I had silenced my phone in the evening then forgot to check it before I went to sleep..."

It's true. I didn't see Pat's text until this morning. It read: Change of plans. Hamptons owner, Mr. Allen, will arrive today. Please prepare the house for his arrival using the PDF checklist I emailed to you.

I wonder if "throw a slipper at his head" was on that list; I'll have to check.

Luke looks relieved to know Pat's not made a mistake. Then *less* relieved when he realizes I'm still touching him.

Oh right. *No putting your hands on your boss.* That's a good rule to live by, something that would have served me well in my *last* job.

I let go and prop my hands on my hips. "So, all's well that ends well, huh?"

He doesn't confirm this. I'd guess he'd say we still have quite a bit of unfinished business.

He clears his throat and rubs the back of his neck. Already, I can hear the guilt seep into his voice when he begins, "So here's the thing, Chloe...you're here, employed as a caretaker for the house, which is slightly redundant now that *I'll* be here for the summer..."

Oh god, I can feel it coming, the axe.

A dejected "Oh" is all I manage.

"And Ned maintains the grounds."

"That's been made abundantly clear," I tell him with a little laugh.

"And a cleaning service will come every other week…"

So you see, you aren't needed. You're fired.

I know that's what he's about to say. I will lose two jobs in less than a month and be right back where I was before, shacking up with Nonna, shoving a chair underneath the bathroom doorknob just for some freaking privacy.

"I can cook!" I exclaim suddenly. "I'm trained and everything!"

I gesture toward the breakfast food littering the counter on the off chance he missed it all on his way into the kitchen. The quiche could use another few minutes, but I don't pass up the chance to whip it out of the oven this very second, swerving close once I have it in hand and wafting the scent his way before I set it down to cool.

Then I smile and boldly put my offer out there. "I understand what you're saying. My duties have changed, but"—I hold up my hand to stop him before he can interrupt me—"perhaps I could maintain *some* caretaker duties, fill in the gaps on the weeks the cleaning crew isn't here, and cook for you and your daughter whenever you'd like."

"Daddy?" A quiet voice sounds from down the hall.

A little girl pads into the kitchen with a stuffed unicorn tucked beneath her arm. She rubs sleep from her eyes and blinks, looking between her dad and me, trying to piece together the scene she's just walked in on.

Luke doesn't hesitate. He hurries over to scoop her up, easily carrying her into the kitchen with her resting in one of his arms.

"Hungry, Harper?"

"Yes. But Daddy, why am I still wearing my clothes from yesterday?"

"You fell asleep in the car last night and I didn't want to

wake you up. You know what else? I didn't brush your teeth either, so I guess we'll have to brush double good this morning."

She laughs. "That's so silly!"

Luke smiles at his daughter, and it completely transforms his features. The hard lines, the sharp angles, they melt away, leaving a man so intoxicatingly handsome it makes my stomach clench.

I'm about to divert my gaze, to somehow try to blend into the background and leave them to their moment when Harper's gaze cuts to me. She's truly an adorable kid. Which, given what her dad looks like, isn't all that surprising. She takes after him in almost every way, including height, it seems.

I smile and give her a little wave, but she doesn't return it. She looks absolutely devastated by the sight of me. Her eyes well with tears, her bottom lip wobbling.

"You said there would be no nannies this summer!" Her small voice shakes with sadness.

Oh no.

I leap forward.

"Nanny? Pfft. I'm *not* a nanny. In fact, I don't know the first thing about kids. I can't even tell your age. You gotta be, what, fifteen? No—*sixteen*?"

Harper snorts with laughter even while tears still linger in her eyes. "I'm six."

"Six?! You're kidding me. What do six-year-olds like to do? You read the newspaper?"

"NO!" Harper exclaims playfully.

"Oh, okay, so you prefer crosswords? I know—I bet you watch *Jeopardy*."

Harper's cute face scrunches with confusion.

"See? I'm no nanny."

She nods then, believing me. "Then what are you?"

"I'm..."

I look to Luke, wondering how exactly I'm meant to

proceed here. If he's about to fire me, I should probably just back away slowly and cut my losses. He returns my gaze with discerning eyes and none of the warmth he shared with his daughter. But then he nods, once, giving me the green light, or so I hope…I guess there's always the chance he could be waiting to fire me in private later.

"I'm a chef! And a caretaker for the house. *And* someone you can come to if you ever need anything."

Judging by his new surly expression, Luke doesn't like this improvised bit I've tacked onto the end.

"Err…if you're hungry or need help cleaning something up that is. Strictly house things only since I'm not good with kids." I give her a reassuring wink. "So what do you like to eat anyway? Raisin Bran?"

"Ewww!" Harper squeals, leaping down from her dad's arms and hurrying over to inspect the cinnamon rolls. "Mmm, they smell so good."

"They have to sit for another half hour or so before I put them in the oven. Normally I like to make them the night before. I can show you next time. Actually, I haven't made the icing yet. You could help me if you want."

"YES!" she squeals, jumping up and down with glee. She looks like I've just asked if she wants to visit a land filled with unicorns and cotton candy and dancing teddy bears. It's impossible not to feel that way too. I'm almost tempted to start jumping up and down myself.

"*Harper*," Luke says sharply.

The teddy bears get their heads cut off as I look back at my boss.

He's got his hands on his hips. "Come on, we need to go unpack, and I need to get you changed out of those clothes."

Harper stamps her foot. "*Why?* They don't even stink or anything! Can't I stay with—" Her sentence cuts off as she looks up at me. "What's your name?"

"Chloe."

"*Ms*. Chloe," Luke amends.

I hold my hand out for her to shake, which she finds absolutely hysterical.

She accepts it, and I wag her limp arm up and down.

"*Ms*. Harper, it's a pleasure to meet you," I say, putting on a fake British accent to sound extra fancy.

She grins, and I can see she's missing her two bottom teeth.

"Ms. Chloe, it is a pleasure to meet you too," she replies, copying my bit with a British accent of her own.

Oh, she's funny! *The kid's funny!*

"Alright, Harper, c'mon," Luke says, sounding exasperated. But when I look up at him, I can tell he's wrestling with something.

Is he really that mad his daughter likes me? I'm a likable gal! It's like the one perk us nice girls get.

Harper grumbles her way over to her dad, and he ruffles her hair. "Go get started unpacking, and I'll be right there. I need to talk to Chloe for a second."

She does as he asks and then it's just us, alone again. He comes farther into the kitchen and walks around the island until we're only a few feet apart. *Phew.* The room gets real hot real fast when his gaze falls right on me. It's like my hormones are swinging wildly in either direction by the second. MORE adrenaline. LESS adrenaline. *Just put all your effort into making her sweat, boys!*

I swallow past the lump in my throat and wonder if I should try wafting more delicious scents in his direction before he begins, "So as you might have guessed, this is really complicated. I don't allow many people around my daughter. I've only ever had a few nannies I trust to care for her, and even then, there's a lengthy interview process, background checks, security screenings—all of it."

I hold up my hands in a gesture of understanding. "Absolutely. You want to protect her. I completely get it."

"If you're staying this summer, it's strictly like you said: you'll cook and care for the house, but you won't look after Harper."

I nod quickly, letting him know that's alright with me. I'm not the least bit offended that he's putting the protection of his daughter above all else.

"Still, seeing as how you'll be staying in the house with us—"

"I could move to the guest house!" I offer, wanting to be helpful.

"No. That's Ned's domain." The way he says it makes it clear he's fully aware of his groundskeeper's *fickle* personality. "You'll have to stay in the house with us, which means I'll need to vet you as I would anyone who's around Harper, just to err on the side of caution. It's okay if I have Pat run a background check?"

"Of course! Yes! I'm not a criminal. I've never so much as hurt a fly."

Just then the back door opens and there's ol' Ned, rake still in his hand.

Did he sleep with it?

He throws me a grouchy look before shaking his head and looking at his boss. "Sir, we need to talk. This girl threatened me with a knife yesterday."

All eyes swivel to me.

The blood drains from my face.

"Right…that…*that's* a funny story."

SEVEN

CHLOE

I CAN'T BELIEVE *I'm working for Luke Allen.*

That's wild.

My brother would lose his mind if he knew. I would never hear the end of it if I told him.

The New York Pinstripes are an institution. All the greats have played for that team. You have your Bobby So-and-Sos, your Ricky Flyballs, your...okay, I admit I know next to nothing about baseball. My family is obsessed with the game, I'm not, so I don't exactly know details, but I know Luke Allen is good. I know the Pinstripes won the World Series last year because there was a parade through the city that made me thirty minutes late for work that day. And I know my new boss is seriously sexy.

That last part I scrub from my brain almost immediately.

Bad bad bad.

There are so many other things to focus on right now. Like, aside from his face, you have his hands, his forearms, his *butt.*

CHLOE.

I'm getting settled into another second-story bedroom, not the one I moved to last night. That one is just too insane, large enough to host a family of ten. I'm more than happy in a small room down the hall with the same view of the pond. I still have a bathroom of my own, and it feels really secluded up here.

Luke and I agreed this is where I'll stay. He walked me up here himself earlier after our run-in with Ned.

I assumed he wouldn't take the knife incident report well, but he actually seemed mildly amused.

"Ned's…interesting. He's used to being here by himself, and I don't think he likes the idea of having to split duties with you," Luke explained.

"Hey, you won't see me trying to wrestle that rake out of his hand, promise. Though, just to be clear, it's not like fused to his hand? He can drop it, right?"

Now, I'm unpacking my things carefully into the dresser beneath the TV, trying to come to terms with the fact that I'll be living in the lap of luxury for the foreseeable future. We haven't talked about all the specifics, but I assume my position here will be seasonal, which is fine by me. I'm just happy to be here. Tomorrow, I'll worry about tomorrow.

I hear peals of laughter outside, and I walk over to the window to see Harper and Luke down by the pool. He's got her in his arms, and he's swinging her back and forth over the water, taunting her like he's about to toss her in.

"No! No!" Harper squeals.

"You're right, I shouldn't…" Then he swings her again, higher than before, and lets her go in the deep end.

Scream of delight.

Huge splash.

"*DAD!* Can you do it again!?"

I feel oddly nostalgic watching them together. It makes me miss being Harper's age, wrapped in that carefree ease of childhood. I might not have ever swum in an Olympic-sized pool rimmed by designer lounge chairs and five acres of private land, but I had a dad who wasn't afraid to be silly with me. Even today, if I were standing by that pool, I'm sure he wouldn't resist the urge to push me in. Some things never change.

While they soak up the early summer sun outside, I'm relegated to a titillating Zoom conference call in my room with a team of Luke's lawyers. They drone on in front of their gray backdrops, asking me question after question in monotone voices until it all seems to blur together. Have I been in this room for thirty minutes or thirty *years*?

On top of everything else Luke and I discussed this morning, his lawyers would also like me to sign an NDA.

"Surely you don't expect me to read this whole thing," I tease.

The stony-faced lawyers blink back at me as if they can't compute my question.

"Because I definitely *did* read every word. Even the hard ones. Okay, some of the hard ones."

"Ms. Ricci, if you would like us to review the document with you, please state that plainly."

Extend this hell? "*No.* It's all good. I got the gist of it. I shouldn't blab about anything I see while working for Mr. Allen. No talking to the media, tabloids, press. I got it, loud and clear. Now where do I leave my electronic signature?"

After the call ends and my room is squared away, everything nice and neat, I change into a sundress and slip on some sandals. I'm going grocery shopping!

My goal for now is to make myself absolutely irreplaceable to Luke. I'm aware that he's not wholly convinced I should be here, so I'll tidy up around the house, throw in a few loads of laundry here and there, and make Luke and Harper the kinds of meals that will make their palates *sing*!

Before I sneak out of the house, I head to the backyard where Harper and Luke are still hanging out. Harper has a row of mermaid Barbies lined up on the top stair in the shallow end of the pool. She's acting out a little play scene, giving them each a different voice, when she spots me and waves eagerly.

"Are you going to swim with us!?"

"Not today." I frown as if I'm as sad about it as she is. And I am. I would love to jump in this pool, but duty calls. "I'm going to the grocery store. I just wanted to come and ask you and your dad about what kind of foods you prefer, your likes and dislikes. Also, do you have any food allergies?"

Harper, overwhelmed, looks to her dad, which means *I* have to look at her dad. It's something I've tried not to do since coming outside.

He's on a lounge chair sans shirt, tan and muscular. His hunter green swim trunks aren't sitting obscenely low or anything, but it doesn't matter. That smattering of hair under his navel that leads down, accompanied by his deep V, proves he is *all* man.

"Ms. Ricci?" he asks.

Ah, so I'm Ms. Ricci now. Interesting.

"I prefer Chloe," I say, smiling. "If that's okay."

He sits up and waves me over, turning his baseball hat around backward so he'll be able to see me better without the brim in the way. My ovaries take note.

I want to stay where I am, safely by Harper, but that means I'd have to all but shout for him to hear me, so I brace myself and walk toward him.

He's just a normal person. His abs are just abs. His chest is just a chest. His shoulders are just so lovely and wide and bronzed.

"You needed to know about allergies?" he asks, prodding me to get on with it.

I blush and look away from his chest, shifting to his face instead.

His eyes are such a light shade of brown, especially in the sun.

"Yes. Allergies, preferences, that sort of thing."

I have a little notebook ready and everything, but it'll be easier if I can sit and rest it on my lap while I write. I gesture to the lounge chair beside his.

"May I?"

He frowns. The idea clearly troubles him.

Oh how mortifying.

"Never mind, let me just—"

With a heavy sigh, he tells me to sit.

I do, quickly.

I go through all the major allergies with him as quickly as possible, relieved that their family doesn't have any concerns.

"Harper's pretty picky though," he warns.

"I don't know any kid who isn't," I reassure him.

He narrows his eyes, taking me in. "You know a lot of kids? What about that whole speech earlier in the kitchen with Harper?"

"Oh." I laugh and lower my voice. "Yeah, I mean, she was clearly upset about the nanny thing and I wanted to reassure her. I probably wasn't *too* far off, though. I'm not like a secret baby whisperer or anything, but I have a lot of cousins. I've changed a lot of diapers and wrangled a lot of toddlers in my time."

"Which is what exactly?"

"Huh?"

"How old are you?"

"Oh. Twenty-seven."

He lifts his brows as if this surprises him.

"You look younger," he supplies when he reads my confusion.

I let his comment marinate for a second before giving in to my curiosity. "Is that...bad?"

He studies me, his gaze roving over my face, then he looks away. "She's good about trying new food, she just might not finish all of it or anything. So you can make whatever you'd like."

Ah, understood. Business only—got it.

I focus back on my task, going through preferences. People are usually most particular about seafood: oysters, no oysters, that kind of thing.

"Does the grill work?"

"Last I checked."

I beam and shoot to my feet. "Great. Well, I'll head to the store and pick up some provisions. I'll try to go every day or at least every other day, that way I can get the freshest ingredients for you and Harper. I haven't had time to do much research yet, but I'll ask around about a fish market. I'm sure there are plenty of them in this area."

He nods then points back toward the house. "Grab the black Amex from my wallet. I think I left it on the kitchen counter by the coffeepot. Use it for household expenses. I don't expect you to cover the cost of our groceries. In fact, anything you need while you're here, use the card."

"Okay, I can do that."

His gaze stalls on my sandals. "Are you walking?"

"Just to the bus stop," I say to reassure him that it's no trouble.

Still, he shakes his head like that won't work.

"Take my car. The keys are next to my wallet."

There's no argument from me. Using his car will make it much easier for me to transport groceries. I thank him and wave goodbye to Harper before heading back inside.

Now, I'm no sleuth, but I can't help myself. When I get his credit card out of his wallet, *oops*, his I.D. accidentally slips out too.

Luke Nathaniel Allen. His birthday is in September, and *oh wow*, he's nine years older than me.

Miles was only *eight* years older than me, though why that matters, I have no idea. Maybe it's my subconscious way of erecting clear boundaries for myself. I have obviously noticed Luke. A blind woman would notice Luke.

Now, that aside, I don't make the same mistake twice. Well, there were those times I tried the at-home wax kit, but *this* particular mistake I will not repeat. I've learned my lesson. Swooning over my older off-limits boss will only land me in hot water. I know this. All I have to do is close my eyes and I can still vividly see Angie and Miles pressed up against Fig & Olive's damn refrigerator, going at it. I do it now, as a reminder to myself, but that same sting isn't there. Truthfully, the betrayal was always lackluster compared to the inconvenience of having to find a new job and uproot my life. I wasn't heartbroken so much as annoyed by the whole situation. I don't want to do it again. So, from now on, every time I see Luke, I'll be picturing him in some kind of funny getup to counteract my burgeoning feelings for him. Big red clown nose. White bushy rabbit tail. Hot wax getting poured slowly over his naked body.

AH.

I grab his keys and credit card and get out of there.

Fortunately, to get to the grocery store, I only have to drive a car worth more than my parents' entire net worth. Luke owns some kind of special edition Range Rover. No Corolla or Camry for Mr. Big League. Because I'm pathetically poor, I don't even know how to open the driver's side door at first. The handle is flush with the side of the car. I wave my hand in front of it like it's a paper towel dispenser in a mall bathroom, but nothing happens, so I wave faster, harder.

Ned, of course, walks by and sees me doing this.

He says nothing, just pins me with an exasperated glare before continuing on his way, his cat trailing behind him with its taunting orange tail. I'm too annoyed to take stock of whether he still has his rake in hand, and by the time I remember to turn and check, he's gone. Dammit.

Out of other options, I ingeniously press unlock on the car's key fob, and the door handle springs out all nice and nifty. Simple as that.

"It wasn't unlocked!" I shout for Ned's benefit.

Once I slide into the smooth black upholstery, I notice how hard my hands are shaking.

To be clear, I have my license; my parents insisted on it even though we barely drive in the city. My uncle Antonio was the one who taught me how to drive. He was patient with me then, and I pretend he's in the car with me now as I head down Ocean Drive at a snail's pace. People lay on their horns, and I wave so they'll go around.

"I'M NOT GOING ANY FASTER!"

The grocery store is less than a mile away, and yet it takes me twenty minutes to get there. When I park and turn off the car, the entire population of the Hamptons sighs with relief.

EIGHT

LUKE

I'M GETTING ready for dinner after swimming with
Harper most of the day. When my sister calls, I've just showered and have my towel wrapped around my waist. I put her
on speakerphone and toss my phone on the bed after I
answer it.

"Hey, can you hear me? I'm getting ready for dinner. I
need to shave and stuff."

"Yeah, it's fine. How's the house? How's Harper?"

"Good. I'll let you FaceTime with her after we eat. I bet
she'll want to show you how she set up her Barbies in her
room."

"Cool, yeah, have her call me."

There's a soft knock on my bedroom door, followed by,
"Luke? Sorry to bother you. I cannot for the life of me get this
jar open."

I look down at my current state of undress. "Uh, just a
second!"

"Who's that?" Tate asks, loudly enough that Chloe must
hear her through the closed bedroom door because she
responds right away.

"NEVER MIND!" she shouts.

Oh hell. I rush over to whip open the door so this situation doesn't turn from bad to worse, never mind that I'm still in my towel. Hopefully this exchange will be so brief Chloe won't notice.

I open the door, take the jar of pesto out of her hand, and pop that lid open on the first try.

Chloe's eyes widen like I've just displayed a superpower. Then her apologetic gaze catches mine.

"I heard a woman's voice. I didn't realize you were busy…"

"EW!" Tate groans.

Chloe looks to the phone on my bed with confusion.

I scratch the side of my jaw. There's some scruff there that I was about to trim. There also might be a smile I'm having a hard time fighting back. "I'm just talking to my sister while I get ready for dinner."

"Hi!" Tate shouts on cue.

"Oh." Chloe shakes her head. Then she tacks on, "*Hi!* I'm Chloe."

"I'm Tate."

Chloe's eyes drift from the phone, to me, down to my towel, then back to the phone. A red blush creeps steadily up her neck.

"Well, cool. See you around!"

"Bye!"

Chloe's already halfway down the hall before I close the door and walk back to retrieve my phone. I recognize immediately that it's in my best interest to take my sister off speakerphone. In fact, I've only just managed it before she starts taunting me like a middle school bully.

"Ooo, who's *Chloooo-ee*?"

"My employee."

"Oh."

Her disappointment is swift. Silence fills the air.

Then, "Are you sure you're not lying?"

"Why would I lie?"

"To get out of having to give me details about your love life."

"Sadly for you, that's not the case. No information to pass along. Chloe is my new employee out in the Hamptons. Nothing more."

"Is she young?"

"Three years older than you."

"Oh! Is she cute?"

I go back into the bathroom so I can start shaving. "Not answering that."

"SHE'S CUTE!"

"Hanging up."

My finger hovers over the red END button just as she screams desperately, "*LUKE! TELL ME! IS SHE CUTE?!*"

When I head to the kitchen a little while later, Chloe won't look me in the eye. In fact, she won't even turn fully in my direction.

"Good evening. Hi. There's some chilled white wine open over there." She points toward the kitchen island while she continues working hard at the stove, tending multiple pots and pans. "The sommelier at the grocery store recommended it to me. *Yes*, there was a sommelier at the grocery store, and not just a teenage employee hanging in the wine aisle, hoping to mooch a bottle off someone. This guy trained at a school in France, *Union de la Sommellerie Française*. I mean, I butchered that, but you get the idea. It's good."

"Chloe."

"Hmm?" she asks while she aggressively stirs and stirs and stirs something on the stove. Whatever it is, surely it's mixed by now.

"Sorry about that. It was inappropriate."

She looks over her shoulder, all fake innocence. "What? Oh! *That?* No big deal at all. Cool to meet your sister. Glad to see you ditched the towel for some jeans. I, for one, think you could have pulled it off with the right shirt, but to each their own."

I lose the battle with myself and laugh. I mean, I have to. Very rarely is a person the perfect combination of smart and silly.

Chloe whips around to face me fully, astonishment evident on her face.

"First laugh unlocked. That felt good."

"I'm sure you'll get another. You're funny."

That endearing red blush is back. "Thank you. I don't get that often."

"No?"

She shakes her head, and a few more pieces of brown hair fall out of the messy bun piled on the top of her head.

"I get a lot of 'You're so nice,' which is annoying because like anyone can be nice. It takes no intelligence to be nice. But funny? That's a real compliment."

The oven timer beeps, and she dashes toward it.

"How can I help?" I ask, already stepping toward her.

"No! Absolutely not. This is my job. Go drink wine. There's a cheeseboard too, just a little something to nibble on. I have a lot planned for you and Harper so I didn't want to ruin your appetites beforehand."

Harper comes barreling into the kitchen wearing mismatched pajamas, her hair still damp from her shower.

"It smells so good in here!"

It does. It reminds me of my mom's kitchen during the holidays, that rich fragrant smell of good food being prepared by skilled hands. When I'm away from Texas for too long, I miss her homecooked meals like nothing else. I've tried to get better at cooking myself. I'm not an idiot; I know how to follow a recipe. It's just not something I'm naturally good at, and I don't really have the time or desire to branch out, so the same few meals get rotated nonstop. I know at this point, Harper's as sick of spaghetti as I am.

"Thanks, Harper," Chloe says, waving her over. "Want to come see what I have cooking? Actually, I could use your help with something important."

Harper puffs with pride. "Really?"

"Yes. I just took this strawberry crisp out of the oven, and I absolutely *need* a taste tester."

"Okay!"

I watch Chloe carefully dip a spoon into the edge of the dessert and then blow on the bite to ensure it's cooled down enough before she passes it off to Harper.

Harper—my picky eater—takes the bite without hesitation, then her eyes squeeze shut as she savors it.

"It's *so* good, Chloe!"

"Ms. Chloe," I remind her.

Chloe beams. "I'm glad you like it. Strawberries are in season right now, and I bought a big ol' carton of them at the store. Tomorrow, I have plans to make a strawberry cake."

Harper passes the spoon back. "Can I help you make it?! I like baking! Can I have an apron like yours too? Only mine could be purple and pink and there could be a unicorn right here."

Chloe fields her questions like a pro, mostly deferring them my way with "If your dad says it's okay," and then she enlists Harper to help put the finishing touches on the table. "I picked these flowers from the garden. Put them wherever you think they'd look best."

It's so natural watching them together. It reminds me of how Harper is with my mom and my sister. Maria's good with her too, but she's older, and while she's incredibly reliable and trustworthy, she can be a little stern. It's probably good for Harper in the end. I can think of a thousand ways to raise a brat in this private-school-trust-fund-baby world I've found myself in.

I like that Chloe seems to be good with Harper. Still, I haven't fully come to terms with the fact that there will be someone else living in the house with us this summer, not quite intruding but *becoming* part of our time together, for better or worse. If you'd asked me before I left the city if I wanted to have a live-in caretaker and chef with us this summer, I would have said absolutely not. These months are about taking it slow and being with Harper, just her and me. We have a lot of lost time to catch up on from my travel days with the Pinstripes.

It was tricky though, finding Chloe here in the middle of the night. I couldn't kick her out then, and by this morning, it was as if the ball was already rolling. I would have felt like an asshole turning down her proposal and telling her to pack her bags.

But now, when Harper asks Chloe to stay and eat dinner with us, it feels like one step too far, and I'm relieved when Chloe shakes her head before I have to be the bad guy.

"That's really nice of you to offer, Harper, but you know what? I'm going to take dinner back to my room and clean up a little. I'm a mess! I think I have strawberries in my hair."

She bends down and insists Harper check for her.

Chloe does look like she's spent the last few hours in the kitchen, but she doesn't look like a mess. Far from it. She's still wearing her sundress beneath her linen apron. Her cheeks are naturally flushed against her tan complexion. She's barefoot and beautiful. I've seen women dressed to the nines after sitting in a hair and makeup chair for five hours, and they don't hold a candle to Chloe.

As if aware that my thoughts have drifted toward an unprofessional place, her attention shifts to me. The light in her eyes doesn't dull, but the edges of her smile grow slightly more guarded.

"Just let me know when you guys are done and I can come do the dishes. I tried to clean up as I cooked, but—"

I shake my head. "Harper and I will do the dishes."

Harper nods enthusiastically. "That's one of the tasks on

my chore chart. We didn't bring it with us, it's in the city, but it's really cool. I spin it and it tells me what job I have that week. If I finish all the tasks before Dad reminds me, I get to pick a little treat from a basket. I got scratch-and-sniff stickers last week!"

Chloe nods appreciatively, looking back at me. "That's a cool idea."

"My sister came up with it," I lie.

Why the hell did I lie?

She pats the front of her apron. "Right, well, you two take a seat, and I'll bring the last dish over then make myself scarce."

Harper pouts slightly, likely because she doesn't want to lose the opportunity to hound Chloe with a million more questions, but she ultimately does as she's asked.

Chloe flits around the kitchen, hurrying over to place a glass of milk in front of Harper and a glass of white wine in front of me. Then she brings over the last serving dish of food before standing back to present her meal.

"Okay, so we have a roasted vegetable salad with feta and a pesto vinaigrette; roasted shrimp with garlic, lemon, and herbs; and pasta with a sauce I made from tomatoes straight from the garden. They're so delicious. Harper, there's a cheeseboard too with a few things you might like."

"I'll eat the pasta and the shrimp and cheese, but I don't like vegetables," Harper declares haughtily, like she's an empress exiling vegetables from her realm.

"She'll try a bite of everything," I reassure Chloe. "It looks great. Thank you."

Chloe bows forward gently then claps her hands together. "*Bon appétit!*"

NINE

CHLOE

EVEN EATING with the *Real Housewives* on in the background doesn't make me feel less lonely in my room. This isolation is new for me. I grew up in a tiny apartment with a family for whom the word privacy meant absolutely nothing. Up until a few weeks ago, I spent most of my waking hours in a restaurant kitchen, surrounded by dozens of opinionated coworkers at all times. Even outside of work, I had Miles.

Now, I have Kyle Richards and Lisa Rinna and it's just not the same. Their on-screen fights don't elicit the same feelings of togetherness as the thoughtful barbs Ernesto and Michael would sling back and forth to each other across the kitchen at Fig & Olive. Those two really knew how to go at it. I miss them.

I eat fast, both because I'm hungry as hell and because my dinner is delicious. I knocked it out of the park (baseball reference for Luke's benefit) on my first night. Once he gets a bite of my strawberry crisp, he'll realize he can never live without me. In a strictly *culinary* sense, of course.

After the episode of *Real Housewives* ends, I shower and indulge in the good water pressure. That's the real luxury rich people have. Back at my parents' apartment, showering feels like you're standing underneath the slow trickle from a garden hose that's almost shut off. This shower is blasting away dirt and grime that's probably been lurking in my crevices for the better part of a decade.

It's so good I linger longer than I should. It's a half hour before I towel off and slip into my pajamas.

I need to take my plate back down to the kitchen, but I'm waiting to make sure Luke and Harper are done with their meal first. I don't want to interrupt them. It doesn't take a rocket scientist to realize Luke wants very little to do with me, and I get it. If I were as famous as he is, I wouldn't want some random person hanging around my family or me either.

At my window, I reach out to draw the drapes closed now that the sun has long since set, but I pause when I see Luke sitting on a lounge chair, illuminated by the warm glow of the pool lights. He's nursing a beer and staring out at the property in the distance. It's later than I thought, close to 9:00 PM. Harper's probably in bed. He must be tired after a long day of single parenting.

"No, Dad, I am *not* trying those vegetables" was the last thing I heard Harper say before I left the kitchen earlier, and it made me laugh under my breath.

Harper seems like a seriously great kid, but parenting is parenting. I don't envy the fact that he has to do it alone. I'd like to know where Harper's mom is, but I don't think I'll be getting that information anytime soon.

Luke's phone lights up with an incoming call on the table beside him. He checks it then lets it go to voicemail before placing his phone back on the table, screen down.

I can't help but be curious.

Guys like him are usually living it up: traveling the world, taking full advantage of their VIP status in life. Maybe he did that in his younger days and has outgrown that life, or maybe he was never that way to begin with. Luke doesn't strike me as the partying type, but that's probably because I've only seen him around his daughter.

I could look into it. Google is merely a few taps away, but I won't.

Already the idea of using his fame to my advantage leaves me with a gross feeling in the pit of my stomach. I'd hate if people could Google me and find all sorts of private information I didn't put out there myself. Public person or not, the guy seems to value his privacy, so I'll give it to him.

Though I'm sad to do it, I close the drapes and block him from view.

For three days, we continue on like this, with me mostly keeping to myself, cooking, cleaning, making myself useful. I start to post a proposed menu on the fridge in the morning so Luke can make any changes if he wants to. By the third day, I already have a request.

Can we get those roasted shrimp again? And I finished the strawberry cake last night…

I practically float off the earth.

Since I'm not around at mealtimes, I don't know what Luke thinks about my cooking. I mean Harper has been raving about it, but Luke's extremely reserved compared to his daughter. If we bump into each other around the house, it's "Hi, how are you?" or "Lunch will be ready in about thirty minutes!" or "I'm headed to the store if you need anything!"

I try to be careful with Harper. It's a balancing act. If she and I had it our way, we'd be together all day, BFF status. I crave her company—*any* company, really—but Luke's never all that enthusiastic about us hanging out together. I try to let her down gently when she invites me to join them for meals or accompany them into town. I did let her help me make the strawberry cake though, as promised. I told her how I fell in love with baking because of Ms. Paulette and all the time I spent sneaking around the Plaza, and she told me all about school.

"I was the tallest girl in the entire first grade," she proclaimed proudly.

"Oh yeah?"

"Yes, and I'm really fast too. *And* athletic. I just finished playing Little League and I hit *three* homers this season. That's more than any of the boys hit."

"People are hitting home runs in Little League?!"

This is frankly astonishing to me.

"Not people, *me*."

"And do you like school?"

She shrugged. "It's tricky sometimes. Reading doesn't come that easy for me, but Dad says that's normal. We work on it together a little every day. Even when he was gone more, we would talk on the phone and I would have to read a few pages aloud to him, no matter if I was tired or in a bad mood. Do you like to read?"

"I love it."

"Yeah, me too," she said as she picked up the frosting spatula. "Could I…"

She asked the question timidly.

"Lick it?" I finished for her.

She looked surprised, like I'd just read her mind.

I gave her a conspiratorial wink. "Go for it."

I'm starting to settle into the quiet life here a little more. I went on a run yesterday.

Well…I put on running shoes and workout clothes and went outside with every intention of running, but I ended up walking most of the way and it took me forty minutes to go two miles, so does that really count? Who cares. I'm going again today, and I'm going for three miles come hell or high water!

I also made a friend.

It's the sommelier from the grocery store—though to

continue calling it a grocery store is a bit misleading. It's like calling Chanel "just some place you can grab a purse". Bridgehampton Market is a luxury supermarket that focuses on niche, locally produced, organic foods at prices that routinely make me do a double take. We're talking $50 bottles of "specialty" barbecue sauce, $17 smoothies, $20 chocolate bars arranged neatly near the checkout. Luke didn't balk at the cost when I showed him the first receipt.

"I didn't realize it would be that expensive. I don't have a problem driving to the Stop & Shop, but their produce selection is lacking. I could still make it work though."

"No, this is fine. Yeah, prices are a little crazy, but that's the way everything is out here."

So Bridgehampton Market is where I head most days. Oliver is always there, steering patrons toward the best bottles of wine while wearing pressed khakis, a button-down, and swanky Italian loafers. He's nice, if a bit snobbish, until I make some offhand remark about one of the wines he recommends being a fan favorite at Fig & Olive.

"Oh, I love that restaurant. I always have a killer time getting reservations, but it's worth it for the dessert alone."

"That's me! I mean…it was. I used to be the pastry chef there."

He seemed skeptical at first, like it wasn't possible that I, a girl with an untidy braid and a mustard stain on her shirt, could possibly have been the source of such delicious delicacies.

"What are you doing out here? Vacationing?"

"Working, actually. Private chef gig."

His brows rose in shock. "I have no doubt it's a lucrative setup, but leaving a place like Fig & Olive?" He shook his head like I was crazy.

Even without getting into all the lurid details, it was easy enough to explain my exit from the popular restaurant. "It's a hard world to be in…"

He held up his hands to reassure me. "Hey, you don't have to tell me. Why do you think I'm a sommelier here rather than at a place in the city? I prefer the hours. Though I kind of straddle both worlds—I consult on the side for a few restaurants around here. Have you tried Pierre's?"

"No. Worth it?"

"It's fantastic. I helped curate their wine offerings. My friends and I are actually headed there this Thursday. We're a foodie crowd—I'm sure you'd fit right in. Want to join? Here, let me grab your number really quick. I see Mrs. Kilpatrick heading over, and once she gets ahold of me, it'll be thirty minutes before I can surface for air."

So that's how I made my first friend here. Oh, second if you count Ned. *Ha.*

My fifth day on the job, I have my AirPods in and I'm jamming out when I walk into the laundry room to fold clothes, only to find that Luke's beat me to it.

"Hey! You don't have to do that."

He shrugs as he continues, "It's fine. You probably don't need to be folding my boxer briefs anyway."

"It's no big deal. They just look like black shorts."

I almost sound convincing.

Truthfully, it *has* been slightly awkward doing Luke's laundry. His workout shirts and shorts are soaked in sweat and drenched in his deodorant and natural musk by the time they make it into the hamper. While I've yet to press the fabric to my face and inhale deeply like a no-holds-barred stalker, I have given the air a hard sniff a time or two.

"Guess it's only appropriate. I've touched your underwear too."

"WHAT?!" The question sputters out of me.

I swear he almost, *almost* looks pleased by my reaction to his casual statement.

"You left a pair in my bathroom the first night you arrived."

"Did I? Where are they now?" I sound panicked by the prospect that they might still be in his possession.

"I put them in your laundry hamper."

I shake my head as I walk into the laundry room and start to get to work beside him. "Jeez, good thing you don't have an HR department. They'd have a field day with me."

"True. Pink thong aside, I think you pulling a knife on Ned would have gotten you axed day one."

So it was my pink thong.

My itty bitty silky pink thong.

"LUKE!"

It's the first time I've said his name, and it charges the air with tension.

My heart's racing like I'm on a first date. A seriously good one.

If I ever want to be able to look at my boss the same way, we cannot keep discussing my *delicates*, so I reroute us.

"Why were you in here doing the laundry anyway?"

He shrugs. "Habit. Pass me that shirt, will you? When I was on the road a lot, it was just me."

I respond with disbelieving side-eye. "You're telling me the MLB doesn't spring for maids and laundry service?"

"It's not as easy as it sounds. I don't generally like people in my space. I've had things stolen, information fed to tabloids…that kind of thing. I can keep things tidy enough on my own."

"God, I can't imagine that way of life. I dated a guy who was marginally famous, at least in the restaurant world, and that was hard enough."

"Not with him anymore?"

"*No*," I say vehemently.

I catch him raising his eyebrows, but he doesn't say anything else on the subject.

There's a beat of silence as we match up different pairs of socks. I swap him a purple one and he hands me a gray one.

We are so ridiculously careful to not make any skin-to-skin contact as we do it. We have the concentration of a bomb squad picking between red and blue wires.

"Just wondering…I am *allowed* to go out, right? After I've finished my duties for the day, I mean. I'm not, like, confined to this house and the supermarket, am I?"

"Of course you can go out," he says, sounding insulted by the idea that he'd ever say otherwise.

I laugh. "Right. Okay, good."

"Big plans?"

Oliver texted me this morning about having dinner at Pierre's. He and two other friends are heading there around 8:30 PM and can add on one more to their reservation if I'm interested. I haven't texted him back yet because I've been too chicken to ask Luke if it's okay if I go.

"I might go to this dinner."

"With a guy from the city?"

"A new friend from here, actually."

I almost clarify that it's not just the two of us going, but it seems odd to point it out. What does Luke care whether it's one guy or ten guys? He's just trying to make polite conversation; he's not prying into my dating life.

We finish off the last pair of socks and step back to admire our neat piles of clean clothes. Then instead of leaving, Luke turns and props a hip against the counter, blocking my exit.

"Do you need to take my car?"

"I'm sure I can bum a ride."

He nods, mulling this over with a look of slight annoyance. I think he's fighting back the urge to give me his two cents, but instead he settles for asking where I'm going to dinner.

"Pierre's?"

I say it like a question, wondering if he's been there.

"Oh yeah? That place has the best onion rings." He pushes off the counter, about to head out. "Should be fun."

TEN
LUKE

OTHER THAN THE strawberry cake earlier in the week, Chloe hasn't enlisted Harper's help much in the kitchen, but Thursday afternoon—a few hours after I helped her fold laundry—she knocks on my open office door.

"Have a sec?"

She's wearing jean shorts and a white t-shirt with her apron on top. Today's apron is covered in a ladybug print. Yesterday's was blue and green polka dots.

I nod, and she wrings her hands as she begins, "I totally understand that you're here this summer to spend time with your daughter and I should make myself scarce…"

Well, when she puts it like that, I sound like a bit of an ass.

"But I thought I would ask, on the off chance you say it's okay…I'm planning on making pizza tonight before I head to Pierre's, and I thought it could be fun if Harper helped. Pizza is a good way to introduce kids to cooking. There are no exact measurements required and she doesn't have to be scared about making a mess since I'll set up everything outside. She did great the other day with the strawberry cake, and she seems really eager to learn."

She finishes all of this with a relieved sigh like she's been rehearsing this speech in her head all morning. That's how badly she wants me to let Harper join her.

I should probably still say no and keep the erected walls exactly as formidable as they have been, but I find myself agreeing anyway.

"Yeah, okay. That's fine."

Chloe's responding smile could melt snow. "Okay! Awesome!" She darts down the hall then curses and flies back to reappear in my open doorway. "Obviously you can help too. I'm not trying to exclude you or anything. I just figured you have better things to do."

I close out the game footage I was watching on my computer.

"I could probably help for a bit."

When Chloe tells Harper she'll be acting as her official sous chef tonight, she accompanies the announcement with the unveiling of an apron she must have picked up in town.

"I know you wanted there to be a unicorn on it, but I couldn't find that on such short notice. However, this apron *is* pink and purple! So I checked two boxes at least."

"I love it!" Harper exclaims, running over to take it from her so she can tug it on over her head right away. "I'll look just like you. A real chef. Dad, take our picture!"

Oh okay, great. Yeah, let me snap a picture of my hot employee posing next to my daughter so I can just keep that on my camera roll. Sounds good.

I do it, and then Harper asks for another.

"Wait, I want to do a silly one too."

Am I in hell?

"Yup. Got it," I lie, already pocketing my phone.

Chloe looks at me, and it feels like she can read my thoughts. Can she tell how strange this is? How simultaneously natural and *unnatural* it feels to have her as part of our small family unit?

There's a pizza oven outside adjacent to the outdoor

kitchen and grill, and that's where Chloe has set everything up for us. She proceeds to run through it all. There are fresh toppings and herbs from the garden, homemade crust, and a sauce she learned to make from her Nonna.

Harper shapes her dough into a heart with Chloe's help. I keep mine the standard circle, but I lay out my pepperoni slices like laces on a baseball, which gets a round of applause from Chloe when she comes over to inspect it.

"*Very* creative."

I raise a taunting brow. "Why do I feel like you're my kindergarten teacher praising my scribbles?"

She acts affronted by the idea that her enthusiasm might not be genuine. "What? *No.* It's cute. I mean sure, the distribution of toppings is completely thrown off by the design, but I'm no critic."

She tosses me a wink before answering Harper's call for help with arranging her shredded cheese. It's several seconds before I realize I'm still staring at her long after she's walked away.

After all the pizzas are out of the oven (the good ones Chloe made and the shitty ones we concocted), Chloe motions toward the house. "Okay, enjoy, you guys! I need to go clean up the kitchen and then shower or I'm going to be late."

"Where are you going?" Harper asks, sounding utterly dejected at the idea that Chloe's leaving us.

"She has dinner plans," I supply, trying to save Chloe the trouble.

Harper sits up in her chair, suddenly interested.

"With who? You never eat with us! How come you're going to eat with someone else?"

The intricacies of Chloe's working and living arrangement are utterly lost on my six-year-old.

"Chloe has a date," I explain, hoping that will solve it once and for all.

Harper looks at me like I'm a complete idiot. "So? *We*

could take her on a date. Dad, don't be such a slob—go put something fancy on and we can go for ice cream, my treat. I have money in my play purse. What does ice cream cost? A dollar? Dollar fifty?"

Chloe doesn't even bother trying to quell her laughter. She's enjoying this far too much.

"Not how it works, kiddo. She can't ditch her friends."

Harper shakes her head. "*We're* her friends."

Chloe looks to me and mouths, "What do I do?"

I wave her off, and when she escapes into the kitchen, I lean over the porch table to explain things to Harper. "Chloe is an employee here. Yes, she's our friend too, but we can't force her to hang out with us."

Harper crosses her arms and leans back in her chair to sulk. "It's because of you and your attitude. That's why she's always running away from us as fast as she can."

"My attitude?"

"Yes! You get quiet when she's around, and sometimes you act like you're better than she is. It's exactly how Amy S. acts when I try to sit by her at lunch at school."

"Okay, well let's just enjoy the pizza, yeah? And later we can watch a movie. Your choice."

Harper grumbles under her breath, only mildly placated by this plan. In fact, she can't resist throwing out one more barb.

"And for the record, she's a way better cook than you, Dad."

"Yeah, well, like I said, it's her job."

"Still, you could never make pizza this good."

Thanks, kid.

Later, we're on the couch, watching *Moana* and sharing a bowl of popcorn with M&Ms when Chloe's light footsteps sound on the stairs.

Harper perks up and spins around so she can poke her face over the back of the couch.

"Wow!" she exclaims.

Chloe's effervescent laugh makes my chest tighten.

"You look *amazing*," Harper tells her. "I've never seen you with makeup on."

I narrow my eyes on the TV, concentrating on the maniacal singing crab like my life depends on it.

"You like my dress?"

"I love it."

"I'll let you borrow it," Chloe teases.

"Okay!"

Chloe makes it down to the bottom stair then walks right behind the couch on her way into the kitchen. Every hair on the back of my neck stands on end as she passes by, and still, my eyes are on the damn Disney movie. I don't think I've so much as blinked in the last few minutes.

Then Harper's bony elbow collides with my rib.

"Aren't you going to say something to Chloe, Dad? You're just like *ignoring* her!" she hisses.

While she might think her voice is quiet, it's not.

"This is what I meant. You can't just sit there in silence. Tell Chloe she looks pretty."

Chloe laughs again. "Harper, give your dad a break. Besides, it's enough that *you* think I'm pretty."

"Dad!"

Dammit.

I'm prepared to whip around and throw out a "You look pretty" remark as fast as I can then refocus my attention on the movie once again. Instead, I turn back, and my voice stalls in my throat.

Chloe stands in the kitchen doorway with her long brown hair tumbling down around her shoulders. On one side, it's tucked enchantingly behind one ear. She's wearing dark mascara that highlights her already large eyes, pink gloss on her lips that makes them look edible, and some blush high on her cheekbones that gives her a healthy glow. She's poured herself into a thigh-length spaghetti-strap dress in a sky blue fabric that's set off by her olive skin tone.

Fuck me.

That's the first thing that pops into my little pea brain.

Chloe fidgets under my intense scrutiny. Her features scrunch up in confusion as her smile spreads just a little wider.

"*Dad.*" Harper reprimands me again.

I clear my throat and barely manage to choke out my words. "You look beautiful."

Her chest and neck flush with color.

"Thank you, Mr. Allen."

Mr. Allen.

I'm her boss, and she's reminding me of that.

"Have a good time at dinner," I say, my voice taking on a stern edge all of a sudden. Then I turn back around, reach for the remote, and turn up the volume on the movie.

When Chloe leaves and the front door closes behind her, Harper shifts to face me, no doubt prepared to give me more unsolicited advice, but I hold up my hand.

"Not now, kid. Let's just watch the movie."

She sighs and steals the popcorn bowl from me, punishing me by taking all the warm M&Ms at the bottom before I can get to them.

Once I put Harper to bed, I busy myself with a few emails, clean up the last of the dishes in the kitchen, and then tidy up around the house.

It's 9:45 PM.

Chloe probably won't be back for a while, and I can't go to sleep because I forgot to give her a spare key and the alarm code. I don't want to lock her out, and I don't feel comfortable going to sleep with our front door unlocked and the alarm not set. Not with Harper in the house.

So you see, my reasons for staying up, sitting on the couch, watching ESPN, are sound. I don't even have to wrestle with my subconscious over the idea that I might be staying up to wait for Chloe for different reasons.

Nope.

It's 10:16 PM when the front door opens. Chloe quietly tiptoes down the hall toward the living room.

"Oh! I was hoping you'd still be awake."

God. Why do her words make all my blood run south? It's an innocent enough statement, but it *could* be nefarious if only she wanted it to be.

I reach for the remote to turn off the TV just as I turn toward her. It's easier to see her now, knowing what to expect, bracing myself for her charm.

Or so I think.

When she produces a small white takeout container from behind her back and waggles it in my direction, all bets are off.

"Onion rings," she proclaims with a knowing twinkle in her eyes.

"You're kidding."

She bites down on her bottom lip to quell her smile. "I waited to order them until we were about to leave, so they're still hot and everything."

"Oh fuck," I say, tossing my throw blanket off my legs and standing up to take the container from her. I'm in the kitchen with that lid open in record time. I grab ketchup from the fridge and enter fried food heaven with a moan of delight.

Chloe followed me into the kitchen, and she stands on the other side of the island, watching me eat with big round eyes.

"What did I do to deserve these?" I ask once I've polished off the first one.

"Who says you had to earn them?"

I cock one eyebrow. "So you routinely do things solely out of the kindness of your heart?"

"I saw them on the menu and thought of you and…" She shrugs. "I couldn't resist."

I grab a second onion ring and wag it in her direction. "Let me tell you, you keep going above and beyond like this and you might just earn yourself the title of employee of the month."

A laugh bursts out of her. She slips her purse off her shoulder, drops it on the counter, and leans toward me.

Saint that I am, I don't even look down the top of her dress despite the fact that it's gaping.

"Does the award come with any perks?" she teases.

Chloe, Chloe, Chloe. Don't make this harder than it has to be.

I sidestep her question, aware that it would only lead us down a dangerous path.

"How was dinner?"

Her shoulders sag with disappointment, like she was hoping I'd continue her thread of banter. "Fine."

"And how was your guy?"

"Fine."

I want to pester her for more details. Who is he? Some trust fund schmuck clad in boat shoes and a Ralph Lauren sweater? How'd she even meet him so fast?

"The restaurant was romantic. Have you ever been there on a date?"

"*Date?*" I ask with laughter in my voice before popping the second onion ring in my mouth.

"Yes, like when two people who are mutually attracted to each other get dolled up to enjoy a meal or a drink together."

"Ah, so *that's* a date. I forgot—it's been so long since I've been on one."

"Oh? You're telling me *Luke Allen* has a hard time finding a date?" She rolls her eyes to emphasize her point.

"I can find a willing woman to fill a night, sure. A date is something else entirely."

"So you're really picky?"

"I'm not looking for love right now. Harper is my full-time

focus."

She nods. "Of course. That's admirable."

Her gaze slides to her purse, and for a moment, I think she's going to call it a night.

I'm not prepared to let that happen just yet. "What about you?"

Her gaze flits back up to me. "What?"

"What are you looking for? Love? With this guy?"

She huffs out an exasperated breath. "*No.*"

"Why do you sound so put off by the idea?"

She stares at her finger as she draws circles on the counter. When she replies, she sounds slightly embarrassed to admit, "I just got out of a weird, bad relationship. He was my boss at the restaurant, and a little older, and there were approximately a million reasons I should not have been with him."

Her older boss.

My stomach twists into a painful angry knot.

"Your boss? Inappropriate, no?"

She looks up at me from beneath her eyelashes. "Don't judge me. It happens all the time. He was impossible to ignore, kind of a celebrity in the food world, and he was really persistent."

"So he's an asshole," I say with a hard edge to my tone.

"*Luke.*"

I sigh and ease up. "Why didn't it work out then? Aside from the fact that he shouldn't have been with you in the first place."

She slices me in two with a pointed stare. "What did I say about judging? Anyway…oh yeah, why didn't it work out? It's simple: he was a terrible boyfriend, but before I could break it off with him, I caught him cheating on me, so that made the ending nice and quick."

She says it all like it's no big deal, just a simple resolution to a simple relationship when in fact it sounds pretty messed up.

"You caught him?"

"Yup. It was in the restaurant kitchen. Hot and heavy. Better sex than he and I ever had from the looks of it."

We're so past the point of propriety I can't even make out how long ago we crossed the line. Talking about her sex life? Asking about her ex-boyfriend? This is just as inappropriate as the relationship I'm chiding her about.

Enough.

I slide the onion ring container off the counter and stow it in the fridge.

"I'm sorry that happened. He sounds like a real asshole. You're better off."

She laughs. "Thanks for that. Practicing for when Harper comes home with a broken heart?"

I could throw up just thinking about Harper dating a scumbag like Chloe's ex.

She shakes her head. "Sorry, that was all probably…a lot. You didn't have to listen to me drone on like that."

The spaghetti strap on her dress slips off her shoulder as she grabs for her purse. It's nothing. Chloe fixes it right away, but it's just another reminder of how tightly wound I feel when she's around. Every little gesture, innocent as it may be, sends me into a tailspin.

"Yeah. Hey, I'm going to head down to the beach tomorrow with Harper. We'll spend the whole day there, I'm sure. There are a lot of places to grab food, so no need to worry about us. You can have the day off."

She looks startled by this announcement.

Maybe it seems as last minute as it actually is. I just plucked the idea out of thin air, but it makes sense. It would probably be a good idea for everyone involved to get some distance, put these feelings on ice.

Chloe just got out of a dysfunctional relationship with her older boss. If that's not a sign, I don't know what is.

ELEVEN

CHLOE

APPARENTLY, I have the day off, so I start by sleeping in until I can no longer ignore the blazing sun creeping through the sides of my drapes and Ned's odd hammering in the backyard. Still, I linger in bed, buried under my covers, reading until my grumbling stomach has had enough.

I fix myself buttered toast and a milky cup of coffee then take both to the kitchen's breakfast nook so I can sit and eat in the warmth of the bay window.

Harper and Luke already left for the beach. I heard them getting ready to head out the door while I was still in bed. Luke was calling out orders.

"You better use the restroom before we leave."

"I can just go in the ocean!"

"Harper!"

"It doesn't even bother the fish!"

On the kitchen counter, there's a pile of beach toys that apparently didn't make the cut: a few cracked sand pails, a shovel that's missing a handle, one of Harper's mermaid Barbies that has somehow lost its head.

For some absurd reason, I feel left out that they're

enjoying the beach without me and I'm stuck here, forgotten like that headless doll.

This job is so weird, the lines so easily crossed. I have a hard time differentiating work time from personal time, professionally appropriate conversations from friendly banter. It doesn't help that my small, easily ignored crush on Luke is quickly morphing into this hugely inconvenient elephant in the room. I can no longer get away with ignoring my attraction to him, so I don't even try. He's hot—there, that's been established. He's also oddly charming and more personable than I would expect a celebrity athlete to be. Okay, so who cares? He's still my boss.

My boss!

Instead of slowly savoring my coffee, I toss it back like it's a shot of hard liquor. Then I tear through my toast with quick aggressive bites before getting on with my day.

Dinner at Pierre's was exactly as I told Luke last night: fine. The food was fantastic and fancy and the company was entertaining enough. Oliver's friends were excited to hear about my background both at Fleur de Sel and Spiced Pear as much as Fig & Olive.

"I read a story about Miles Wilson in *The New Yorker*. It mentioned he can be a real asshole in the kitchen," Oliver mentioned. "Is that true?"

Miles *was* a terror in the kitchen sometimes, but never with me.

"If you got your work done, he mostly laid off," I replied, unwilling to divulge any more details than that. The restaurant world is small, and while I might be taking a hiatus from working in the city for now, I want to be careful not to burn any bridges permanently by running my mouth to veritable strangers. All I need is for word to get back to my old boss…

It's still brisk in the mornings here, which I love. I want to take full advantage, so after breakfast, I head out on a run. Then I spend time in the garden, harvesting huge sun-ripened tomatoes and zucchinis. After, I fertilize, water, and clean up the beds a bit so it's easier to tell what's growing where. A few times, I need to get tools from the backyard shed. Ned, of course, hates this.

"I've got it all organized in here" is his explanation for why he doesn't want me invading his space.

I look into the shed to find it's a complete war zone. There's no rhyme or reason to any of it.

"Ned, I could help you clean this up."

"Now, don't start changing it. I like how I have it."

"But you can't actually see anything in here. It's a mess."

A hammer that was precariously placed on the edge of a table falls to the ground, punctuating my point.

It takes some arguing, but I do manage to convince him to let me organize the shed.

"Just a little," I promise.

It ends up taking me two hours. By the time everything is in a state of cleanliness I deem acceptable, I have dirt caked under every fingernail, dust in my hair, and enough spider webs sticking to my body that I can't help a shiver of disgust from running down my spine.

"What do you think?" I ask Ned as we stand back to examine my handiwork.

"It's okay," he says with a disgruntled frown.

"See how all your rakes and shovels are hanging nicely now, and your trowels are all set there. I bet you didn't realize you had six of them, did you?"

His glare tells me I'm not getting the thanks I'm searching for.

"Right."

Ned leaves me to go into town. Now I'm *alone* alone. Instead of showering, I change into my bikini and head straight for the pool. I swim a few laps and luxuriate in the water, floating on my back with my face tipped up toward the sun. I'm out there for an hour before I take a break, wrap a towel around my waist, and head into the kitchen.

Summer calls for focaccia bread, so I make two batches. One I'll let rest in the fridge until tomorrow like you're really supposed to. The other I'll bake today. While I wait for them to rise, I head back outside. I lie by the pool and read, only ever bothering to pry myself off the lounger when I get too overheated. I take another dip, then I check my focaccia and let it rise for another hour.

Once the dough is ready to go in the oven, I add some toppings. Though it's tempting to go overboard, I keep it simple so Harper won't be scared off. Just the universal favorites: olive oil, minced garlic, freshly chopped basil, thyme, and rosemary, and then a liberal sprinkle of coarse salt and freshly ground pepper. Already my mouth is watering thinking about taking the first savory bite.

It'll only need to bake for half an hour, so I stay inside and fix myself a big green salad for lunch with beans from the garden and enough tomatoes to have one on my fork for every bite.

My timer for my focaccia goes off right when I'm in the good part of my salad and my book: i.e. lover boy has finally admitted his feelings for the heroine and now he has to grovel and chase her. Ah, *bliss*.

I take a slice of bread and my book back out to the pool, where I read until the afternoon sun proves too powerful for my heavy lids. I turn on my stomach and close my eyes, promising myself I'll only be out for a few minutes.

Harper's face is the first thing I see when I stir awake hours later. Her little nose is nearly pressed right up to mine.

"It's okay, Dad—she's not dead!"

I startle and sit up. "*Dead?*"

Harper laughs and sits back on her heels. "Yeah, you were laying so weird."

"I was asleep."

She shrugs, unperturbed by the truth. "We went to the beach today."

"I can tell," I say, wiping sleep from my eyes.

I'm slightly disoriented. *What time is it?* I reach for my phone to check and see it's well past 7:00 PM. I also have three missed calls from my dad and a slew of texts from my mom. I tried to call them earlier while I was making my focaccia dough, but they were out at lunch. Knowing they're probably worried, I fire off a quick "All is good, I'll call later" text.

I press send on it just as Luke steps into the doorway looking like a true beach bum. He and Harper both got a lot of color today. His hair is still damp, his swim trunks and t-shirt both still sandy. Harper leaps to her feet, cutting back into view so she can tell me more about their day.

"It was so fun. My dad and I built a sandcastle almost as tall as me!"

"We did not," Luke corrects with a laugh.

"Okay, not that tall, but it *did* almost go up to my knee before it accidentally got washed away."

"Sounds awesome. I wish you'd snapped a picture so I could have seen it."

Her shoulders sag. "I know." Then she perks right back up again. "We ate hot dogs and French fries for lunch, and me and Dad both said we missed your cooking."

I peer over at Luke to see he's watching me, and upon hearing this, he nods, not bothering to refute Harper's claim. Pride stretches a smile across my face.

"Next time, maybe you can come with us and we can pack a picnic with your food."

I don't have the heart to tell her that likely won't be happening.

"Well are you hungry now? I could make you something."

"You have the day off," Luke reminds me. "No cooking."

I can't find the courage to meet his gaze again for some

reason—maybe it's the tousled hair, maybe it's the warm tan —so I tell my response to Harper instead. "Sorry to report, but I couldn't resist. There's some focaccia bread in the kitchen that will knock your socks off."

"Knock your socks off?" Harper repeats with a laugh of delight. "What does *that* mean?"

I stand up so I can show them the bread, and only then do I become acutely aware of how much of my body my bikini reveals.

"*Ooh*, I like your swimsuit. I want to wear a two-piece like that, but Dad says not until I'm older."

All eyes are on me, or so it feels, so I grab my towel and wrap it around my chest, grateful that it goes all the way to the top of my thighs.

"That sounds like a good rule. You want to protect your skin from the sun, and it's hard to do that in a two-piece."

I'm saying this because it's absolutely obvious that I've done what no Italian has done before: gotten a sunburn. My back feels hot and tight, and I wince when the scratchy towel rubs across my bare skin. Even so, I have no choice but to keep it on while in Luke's presence.

That's what I get for falling asleep on a lounge chair like some pasty uncle on a cruise ship.

"If it's any consolation, I got too much sun today too," Luke tells me as I lead Harper toward the kitchen to try the bread.

He must have caught my wince, or maybe my red back is visible even from space. Astronauts are up there saying, *Look, there's the Great Wall of China and that dumbass who fell asleep by the pool.*

"We'll be in a world of hurt later," I lament.

"I have some aloe around here somewhere."

Keeping his promise, he knocks on my bedroom door later that evening, after Harper's gone to bed. I'm in my bathroom, assessing the damage to my shoulders when I hear him through the door.

"Did you want this aloe, Chloe?"

"Yes!"

I rush to throw a t-shirt on, hissing as the cotton fabric rubs against my skin. The aloe will help.

I whip the door open and Luke stands there, tall and imposing, with the bottle of aloe cradled in his palm. With this offering in his hand, I swear he's never looked sexier.

"Need this?"

"*Yes,*" I sigh, greedily accepting it when he hands the bottle to me. "I've never been burned. This is horrible. My Italian ancestors are looking down and laughing at me."

He chuckles. "Hopefully you fare better than me. I had a hell of a time getting it on my back. I just kind of slapped it on blindly."

"Oh god. Here, I can help."

Without thinking, I motion for him to turn around, fully prepared to rub aloe cream all over him until Luke grimaces like he's uncomfortable and brings his hand up to rub the back of his neck.

"I don't think that's a good idea, Chloe."

I flush, doubly embarrassed, not only for being so thoughtless as to suggest it in the first place but also because of his rejection.

"Oh god, sorry," I rush out, worried I've put him in an awkward spot. "I wasn't trying to cross a line."

"No. It's just…you know, I'm trying to keep things semi-normal for you. Most jobs don't entail rubbing lotion on your creepy boss."

I frown. "You're not creepy."

His eyes look so sad when he replies, "But I am your boss."

Neither of us has a reply for that.

I look down, adjust the aloe bottle in my hand, and try to

swallow down my nerves. I only gather the courage to peer up at him again when he says my name.

"Chloe—"

I panic and hold out my hand. "Whatever you're about to say, don't. Let's just…let's keep things like they are, okay?"

I'm so scared of what's about to come out of his mouth. It could be anything: *Listen, weirdo, you've made this all really difficult; we've crossed a line; I don't feel comfortable having you in my home anymore.* Something like that is coming, I know it. It's why he looks so remorseful, like he's already queuing up his apology.

But fortunately, if he's planning to send me packing, I've apparently stalled him at least for another day because he nods in agreement. Then he steps back.

"Hopefully that helps," he says, pointing to the lotion.

I hold it up. "Yeah, it will. Thanks."

I close my door, squeeze my eyes shut, and try to figure out how it's possible to wipe the last few minutes from my memory.

TWELVE

LUKE

I GO to sleep with visions of Chloe in her bikini dancing in my head like she's the goddamn Sugar Plum Fairy in an X-rated rendition of *The Nutcracker*. I try a different position, rolling onto my side, but she's still there, hot as hell.

Worse, I'm not even remembering her with rose-colored glasses or dreamy delusions. She was absolutely sucker-punch-to-the-gut sexy in her white bikini. I must have made a complete fool of myself when we arrived back from the beach. Harper was chattering on with her by that lounge chair, but I doubt I put two words together: me, hi, beach, we, back.

I stumbled out onto the porch, saw her, and froze. It was all too much for my brain to compute at once: her bare skin, slender calves, curled toes. I looked at her stretched across the lounge chair like I was standing in front of the *Mona Lisa*, admiring every inch. Then I remembered that I was fawning over my very young employee in the presence of my child, and I gave myself a stern rebuke and looked away. Up to the sky, a swaying tree, a passing bird—I would have stared right at the sun if only it would have saved me from being an inappropriate asshole.

Less than twenty-four hours ago, Chloe confided in me about her last job, and it sounded like a really toxic situation. Now she's landed here—out of the frying pan and into the fire with me. I looked up her boss at Fig & Olive. Miles Wilson is older than Chloe, yes, but younger than me. *Younger.* How's that for a wakeup call?

I throw off my blanket and sit up, knowing my brain is intent on acting as a saboteur. If I keep lying here, daydreaming about Chloe in her bikini, I'll slide a hand past the waistband of my boxer briefs and give in to the fantasy then feel like an absolute jerk for it in the morning.

Instead, I head out to the kitchen for a late-night snack. There, resting on the counter, is Chloe's homemade focaccia bread. I tell myself I'll just cut off a bite, but I black out from the sheer pleasure of the taste and nearly eat half before I come to.

How does she do it? How does she touch food and make it so special?

The next day, after breakfast, Harper gathers us into the living room to proclaim that today, we all have one collective goal.

"*Lemonade stand,*" Harper says, swiping her hand across the air above her head like the words are printed on a marquee.

She has Chloe and me sitting side by side on the living room couch. We haven't so much as looked at each other since we sat down.

When Harper first called this "very important meeting!" I tried to sit on a chair in the corner. No. Harper needed us both on the couch so we could see her presentation clearly. Then when I tried to sit on the opposite end, far away from Chloe, Harper gave me a look that foreshadowed what an interesting time I'll have parenting her through her teenage years. She mouthed, "*Stop being weird!*"

"Okay, so here's the plan. We're going to do a real lemonade stand, not this *crap*—"

"*Harper.*"

"Not this *crud* you see from other kids with no business sense."

She slaps her marker against her presentation board. It's completely covered in drawings and schematics, logo ideas, and potential menu offerings. She's clearly put a lot of thought into this.

"Our goal?" Harper lifts a flap that was concealing a picture of an adorable golden retriever puppy. "Earn enough money to buy a dog."

"No," I answer simply. We've gone over this a thousand times. We're not getting a dog right now. Maybe at some point in the future, but I have a hard enough time being responsible for one living thing at the moment, let alone two.

"Right," Harper says, unbothered as she rips the dog picture away to reveal a Barbie Dreamhouse. "New goal."

Chloe leans forward. "Does that thing have a *jacuzzi*?"

"Oh yes, and a working elevator," Harper notes, tapping the picture with her marker.

I look at Chloe to see what she thinks about all of this. She shyly looks back over at me, and we share a glance that feels like it's chock-full of a whole year's worth of conversation.

Are we okay?

Was last night too weird?

Let's just reset.

"I'm in if you are?" Chloe says with a shrug. "I can help make the lemonade, obviously." She looks back at Harper. "But it looks like you'd like to offer some food as well?"

"Oh yes, muffins, croissants—"

"I wouldn't do croissants. They're too time-consuming to make, and they're not as profitable as muffins. What about cookies?"

Harper snaps with enthusiasm then rips off the cap of her

marker with her teeth like some power-crazed corporate exec so she can scribble down "cookies" on her board. "That's good. *Good.* What else?"

While they tackle the menu items, I get tasked with construction of the lemonade stand. Harper's printed out inspiration photos for me.

"Harper, this took a team of carpenters two weeks to build," I say, pointing to the *least* elaborate of them. "And this one is housed inside an actual Airstream."

"Okay fine, it doesn't have to be that fancy, but it does need to—hold on." She references her notes and starts to read from them. "'Represent our brand well and set the right tone for our consumer.'" Then she looks back to me with a confused frown. "What's a consumer?"

I run down to the small hardware store near our house, and after the shop owner gets a picture with me and talks my head off about a home run I hit five years ago during a game against the Astros, he walks me through what I should purchase.

"You're gonna lay these wooden crates on their sides, and the bottom slats will make it look real fancy for your kiddo. It'll also form the top of your counter. Then you just nail in your supports, add the tall boards to either side, and tack on your board up top where she can write her name. Won't take you but an hour. The painting will be a headache though. I'd use spray paint. Here, I'll show you where it is."

Once I get back to the house, I unload everything near the shed. I'm sure I'm supposed to be annoyed that Harper has given me this task, but I'm enjoying it. I used to tinker around with stuff when I was a kid, before baseball started to consume so much of my life. I like to build things and use my hands.

Ned lets me into the shed so I can grab some tools.

"Oh, you organized it," I say with an impressed nod.

He grumbles and points me in the direction of the nails and hammers.

"Don't like it one bit. Used to keep a pile of nails right underneath my hammers. Now she put them up all neat so I can barely see them."

There's no need to ask who *she* is.

Before I get started, I check in on the girls to see how they're doing. The kitchen is absolutely littered with cooking ingredients: sugar and flour, eggs and milk. Harper has a dusting of flour across her cheek and her hair. She's adding a liberal pour of chocolate chips into a mixing bowl when she looks up and waves.

"You're back!"

"It smells like a real bakery in here," I tell them, amazed.

Chloe finishes taking a tray of cookies out of the oven. There's already a pile on a cooling rack nearby, and she walks over to pick one up so she can bring it to me.

"Chocolate chip cookie courtesy of Sugar Stand by Harper."

Harper jumps up and down behind her, giddy with excitement. "That's the name! Sugar because of the lemonade and treats and Stand because it's a stand!"

Chloe laughs. "Genius, right?"

"We'll paint Sugar Stand really big at the top and then 'by Harper' smaller underneath," Harper adds.

"Genius," I confirm before I take a bite of the cookie.

As I assumed it would be, it's delicious, that perfect middle ground between gooey and crunchy.

I wag the second half of my cookie at Chloe. "How do you do it?"

Her smile spreads wide. "Chef's secrets."

Harper thinks this is wildly funny.

We spend the rest of our day at our battle stations. It doesn't take me long to build the actual stand. The method the guy at the hardware store suggested works out seamlessly, but painting is tricky, especially once I try my hand at hand-lettering Sugar Stand at the top in pink paint. The first go-around looks horrific, as if I painted with my eyes closed, so I spray paint over it all and try again, slower the second time.

Chloe whips up shrimp po-boys for dinner, and we eat them outside on the porch, talking over our strategy for tomorrow.

"What time do you guys think we should open? 6:00 AM?" Harper asks.

Chloe chokes on her bite.

"If you're opening that early, kid, you better be serving straight espresso shots, not lemonade," I tell her.

"Okay fine. We'll cut the grand opening ribbon around 10:00 AM. Hopefully there are a lot of people. Maybe I should call the local paper? They could send a news crew."

Chloe looks at me. We're both obviously fighting down our laughter.

"Why don't we just do a soft opening tomorrow?" Chloe suggests with a reassuring hand on Harper's arm. "That's really common in the restaurant world, and it gives you time to work out any kinks you might have before the place gets *really* busy."

Harper agrees.

Now the tricky thing about running a lemonade stand in the Hamptons is that most of the time people like to stick to themselves out here. Jerry Seinfeld isn't exactly inviting people onto his property for a drink and a pastry.

The next morning, we set up Sugar Stand at the end of our long driveway, and Harper expects ten people to be lined up right away. I bring out two chairs, one for her and one for me, and we sit in the shade under a tree and wait.

Harper checks her pink Barbie watch every few minutes. By 10:10, she's up pacing. Then she rearranges the cookies so the best ones are on top. Feeling as though that still might not be enough, she lines up the muffins so the ones that look to have the most blueberries are right up front.

She stirs the lemonade, then takes a seat and crosses her arms.

"Are we *ever* going to get a customer?"

"Sure, we just have to be patient. C'mon, Rome wasn't built in a day."

"Whatever that means, it's annoying."

Noted.

Chloe brings us a midmorning snack and offers to take over for me so I can go get a workout in. She gestures over Harper's head so my daughter can't see her.

"Any customers?" she mouths.

I give my head an infinitesimal shake, and Chloe cringes.

By the time I'm back, a little over an hour later, they still haven't had a single patron.

Then Ned wanders up with his cat. He's been out back all morning weeding and tending the flower beds around the pool. He looks like he could use a pick-me-up.

"How much for a cup?"

"Fifty dollars," Harper says with a completely straight face.

"*Fifty dollars?!*"

"Okay, three dollars," she counters, clearly still working out her pricing strategy. "But you get to pick a treat too."

Ned slips three dollars out of his wallet and hands the cash to Harper. She passes him a cup of lemonade and lets him take any baked good he wants.

"These have nuts?" he says, pointing to the cookies.

"No."

"They vegan?"

He pronounces it *vay-gan*.

"Uh..." Harper looks to Chloe, and Chloe shakes her head.

"Alright then. Thank you, miss," he says, tipping his

imaginary hat to Harper as he downs his lemonade in one go then nabs a cookie off the top of the pile to eat on his way back to work.

After that, it's thirty minutes of tumbleweeds. A lot of cars pass by on Ocean Drive, but no one stops.

"This is embarrassing," Harper says, kicking her foot out dejectedly. "My business is the worst."

I don't have the right words on the tip of my tongue to make her feel better, but Chloe does.

She springs into action and reroutes Harper's mood like it's the most natural thing in the world to her. "You know what I was thinking, Harper? We need signage! Something we can put out on the road. How are people going to know about our stand otherwise?"

Harper perks up. "I do have a bunch of paper and markers inside! *Oh!* I could even use the back of that poster board from my presentation. I'll go grab it!" She takes off in a full-out sprint back toward the house.

Chloe and I watch her go, then in sync, we turn back toward the road, watching the cars drive by and pretending the other person doesn't exist. I damn near start whistling to cut the tension.

"Any requests for dinner? I was going to head to the market soon."

Still no eye contact.

I drag my hand through my hair. "No. I mean, just…whatever you want to fix, I know it'll be great."

She tucks her hands into the back pockets of her jean shorts and rocks back on her heels. "*Sounds good.*"

"Right. I didn't mean to make that sound so flippant. It's more like, I trust you to make something delicious. I never got the chance to tell you how good your pizza was." I could groan with pleasure just thinking about it. "*God*, it was good."

"Oh yeah?" Her voice comes out a little higher than usual. "I'm so happy to hear that. You never know. I might like things one way, you might prefer them some other way. Finding a good chef is a lot like finding a good bedmate."

My eyes nearly bug out of my head. I've lost the battle of trying to keep my eyes off her.

When I look over, she's the color of a tomato.

"I only meant, it can be difficult," she amends hurriedly. "Probably not for you, though. You've likely had *dozens* of amazing girlfriends." Her jaw goes slack and her eyes widen as she looks over at me as if she might have just put her foot in her mouth. "*Or boyfriends.*"

"Girlfriends," I confirm.

She nods and rushes to continue burying herself deeper into this hole. I could help her, of course, by diverting us to some other topic of conversation, but she's just too damn cute when she gets like this. I like her flustered. It's innocent and sweet.

"Have you had a hard time? I mean, outside of Miles."

She frowns. "Did I tell you his name?"

"Sorry, I looked him up. Couldn't resist."

She blanches. "Oh god, that's embarrassing. I hope you don't think less of me."

"Not at all. We're all fools for love sometimes."

She puffs out an exasperated scoff. "It was *not* love. Lust, maybe, for like a week. Then mostly it was just awe of his talent in the kitchen. There aren't many chefs like him."

Hearing her speak so highly of him raises my hackles.

"Good chef?" I shrug. "Big deal. He's a shitty person from the sound of it."

She looks over at me like I'm the first person to ever refer to him this way. She's a little amazed, maybe even a bit scared by it, which really pisses me off.

"There are people like Miles in every industry. I can't tell you how many guys play ball well and therefore get away with murder off the field. They usually get what's coming in the end, though. Coaches end their contracts early because they're too hard to work with. Wives divorce them and take them to the cleaners. It'll be the same for Miles, you watch."

She looks momentarily alarmed. "I don't want anything bad to happen to him."

Of course she doesn't. He took advantage of her, seduced her, cheated on her, but she still cares about his well-being. If that doesn't spell out exactly the kind of person Chloe is, I don't know what does.

"Look!" Harper shouts from behind us. "I found some construction paper too! We can cut it up and make big lemons for our signs!" she says excitedly.

I glance back at Chloe, and she offers a little smile of thanks.

"While you two work on that, I'll head to the store—but I'm happy to pick up a shift out here when I get back, don't you worry," she says, tousling Harper's hair as she walks by.

"Okay, but hurry back, *Clo-Clo*!" Harper says.

"Will do, *Hay-Hay*!"

Harper beams at me. "You like our nicknames? We came up with them while you were working out. We've got a secret handshake too. I'll teach you after we make the signs."

Just then, a dark gray Mercedes slows to a stop and pulls into our driveway. I recognize the driver right away.

"Ooh! A customer!"

No.

Unfortunately, this guy's not a customer.

THIRTEEN
CHLOE

WHEN I ARRIVE BACK at Luke's house, the lemonade stand is gone. Harper's nowhere in sight, and there's a gray Mercedes parked in the driveway, the one I saw as I was leaving for Bridgehampton Market. The driver waved at me as we passed one another in the driveway. I assumed it was finally someone wanting lemonade, but when I head inside with an armful of grocery bags and hear two male voices, I realize I was wrong.

I almost announce myself in some way, like "Hey! I'm back!" but then it's probably better to blend into the background like I'm just a fly on the wall.

I turn the corner from the mudroom and walk into the kitchen. Luke is sitting at the breakfast table with a guy who looks to be close to his age, clean-cut, suited up, and handsome in a suave way. Where Luke is broad shoulders and a day's worth of stubble, this guy is meticulously groomed and smooth. Both men notice me walk in with the groceries, and they immediately push to stand so they can offer help. Luke's friend reaches me first.

"Let me get those for you."

"Oh." I laugh, slightly uncomfortable and unsure of what

I'm supposed to do in this situation. He's a guest of Luke's and I'm an employee. I'm not supposed to accept help, but it's too late. He hefts the bags over to the counter and sets them down neatly.

"Are there any more in the car?" he asks.

"No. *No.* This is all. Thank you."

He shoots me a charismatic, practiced smile. "No problem. I'm David, by the way." He extends his hand for me to shake.

"Chloe."

While he still has my hand firmly in his, he glances over his shoulder toward Luke, whose brows are furrowed as he looks at us.

"No wonder you haven't been returning my phone calls," he tells Luke. "You've been *busy.*"

Oh.

I yank my hand away before I think better of it. Then, aware that I'm an employee and he's a guest, I force out a laugh to help smooth over any ruffled feathers my quick retreat might have caused. I don't want to insult him by being rude.

"I haven't returned your calls," Luke replies, "because you've been hounding me day and night and I don't have a different answer for you."

David completely ignores him, pinning his attention on me. "Tell me, Chloe, what's in all the bags?"

"Dinner."

"Ah. You must be some chef," David notes as he helps to unload my ingredients for tonight. I'll be making skirt steak fajitas. I've been marinating the meat since this morning, but I needed to go grab the rest of the items from the store: cilantro, lime, jalapeños, avocado, sour cream—the works.

"She's *the* chef," Luke tells him.

Realization dawns on David's face and for a brief moment he looks absolutely filled to the brim with lewd thoughts, but then I blink and they're gone. He's back to smiling in that perfect way.

"I'm pretty good in the kitchen myself. No girlfriend or wife to rely on so I've had to teach myself a few things. What will you be making tonight?"

I look to Luke for input on how to proceed here. The tension in this kitchen is palpable. Luke might have accepted this man into his home, but I'm not sure why. His face looks damn near murderous as he stares at the back of David's head.

"Fajitas," I answer simply, just trying to keep the peace.

David groans and pats his stomach. "I *love* fajitas. Chicken or steak?"

"Steak."

"Well it's a good thing I'm here so close to dinner time," David says, turning back to Luke. "Should we go out back and have a beer? Get out of Chloe's hair so she can cook?"

"Don't you need to get back to the city?" Luke asks.

"It's Saturday evening—what do I need to rush home for?" Then he looks back at me with a twinkle of mischief in his eyes. "Besides, I'd much rather taste Chloe's food. Something tells me she really knows how to impress a man."

"What the hell is that supposed to mean?" Luke asks gruffly.

So gruffly, in fact, that it startles me.

"*Nothing.*" David walks over to clap Luke on the shoulder like they're just a couple of good ol' boys having a laugh. "God. Ease up, will you? Let's go have that beer."

I stare daggers at David as he walks away. I hate him and there's no convincing me otherwise. I've been around plenty of men like him, the smarmy rich types who think the world should be laid at their feet. Never mind that I'm a real human, flesh and blood like him. He only sees me as a plaything, something to toss around and tease for the enjoyment of himself and others.

I start aggressively washing and chopping vegetables, glad for the task. My cutting board bears the brunt of my anger. I'm putting so much force behind every slice I'm surprised the wood doesn't splinter in two.

I hear the TV on in the game room down the hall. I know Harper's in there watching a show, and I'm glad she was absent for that whole exchange. Maybe Luke tucked her away in there on purpose to save her from having to be around David.

It's actually kind of disappointing that Luke would associate with a man like that. I would have thought he had better taste in friends.

Luke and David take their beers out onto the back porch, and I hear their muffled conversation. Well, *David's* muffled conversation. My ears are pricked, trying to hear Luke, but he's being quiet out there.

I fix an appetizer of chips and salsa with tomatoes from the garden, deliver a little serving to Harper in the game room, and then take some out to the guys. David is midsentence as I hurriedly set everything down, being sure to stick close to Luke as I lean over the table.

"—regret your decision. Look at Tom Brady and Michael Jordan. Brett Favre too, man. They all came out of retirement because they missed the game. Oh, what'd you bring us, Chloe?"

He adds the last part with a flirtatious tone.

"Just a little appetizer. Dinner shouldn't be much longer."

His lascivious gaze roves lazily over my body. Never mind that I'm fully dressed with my apron on; it's like he can see straight through everything. *Gross.*

I make my escape as fast as possible and get back to work.

When I deliver the fajitas, David doesn't miss the opportunity to ask me to sit and eat with them. He even tugs out the chair beside him.

I don't even wait for Luke to cut in. My excuse flies as fast as a bullet.

"Oh, that is so nice of you! But I actually ate while I was preparing dinner, and I have a whole messy kitchen to clean now. I hope you two enjoy the food though!"

And I don't wait for him to argue.

I lied, of course. I haven't eaten, so I make my plate and take it into the game room. Harper and I eat together on the couch while she walks me through her favorite characters in her show. Then after, I take our empty plates into the kitchen so I can get started on cleaning. I'm standing in front of the sink that's filled to the brim with soapy bubbles and dishes when the door to the porch slides open.

I assume it's Luke coming in to check on Harper or use the restroom, which is why I don't turn around. Then David's voice sounds from right behind me.

"Such a hard little worker…"

I flinch in surprise and the plate slips out of my hand, clattering loudly as it crashes against the other dishes in the soapy water. I move to turn around, but David is there, pressing me against the side of the sink, his chest to my back, his hands caging me in on either side.

He laughs at my reaction; he likes it.

"No need to freak out. I just want to talk."

My mouth opens but I can't get a single word out. My mind has gone completely mute. My arms are useless. Whatever I'm supposed to do now, it doesn't come.

He grips my hip, and all I can feel is my heart racing in my chest a mile a minute.

David is there, right up against my back one second, then in an instant, he's wrenched away from me.

He gasps in surprise, but it comes out slightly strained and gargled like he's being choked. "*What—*"

"Get the fuck out of my house."

Luke's voice is deadly.

I whirl around in a panic. Luke's got David by the back of his shirt collar. It's twisted around his fist, and he's using it to lead David toward the kitchen doorway.

"Relax," David chokes out.

"*Relax?* Be glad I'm not calling the police, you fucking prick." Luke releases his collar and shoves David away like he's disgusted to even have to touch him.

David catches himself, laughs, and then holds up his hands in innocence. "She wasn't exactly resisting, if you know what I mean…"

Before I can even react to this, to defend myself in some way, Luke rears back and punches him. I flinch, glad at least that I quelled my scream. The sound of his fist colliding with David's face makes me almost sick to my stomach. He put the full force of his body behind it; I wouldn't be surprised if he broke the guy's nose.

David groans in pain and starts cursing as blood rains down his lips and chin. Threats tumble out of him, one after another. "I'll sue you for all you're worth! I'll take you to court! I'll call every reporter I know!"

"Good. *Do it*," Luke says, utterly unfazed. "In fact, I welcome it. Now get out."

David spits blood and turns, leaving in an angry huff. Then, just before he reaches the front door, he calls back over his shoulder, "Oh and just to be clear, we're done. Find yourself a new agent."

Luke laughs like this last remark is absolutely hilarious.

David slams the front door, and a few moments later, his tires squeal down the driveway.

I'm frozen in place.

That was his agent, not a friend.

Oh god. Oh god. Oh god.

My shaking hands grip the kitchen counter on either side of my hips. I'm in shock; I think that's what this is. My eyes home in on the wet blood stains on the floor. Then I flinch as I remember the feel of David's hand sliding up my waist. That possessive grip. The fact that I stayed silent instead of defending myself. I could have pushed him away, argued, screamed, done *something*, and I didn't.

Luke is looking at me. I feel his warm gaze on the side of my cheek, my body. Maybe he's looking for damage. Maybe he's just waiting for me to show some sign of life.

"I'm so sorry," he says.

His earnest apology makes me squeeze my eyes shut with guilt.

Was David serious about all those threats? Is he really going to sue Luke?

"It was my fault," I whisper weakly.

None of this would have happened had I not been here, or at least it wouldn't have gotten as bad as it did if I'd just put my foot down with David from the get-go instead of trying to placate him.

I grab a dish rag, wet it, and hurry over to wipe up as much blood as I can before it stains the floor.

"Dad?" Harper's voice comes from down the hall. "What's going on? Was someone yelling?"

Luke curses under his breath and rushes to cut Harper off before she can make it into the kitchen. There's not much blood, but there's some, and if I were him, I'd want to shield her from it too. Hopefully with her show on and the door only slightly ajar, she didn't hear much of what just happened.

I get to work cleaning the floor with the rag while Luke escorts Harper back to the game room, hurrying like it's my blood, like I'm embarrassed it's there in the first place. In normal circumstances, I can't stand the sight of blood, but these aren't normal circumstances. I don't even feel like I'm in my body. I'm cleaning and mopping, starting from the sink and going all the way to the front door like I'm on autopilot. I even check the front porch and hose that off too.

All evidence of David is gone soon enough, but I'm still rattled.

I hear the telltale signs of Luke helping Harper get ready for bed. I could so easily be lulled by the quiet cadence of his voice as he reads her a bedtime story, and because of it I can't stay in the house another second. I go upstairs and yank off my apron and clothes, swap into running gear, and head out. It's dark and I'm being stupid running along the road, but I stick to the grass as much as possible. I make it all the way down to the deserted beach and I stand on the shoreline, listening to the sound of the waves crashing in. Their heavy presence is a welcome reprieve. I feel as insignificant as I am. A speck. Dust.

The wind whips my hair and I feel David's breath on the back of my neck…the counter biting into my hips as he presses closer to me…

It could have been worse isn't a soothing thought.

The waves are so loud, relentless, angry. It's like they rage on my behalf. I open my mouth to scream like I should have screamed at David, and I still can't. It's only a silent cry that escapes.

I run as fast as I can back to the house, but I still feel weak when I open the door and quietly pad inside. Luke's sitting at the kitchen table with his head in his hands, staring down at his phone.

I don't think he hears me come in, but he looks up and relief floods his face. He stands, the chair screeching back, and I realize he must have been worried about me. His hair is mussed up from his hands. His eyes are still wide and a little wild.

"Where'd you go? I went to your room. I thought…"

I give him time to finish, but he doesn't. He just shakes his head.

"I went down to the beach. I just wanted to run for a bit… wanted to clear my head."

"Did it work?"

"No."

I walk over to fill a glass with water and find the sink is empty and clean. In fact, the entire kitchen has been restored to its factory setting.

It doesn't make me feel better. I can't look at him as I fill my glass.

"I'm sorry to have left that mess. I was planning to come home and get to it right away."

"Chloe?" His voice is gentle, like he's trying to coax a baby bird into trusting him.

I peer back at him over my shoulder.

"Are you all right?"

"He didn't hurt me at all," I say with emphasis. "And to clarify, it was *not* like he insinuated. I was not flirting with him or anything."

I didn't want it.

"Of course. I know that." Luke looks like he's found some new font of fury. "He shouldn't have touched you. No matter what."

"No, I know that. Only, I don't want to be overly dramatic. He barely put his hands on me."

Luke's mouth pulls into a tight line and his hands turn into fists. For a second, I think he might hit something, but then he lets his arms fall back limp at his sides like he's utterly defeated.

That makes two of us.

I turn toward him fully, take a sip of my water, and then stare down at my glass as I ask the question I've been worried about since David left.

"Is he going to do all that? Everything he threatened you with?"

"No, he won't. I have a team of lawyers backing me—he doesn't want this to end up in court. And he's too chickenshit to run to the press. He must realize it's his word against ours."

He says ours like we're a team.

Guilt hangs heavy around my neck.

"I'm appreciative that you stepped in when you did. And though I usually wouldn't condone violence, well, I won't lie and say I wasn't glad you punched him like that. God, I wish I could have been the one to do it." My shoulders sag. "I had the chance. He wasn't being that forceful. I just froze…"

"That doesn't make you a coward."

I look away as tears prick the corners of my eyes. Emotion makes my throat so scratchy I don't think I could talk even if I tried, so I merely nod.

"Hey," Luke says, striding over to lift my chin so I'll look at him, but then once I do, he backs off and steps away. It's like he's scared to touch me now more than ever. "You didn't cause that, and there is nothing you should have done. He's in the wrong. While he might not pursue a lawsuit, I sure as shit won't let him get away with it."

"You don't have to do that on my account," I rush out. "You already have enough on your plate."

He tips his head, studying me with a solemn expression.

"My mind is already made up. He did that in my house, knowing I was right there, and he was so damn sure of himself, which makes me wonder how many other women he's harassed. Jesus. I could never live with myself if I don't say something. I'll call my lawyers in the morning and see what we can do. Beyond that, I just want to make sure you're okay."

I hold up two thumbs and force a smile. "Never been better."

He's less than convinced. He stares at me like he's waiting for me to splinter and crack before his eyes. His heady expression is so invasive, so close to the mark that all I can do is deflect.

"C'mon, you've gone above and beyond. Boss of the year, I swear. So let's just drop it."

Luke's face doesn't relax though. He looks so torn.

He rubs the back of his neck, his brows drawing together in anguish. "I can't believe I let him in my house. I put you in that situation…"

"*David* put me in that situation."

His brown eyes are so sad I can't just stand here across the kitchen from him another second. Since I know he won't bridge this gap between us, I do it.

I step forward, wrap my arms around his middle, and hug him before I decide against it. It's rooted in innocence, a hug any person would bestow upon their hero. A hug of gratitude, of sheer appreciation. At first, he doesn't reciprocate. His hands hover in the air, his body remains rigid. But then he must sense how much I need this and that I'm not exactly going anywhere, and his heavy arms come to rest gently around my shoulders.

"Tell me, really…are you okay?" he asks quietly.

"Yes. I promise."

He's so much taller than me, wider in every regard. His biceps feel like they could boa-constrict the life right out of me if that were his goal. Instead, he tugs me closer until we're flush against each other and I'm surrounded by his warmth. I feel like a small child, insulated from the world. God, it feels good.

FOURTEEN

CHLOE

WEE-OH, *wee-oh, wee-oh*. Oh what's that? The thought police have come to arrest me? I'm not even surprised. I'm up to no good, a grade-A deviant. I'm lying on my bed fantasizing about Luke when I should be sleeping. And I know it's wrong! No one needs to remind me of that. I haven't forgotten all the rules surrounding my relationship with him. Do this. Do that. Don't picture him without pants. Do not imagine what it would have felt like if that hug had lingered a little longer, if his hands had traveled south. Yada yada, I get it. Usually, the urge is easy enough to bat away, but not tonight.

In fact, tonight, I've leaned into thinking of Luke because it's helped replace looming thoughts of David—*ew, David*—as I try to go to sleep.

I tell myself it's innocent, but there is *nothing* innocent about my growing crush on Luke. It colors everything I do, everything he does. If he's extra nice to me, I can't help but think, *Oh, well, obviously he's obsessed with me.* If we're in the same room at the same time, there's *always* tension. Am I likely reading too much into things? Maybe. Could the tension exist solely in my head? Magic 8 ball says it's likely.

Honestly, it's probably just been too long since I've had physical affection and I'm starved for it.

Miles was never one to be touchy-feely. He liked his space, and I was okay with that because—and I kind of feel bad admitting this—he wasn't all that fun to cuddle. He's very boney and lanky. Not at all like Luke. Luke is a hunky muscular bear of a man. If I were one of those ladies who, I don't know, (I haven't put a ton of thought into this or anything) enjoyed getting tossed around the bedroom, Luke would be able to deliver on that. And if I were someone who liked my men to be on the *larger* side in the crotch department, Luke would have that covered too.

I know, I know—you can't just assume that kind of thing. Small guys can pack heat too, yes, but I'm not assuming. No, no, no. That first day Luke swam with Harper in the pool, my suspicion was confirmed. I saw the outline of *it*, y'know… beneath his swim trunks. I didn't look for long—I'm classy, after all—so I merely glanced back at it five or six times to verify my findings were accurate. And they were.

At this point, any thought of Luke is accompanied by fluttering butterflies and flute-filled serenades. I'm in so deep there's no going back.

But consequences are for the light of day, so I close my eyes and give in to the indulgence. This sweet pretending is oh so fun. I fall right back into that moment in the kitchen, only this time, it ends differently: Luke hugs me a little tighter, the air shifts between us. His hands grip my waist and, *plop*, he sets me on the counter so he can nestle himself right in between my legs. Then I—

Wait. What am I wearing? Not those jean shorts I had on earlier. A silky negligee. Yes. Black—no, *red*. Oo la la.

Luke compliments me on it. "Red is definitely your color."

No, that's not hot enough. That's something my mom would say to me.

I try again.

"I like this lace, but I'd like it a lot better on the floor."

Still not great considering it sounds like dialogue from an '80s porno, but we'll take it. Moving on.

He starts to slip my apron off. *Apron!?* Yes, apron. I would never cook in a negligee. That's asking for trouble.

But tonight, in my fantasy, whatever, I make an exception. No apron. Luke slips the straps of my red negligee off my shoulders, kissing a path down my neck as he does it.

Oh, this is getting good.

In real life, my hand finds its way underneath my covers, but I have a hell of a time undoing the knot on my pajama pants. I have to sit up and use two hands, and by the time I get it, I've lost the thread of my story. Were we on the counter or the floor?

Counter. Red negligee. Luke's mouth on my neck, now my chest. *Yes.*

Knock-knock.

"Crap."

I sit up in bed as a little fist taps on my bedroom door again.

"Chloe?" Harper asks with a timid voice. "I'm hungry. Could you make me a snack?"

My hand is literally down the front of my pants.

I yank it out.

"Uh…*uh*…" I'm looking around for something, but there's nothing to find except my freaking common sense. "Sure! Yes! Just give me a sec."

I go into the bathroom and thoroughly wash my hands, unable to look up and meet my reflection in the mirror. I'm so embarrassed. I was just fantasizing about her dad! HER DAD! Surely I have more dignity than that. *Narrator: Unfortunately, Chloe does not have more dignity than that.*

I walk back out into my bedroom as I double-knot the front of my pajama pants. There, it's like Fort Knox down there. No more dreaming of Luke for me.

I open my bedroom door, and there's Harper in her cupcake-patterned pajamas with her ratty stuffed unicorn tucked up underneath her arm. Her sleepy brown eyes have never looked more doe-like and innocent.

I tuck her against me as we head back toward the stairs. "I can fix you whatever you'd like. What sounds good?"

———

SUNDAY MORNING, I make breakfast while Luke works out in the facility he has out back. Then while Harper and Luke set up shop at the lemonade stand, I stroll through a farmers' market in town and pick up a ton of fresh organic produce. It's the season of abundance, and I can't wait to put everything to good use.

Harper and Luke actually have customers when I return. Two little blonde girls are passing cash over to Harper while their mom talks to Luke. Oh wait, she's not talking. She's hand-twirling-hair, teeth-biting-lip *flirting* with him.

I nearly slam on my brakes to get a longer look at them together. Why does the sight of it shock me so much?

Oh right, because Luke and I have existed in a weird microcosm of real life. I'm sure women throw themselves at his feet on a daily basis. My experience (i.e. crushing on him hardcore) is not unique, so it seems. I feel oddly sad to realize I'm just one of many.

Harper waves at me as I drive by the lemonade stand at a snail's pace (for safety reasons, I swear), but Luke doesn't look up. He's apparently enthralled in his conversation.

No matter. I throw myself into my cooking. I lay out everything I procured from the farmers' market and grab my recipe books. I have a few tried-and-true favorites: Ina Garten's *The Barefoot Contessa Cookbook*; *The Art of Simple Food* by Alice Waters; and lastly, a stained, creased, truly on its last leg compilation of Italian recipes from Nonna.

Lunch is a tomato-lemon tart with puff pastry I prepared this morning, a cobb salad with a fresh mango and lime vinaigrette, and baked white fish.

I call out to let them know to come eat. When Harper walks in with Luke, she's in a rush.

"I want to take my plate back outside. I can have a picnic underneath the shady tree by the lemonade stand. I'd hate to miss a customer on my lunch break. We've already sold four cups of lemonade today!"

Luke shakes his head. "You'll have to take a break for a bit, Harper. I need to get some work done in my office."

"I could go out with her," I suggest. After all, I did it yesterday.

Luke looks over at me, and if I was expecting him to be relieved, I'm wrong. In fact, he seems almost exasperated with me for stepping in.

"You don't need to do that. You've spent the whole morning working. You deserve a lunch break. Also, I don't expect you to act as Harper's nanny any time I need it."

"She's not my nanny, she's my friend," Harper declares with a big smile. "Last night she even made me a grilled cheese when I couldn't sleep."

Luke shakes his head, confused. "She what?"

"She made me a grilled cheese. I was hungry at bedtime. My tummy was grumbling and grumbling nonstop!"

Luke's eyebrows furrow in a clear sign of annoyance.

"It was really quick. I had her back in bed in no time," I say, hoping to assuage some of his worry. I don't want him thinking I kept her up really late partying or anything. It was a grilled cheese, a small glass of milk, and then right back to sleep. Well, *after* I read her a quick bedtime story.

"Next time, come get me, Harper."

"But Chloe is better at cooking."

Luke closes his eyes and squeezes the bridge of his nose.

"That's not the point. Chloe is an employee here, Harper. She doesn't work for us around the clock."

Harper's bottom lip quivers as he reprimands her with a hard tone.

I jump forward, holding out my hands between them like I'm trying to keep the peace. "No! It's totally okay. Harper can come wake me up at 3:00 AM for all I care," I say with a little laugh.

But I'm not helping, which I realize too late. Luke is trying to get a point across to his daughter, and I'm undermining his authority by butting in with my two cents.

"Harper," Luke says, more sternly, completely ignoring me. "Do not pester Chloe. She's the chef here, that's all. Do you understand?"

We both understand, loud and clear. That speech was as much for me as it was for her, and my cheeks heat with the knowledge that I've messed up.

"Now, I'm going to go work for a little while. The lemonade stand will have to wait. I have a phone call at 1:00 that I can't be late for. After I'm done, we'll head into town to that playground you like, and then we can go to The Pizza Palace for dinner." He turns, barely looking in my direction. "Chloe, there's no need to cook."

Roger that.

The house is deadly quiet later that afternoon and early evening. I'm about ready to invite Ned in for some company.

Fortunately, I have Sunday dinner to look forward to. Per my promise to my parents, I make myself a simple bowl of spaghetti and sit down to eat it with my phone propped up in front of me so I can be on FaceTime with my family.

"Can you see us?" my mom asks once the call connects. "Gio's trying to set it up so we can see you on the big TV this time."

"Nothing yet."

The screen's black as they all chatter in the background,

chiming in with advice for Gio. *Maybe you don't have the right cable? Maybe the TV needs to be on a different channel? Maybe you're supposed to press that button there, Gio?*

"Would you all freaking shut it? I got it here."

Sure enough, a second later, my entire family pops up on the screen: Mom, Dad, Gio, Nonna, aunts, uncles, and cousins.

"Hey!" they erupt. "There she is!"

I wave excitedly and hold up my bowl of spaghetti.

"Looks good, kiddo," my dad says. "Have you made that for your fancy clients yet?"

I smile and shake my head. "Not yet. I would have made it for them tonight, but they went into town for dinner."

"Who's 'they'?" nosy Aunt Amara asks, turning to the group. "Why can't we know who she's working for?"

"It's part of the business," Uncle Antonio says in my defense. "Lay off her. She's not allowed to spill the beans or she'll be sacked."

"It's true. I signed an NDA."

"An indie-what?" my dad asks.

"Doesn't matter," Gio cuts in. "I can tell from the background that the house you're living in is *sick*. Bet the family drives a Bentley or some shit. Is the mom hot?"

"Gio!"

My aunts erupt in protest; my uncles just chuckle.

Then my little cousin Luca runs into frame, takes aim at the TV with his Nerf gun, and fires. The FaceTime screen goes black while everyone starts cursing at him.

His wild laughter dies out swiftly as soon as his mom gets ahold of her son.

"That's it. The Nerf gun is mine!"

"I bought it with my own allowance!"

Gio gets the camera figured out again, and then it's like I'm really right there with them. They serve dinner. Nonna blesses the food in Italian, and everyone tucks in. Tonight, it's

Nonna's tagliatelle al ragù, lasagna, polenta, and cacio e pepe, followed up with cannoli and coffee. My bowl of spaghetti doesn't cut it, and the homesickness feels so heavy I can barely stand it. Everyone's sitting around the table, chattering about nothing really—all the same things they chatter on about every Sunday—but it's enough just to sit and listen.

I hear the front door open, and I mute myself on FaceTime and turn the volume down so my crazy family is nothing but a soft murmur in the background. Luke and Harper walk into the kitchen. Harper has what look to be chocolate stains on the front of her white dress and a nice big chocolate mustache above her top lip. Luke is carrying a takeout container and a pint of ice cream. He's dressed casual in jeans, a simple gray t-shirt, and cool sneakers, and he's still the most delectable man I have ever laid eyes on.

He holds the pint up. "For you. We stopped after dinner and Harper thought you might want some. Hope chocolate's okay."

"Oh thanks! That was really nice of you. I'm actually Face-Timing with my family."

"Really!?" Harper asks excitedly. "Can I meet them?"

She's already running over, but I figure Luke wouldn't be totally comfortable with that.

"Here, why don't you stand here, off camera so you can see them. I have it muted so they won't be able to hear you if you say anything."

She gasps. "Oh my gosh! There are so many of them!"

I laugh. "This isn't even everyone. My cousins are off playing somewhere. That guy right there is my brother."

"Really?" She sounds like she's in disbelief. "He's so big. He doesn't even look like you."

"We have the same complexion and the same eyes, but yeah, he's huge. That's my dad and my mom there."

"Aw, and is that your grandma?"

I smile. "Yeah, that's Nonna at the head of the table."

"Everyone lives together like this?"

"No no, this is just our Sunday dinner. Everyone comes over to my parents' house on Sundays to cook and eat Italian food together. It lasts for hours."

"Oh that sounds fun. I want to go."

I smile. "Yeah. You'd like it."

"Can I say hi to them?"

"How about I say hi instead?" Luke suggests.

I've been aware of his presence this whole time. He came over soon after Harper did, leaning down to look at my screen, to see what his daughter was seeing, I'm sure. Now, he stands just behind her with his hands tucked into the pockets of his jeans. There's a timid smile stretched across his handsome face. This might be his way of apologizing for how stern he was with Harper and me earlier.

My jaw drops at his suggestion. "Are you serious? I signed all that paperwork. I thought I couldn't tell anyone who I was working for."

He grimaces. God, he almost looks embarrassed by his celebrity.

"That's mostly my lawyers being overly cautious. I don't really mind if they know."

"You don't understand." I laugh. "They're going to flip out."

His eyes widen in alarm.

"I mean in a good way! They're like huge *huge* fans."

Harper laughs. "Yes! Do it, Chloe!"

Before Luke can chicken out, I unmute my microphone and turn up the volume on my phone once again. Everyone is still talking, none the wiser that I've been quiet for the last few minutes. Now, it takes me a second to get everyone's attention.

"Hey! Guys!"

"We're talkin' here, Clo," my brother says.

My mom tells him off. "Gio, be nice to your sister. What, Chloe?"

I grab Luke's arm and tug him into the frame. Well, I tug his torso into the frame. Since I'm sitting down and he's so tall, he has to bend down so they can see him. Once his face fills that little rectangle on my screen, I let loose a gloating smile.

"Say hello to my boss."

He doesn't say anything. Not one word, but it doesn't matter.

That entire room goes dead quiet.

My mother does the sign of the cross.

My dad screams like a little girl.

One of my uncles falls back in his chair as another spits out his drink.

My brother's jaw drops, and then I know without a shadow of a doubt he's about to let loose a curse word, so I reach over and cover Harper's ears just before he lets it rip.

"SHE'S WORKIN' FOR LUKE *FUCKING* ALLEN!"

FIFTEEN

LUKE

I RUB my thumb across the calluses on my palm then down over the surgical scar from when I broke my middle finger at the tail end of my fifth season with the Pinstripes. It still aches occasionally, but it's nothing compared to the pain I felt that first time back on the mound. I thought my hand was going to break in two, thought I'd have to walk away from the game for good then. I was wrong. I played another eight seasons after that.

I miss the sport more than I thought I would. I know the season's well underway. I've caught a few minutes of a game here and there in my office, but mostly, I can't stand to watch it. Jealousy rages inside me.

No one understands my choice to walk away. Not my coaches, not my manager, not my *ex*-agent.

"I can see why you've been holed up in retirement," David said to me at dinner the other night. "Choice piece of meat you have there."

Considering I had a hunk of fajita meat on my plate, it took me a second to realize he was referring to Chloe.

I don't know why I felt compelled to answer him. "She and I aren't together."

He laughed at that. "Really? Damn, you're being serious, aren't you?" He shook his head. "You're a better man than me. She's sexy and convenient. Just right there, cooking all your meals every day, looking like *that*."

I should have rearranged his face right then instead of waiting until later. Then he wouldn't have had a chance to put his hands on Chloe. I can't even think about that night without my blood boiling. I grab another baseball, wind up, and throw. It slams against the target at the end of the cage. Its speed flashes in red on the monitor, confirming I'm just as fast as I've always been.

It'll be easy enough to find a new agent. I haven't been with David for long. His dad was my agent before he retired and he'd been grooming David to take over for him, so I signed on with David because I trusted his dad. Well...I learned my lesson, didn't I?

I take another ball out of the basket at my side. I throw at that target until my shoulder tells me to quit.

Besides, Harper will be awake soon anyway. I don't want her wondering where I am.

I had this training facility built on the back of my property when I first purchased the land. It's disguised to look like an auxiliary building in the same style as the main house. It's tucked to the side of the pond, out of view from the road. There's a gym, sauna, physical therapy room, batting cages, you name it. Seems like a pity to let it go to waste, so I've been sneaking out here every morning, practicing and staying in shape.

It's been hard for me to walk away from the game. Harder than I could have imagined, in fact. If I didn't have Harper, I don't think I'd last. But then again, if I didn't have Harper, I wouldn't be walking away in the first place.

I swipe sweat off my brow and head back toward the house, passing near the garden. It's not even 8:00 AM and

Chloe's already out there. She loves that garden and tends to it often, but has she realized Ned's been helping her with it too? He's been watering and pruning the plants, adding fertilizer and such, even though gardening isn't his favorite pastime.

Ned's actually my great-uncle. He used to drive trucks, and anytime he'd come through central Texas, he'd make sure his route included a stop-off to visit our family. When those long days on the road got to be too much, I offered him a position with me here.

I guess Chloe doesn't realize he's not just some employee. I can see her reaction now. Her jaw would drop, her eyes would go wide. "You're related to Satan!?"

It makes me smile just thinking about it.

I stop for a second, back in the tree line, watching while she slowly strolls down the aisles with their overflowing beds. She has a cup of coffee in her hand and she's wearing a sweater and yoga pants. Her long hair is loose and getting slightly mussed by the early morning breeze. She tucks a few unruly strands behind her ear then grabs for her basket. She's picking off a few things as she goes, planning her creations in her head, I'm sure. My mouth waters just thinking about it.

Or maybe just thinking about her.

I've been hard on myself where she's concerned. For four weeks, I've slammed that door shut and locked it with a deadbolt for good measure. But here I am, staring at her like a freaking weirdo, just wanting a glimpse of her like this. She's so golden in the morning light, tan and fresh-faced.

She leans down to inspect the tomato plant in front of her, and then she calls out over her shoulder. I scowl, wondering who she's talking to, then Harper's head pokes out from behind the huge zucchini plants at the end of the flower bed.

I didn't see her. She must have been leaned down, picking something from the garden.

She comes running toward Chloe, and I watch as Chloe instructs her on which tomatoes she should pluck from the vine. Harper excitedly harvests a few cherry tomatoes and drops them into the basket at Chloe's feet.

Trying to keep them apart feels futile, but important.

Neither one of them seems to realize this arrangement is a little strange. If Maria were here, the lines in the sand would be more obvious. She would step in and help out when I need it. She'd redirect Harper away from Chloe. But without Maria here, it's just me trying to convince my daughter to stay away from the woman we're both desperate to spend time with.

Though I could stand there all day watching them, I make myself get a move on. It's not exactly normal to be lingering like I am.

Chloe notices me first and gives me a little wave. She made a point to thank me after I FaceTimed with her family for a few minutes the other week. There was no escaping their millions of questions. I sat down in Chloe's chair and felt like I was facing a team of seasoned reporters.

"What's your plan now?"

"You can't just quit baseball for good!"

"I can see you've still got it, man!"

Chloe acted like my manager, shooing away their more intrusive questions until she could tell I needed a break.

"I'm sorry, he has to go! No, Luca, no. Stop with the puppy dog eyes, he's not going to sign anything for you."

She pressed end on the call while they were all still trying to get my attention. Then she turned to me with an exhausted laugh.

"Sorry. They can be…a lot."

"Big family, huh?"

"Huge. Annoying. Loud. You want them?"

I smiled. "I know you appreciate having them so close."

She nodded with a wistful look in her eyes. "Yeah, I actually miss them, which I know is insane since we're not all that far away, but it's hard when I'm used to seeing them so much. If you think I'm a good cook, you should eat my Nonna's food." She let her eyes roll back as if she were in rapture, and I felt her little groan of delight deep in my stomach. "Anyway, you have no idea what you just started. I'm sure every conversation I have with my uncles and cousins for the next five years will somehow involve *you*."

Now, Harper spots me and comes running. She wraps her arms around my middle and squeezes me tight, but it doesn't last long.

"Ew! You're smelly!"

"It's just sweat."

"*Yuuuuck.*"

Chloe shoots me a knowing smile over Harper's head. "Morning. Harper here wanted to help me make a vegetable frittata, so we're grabbing some things from the garden. Hope that's okay," Chloe says. Then she points back toward the house. "I just made a fresh pot of coffee in the kitchen. Bet you need some."

"Like you wouldn't believe."

I wave for her to lead the way, and then Harper falls in step beside her instead of me. My daughter is talking like she's just found the pleasure of language for the very first time. Chloe doesn't mind though. She keeps up with her easily enough. Meanwhile, I focus on the ground, wondering why it's so damn hard to see Chloe in a pair of form-fitting yoga pants. What's the big deal? I've seen her in less and survived. Barely.

At the house, Chloe holds the back door open and waits for me to catch up to them. I lift a taunting brow and take the door from her.

"After you," I tell her.

"After *you*," she teases right back, waving her arm for me to go ahead.

"You won't win this battle."

She smiles so damn sweetly I almost forget all rhyme or reason and just lean down and kiss her, there with her chin tilted up toward me and her face cast in warm sunlight.

"No, no, no, *I insist*."

Harper's smiling now, watching our exchange.

"I could force the issue, you know," I goad.

"Oh really?"

"Oh yeah. I could pluck you up with one hand."

"DAD." Harper loses it to a fit of laughter.

Chloe leans in closer to me, dropping her voice. "You know some ladies go gaga for that sort of thing."

I lean in too. "Are you one of them?"

Then her smile drops as we both realize at the same moment what we're doing: flirting right in front of Harper. We've lost our goddamn minds.

"You win," Chloe says with a flat tone, walking away from the door and letting me take its full weight. "I'll get you that coffee."

She knows how I like it, with just a touch of milk, and after she fixes my cup, she brings it over to me. She doesn't meet my eyes though. Her gaze is squarely on my chest.

Don't play coy now, Chloe.

"You can go and shower if you want. Harper can help me make breakfast, and it should be ready by the time you're done."

I look over her shoulder at my daughter, who's organizing all the produce they just harvested from the garden. "Harper, why don't you let Chloe get on—"

She whirls around and looks at me like I'm trying to ruin her life, sad eyes and all. "She wants my help, Dad! I'm not bothering her! I swear!"

Chloe has the good sense to stay quiet.

I'm trying to erect boundaries here, but I seem to be failing at every turn.

"Fine. You can help with breakfast, but that's it."

"Fine," she says with a little stomp of her foot.

Fine.

SIXTEEN

CHLOE

WE ALL FALL into an easy summer routine. I try to run every day, or at least every other day in the mornings when it's still cool out. Then I come home, shower, and put on a pot of coffee while I get to work in the kitchen.

It's so quiet in the mornings while Harper sleeps. Luke is up then, usually training out back, but he avoids the kitchen like the plague either because he's not a morning person or he doesn't want to chitchat with me. We're careful about bumping into each other when Harper's not around. Alone time is dangerous, at least on my end. I'm liable to jump his bones any minute. Truly, given the right opportunity, the man could find me surgically attached to him.

As such, I'm all too happy to have the kitchen to myself while I make something light and fresh for breakfast. Usually while the two of them eat, I head out to the garden to check on what's ripe. Then once they clear out and I have the dishes done, I'll start on a bread or pastry. Some days, it's a fresh brioche I can use for French toast or a sourdough to make BLT sandwiches. It's been a long time since I've spent so much time in the kitchen purely for the joy of it. I know I could simply make breakfast, lunch, and dinner for Luke and

Harper and that would suffice. In fact, Luke would probably be happy to eat leftovers half the time, but I'm enjoying it all too much.

After lunch, Harper usually has quiet time while Luke gets some work done in his office. When they reemerge in the afternoons, I like to have a treat set out for them to snack on: cookies, scones, almond croissants, cherry Danishes, banana nut muffins. Any extras get doled out to Ned. I find he's best handled like a wild animal. I coax him a little closer every day with the promise of treats, and every day, he's slightly less grumpy than the day before. Soon, we'll be chatting over coffee, playing cards. I can see it now.

Some days Harper and Luke head down to the beach, other days they stick to the pool. They're both getting tan and lovely, and if I have to endure seeing Luke in his bathing suit one more time, I'm going to spontaneously combust. It's just that the kitchen has these sprawling windows that face the backyard, and I can see right out to the pool. It's so easy to see him in all his glory even when I'm not trying to! It's going to be death by a thousand sightings of rock-hard abs, let me tell you.

One afternoon I pass by Luke's office and overhear him talking to his lawyers about David. I don't linger, but it sounds as if the MLBPA is going to take action against him. I have to look up what MLBPA is later: a governing body for sports agents within the MLB. Damn. I almost feel bad for him, but nope. I snuff out that bit of sympathy. Guys like him so rarely get what they deserve. I'm glad Luke is willing to take a stand. Harper doesn't realize how lucky she is to have a dad like him.

Another afternoon, I'm in the kitchen prepping dinner when Harper and Luke get home from a long day out. I'm totally minding my own business when Luke waltzes in wearing a full Batman costume. Head to toe black, the mask, tactical belt, *everything*.

"Should I ask?" I arch a teasing brow.

Harper proudly tells me they spent most of their day at the children's hospital. Luke dropped off toys, took pictures, and signed autographs for the patients.

"But why the getup? Surely you're famous enough as it is."

Luke shoots his daughter an unamused glare as he tugs the mask off with a relieved sigh. "Harper's idea. She didn't think the kids would be impressed to see me otherwise."

Harper clearly still stands by her theory. "You're just a guy! Who cares if you walk into a room! Now, if *Batman* walks into a room…that's really something."

Luke looks at me like, *Can you believe this?*

"She's right, you know. It's just a couple of World Series wins," I tease. "No big deal."

"*Pfft.* Just a regular Joe."

"Boring, really. I'm yawning just thinking about it."

Harper cuts in here. "What are you two doing?"

Luke tousles her hair. "Riffing, kid. We're riffing. Now if you'll excuse me, I'm going to change out of this costume. It's chafing."

Harper continues to open Sugar Stand every few days, whenever the weather is nice or Luke doesn't have something else planned for them. Before she heads out, I help her prepare fresh baked goods to sell, but I try to let her do most of the work herself so she really feels as if she's earning every bit of her profits. Which to date is only $19.

"How much is a Barbie Dreamhouse anyway?" she asks while we bake. "I've gotta be getting close to my goal."

I look it up on my phone.

"Says it's $150 at Target."

Her face falls. "*$150!?* That'll take me all summer! I have to step up my game."

She proceeds to dump two entire bags of chocolate chips

into the stand mixer and turn it up to its highest setting. Chips go flying, pinging around the kitchen like bullets.

The next day, Harper has a playdate. Peyton, a friend from her private school in the city, comes over to the house with her nanny. Peyton is a chubby-cheeked redhead with glasses and a big toothy smile. Her nanny is a supermodel-tall, svelte-thin, hyper-blonde bombshell named Alexia.

Luke lets them in and gives them the lay of the land. I hear giggling from down the hall.

"You have such good taste!" Alexia coos. "Look at this furniture! You should be an interior designer."

Look at this furniture, I mimic to myself bitterly.

"Oh." He forces an awkward laugh. "The place came pre-furnished, actually."

"No, you're kidding! What a find."

What a find! she says while hoping she'll *find* him bending down on one knee and proposing to her on the spot.

Their conversation dwindles as they disappear farther down the hall and, *unrelated*, I accidentally burn some onions I had going on the stove because I'm standing clear across the kitchen with my ear tilted toward the hallway, trying to listen. It's pure happenstance.

I toss the burned onions and start over chopping with vigor. Then the bombshell herself lets herself into the kitchen. *My* kitchen. Her charge is nowhere in sight.

"Anything good to eat around here?" she asks, all formal accent dropped now that she's only talking to me, the fellow help.

"Um, I mean, I'd be happy to get you something. If you can wait a bit, I'm making lunch. There will be more than enough for everyone."

"Yes, that'd be great. It's all almonds and bird seed in the pantry at Peyton's house. Her parents are totally wacko." She suddenly whirls around to face me, eyes alarmed. "*Don't* tell them I said that."

I mime turning a key in a lock on my lips. "Secret's safe with me. I don't even know them."

She tosses her hand into the air as if to say, *It doesn't even matter.*

"The dad's in hedge funds. The mom's like some famous yoga lady. Your setup is way better. How'd you get this gig anyway?"

At this point, she has let herself into the pantry and is rifling around the snack drawers. I just organized things in there yesterday, so it pains me to see her haphazardly pulling stuff out and putting it away wherever she wants. Even Harper knows better than that.

"The job sort of fell into my lap," I answer.

"God, you're lucky." She holds up some Cheez-Its. "Can I open these?"

I nod. It's not like I can tell her no.

"Working for *Luke Allen*." She whistles long and low then pops four crackers into her mouth and proceeds to talk while she chews. "Jesus, I'd die if I got to look at that man every day. Where is he anyway? The girls set up shop in the playroom and then he ran for the hills."

Interesting. So he's not dying for more alone time with mommy long legs over here? I'm shocked.

"I'm not sure. I thought I saw him heading to work out."

It's not true. I haven't seen him, but I don't want her to search him out, so I came up with a tiny white lie. Sue me.

"Right." She crams another fistful of crackers into her mouth. They really must not feed her over there at Peyton's house. "So is he dating anyone?"

I spin back to tend to my food. "I have no idea."

"Really? There aren't like women over here at the house on the weekends?"

She can't see me grimace. Thank god.

When I reply, I've taken on a hard tone. "Sorry. I'm really

not allowed to talk about this stuff. No offense, but for all I know, you'll sell the information to some tabloid."

She walks over so she's back in my line of sight and props herself up on the counter beside me. "Hey, I get it. I mean, I wouldn't, of course. I'm asking purely for personal reasons, trying to get a feel for if I have a chance or not."

"With Luke?"

"Uh yeah. He's so freaking hot. And"—she rubs her fingers against her thumb like she's rubbing dollar bills together—"*loaded*. No more nannying rich entitled brats."

Sheesh.

"Peyton seems sweet I thought?"

She shrugs. "Whatever. She's fine. I've nannied for kids way worse than her, believe me. But like I said, her parents are insane and overbearing. They want her in bed by the same time every night and they don't want her watching more than an hour of TV a day. Are you kidding? I'm supposed to entertain her otherwise? How?"

I try to think of how much TV Harper watches in a day. Usually she's outside swimming or playing with her Barbies or manning her lemonade stand.

Still, I nod as if I understand her dilemma.

"And don't even get me started on all the other rules. No, I'll be with them for another month or two and then it's sayonara, on to the next. I want a cushy job like yours. What training did you say you have?"

"I have my culinary degree and quite a few years of restaurant work under my belt."

Never mind the fact that I worked in extremely prestigious kitchens. We're not talking Wendy's, people—though don't get me wrong, I can get *down* with some Wendy's. Dipping salty fries into a thick chocolate frosty? *Oh my gawwwd.*

She rolls her eyes. "Kill me. I'm *not* going back to school." Then she brightens as she thinks of something. "You think

Luke is in need of a nanny? I haven't seen one here. Did I miss her?"

"He gave Maria the summer off. Usually, she's with him in the city. He might even have more than one, I'm not sure."

She smiles wider and waggles her shoulders. "Well it never hurts to ask if he's interested in hiring another."

She hops off the counter with her Cheez-Its in hand and heads out of the kitchen. I'd guess she's planning to hunt Luke down right now and talk things over. I'll be working alongside Alexia before the day's out.

No.

I'm down the hall, rushing toward Luke's office.

Tap, tap, tap.

"Luke?"

No answer.

I spin around and head back toward the playroom. Alexia is in there with the girls, her feet propped up on the coffee table, her eyes on her phone's screen as she scrolls without a care in the world. Harper and Peyton play pretend store in the corner with a cash register.

No sign of Luke though.

I head toward his bedroom on the other side of the house.

The door's closed, but I'm on a mission.

"Luke?"

"Yeah, give me a second."

He shuffles around for another moment and then the door opens. I see the last few inches of his toned stomach before he finishes putting on his shirt. I'm rendered senseless.

"Chloe?"

My blinking does nothing. I'm a sack of potatoes on his doorstep. A bump on a log.

"Are you sick?"

That does it.

I shake my head and glance back toward the playroom. I can still hear the girls playing, which means it's not out of the question that Alexia could hear me talking to Luke here in the hall. I take matters into my own hands, push him back, and close his bedroom door behind us.

"Hi, can I come in?" I ask once we're already locked away in his room together.

He immediately protests, but I hold up my hands.

"This isn't what you think."

Surely, what he thinks is, *This is it. Chloe has lost her marbles and she's going to tie me up and have her way with me.*

Well, buddy boy, on another day, I just *might.*

"You cannot hire Alexia."

He's slow on the uptake, but eventually, he lets his arms fall back by his sides. He's no longer concerned about bodily harm.

"*Okay.*"

"Yeah, she came into the kitchen blabbering on about how she would kill for a job with you, but you cannot let that happen. And to be clear, it's not even about her being hot. It's about her personality and her being an endangerment to children. I haven't confirmed it, obviously, but she totally seems negligent. I would never want a nanny like that around Harper."

He doesn't look as worried as he should. "Oh really?"

"Yes."

A little smile starts to spread across his lips. Those white teeth are taunting me.

"Whatever you're thinking, stop. I came in here because I was worried about Harper's well-being. I don't want you thinking anything else. It's not about her looks. It's not like I'm acting like some jealous girlfriend."

When he doesn't say anything, I'm forced to add, "Which I'm not."

"Of which I'm well aware."

"As such, we should stop talking about it now."

He cocks his head to the side and narrows his gaze. "I'm

curious why you want me to know you're *definitely* not jealous."

I'm practically panting.

"I've lost the thread of this conversation," I say dumbly.

How are we here again, staring at each other's mouth? Why are my hands fisted at my sides, my thoughts in the gutter?

His bed is right there. Hell, who says we even need a bed? I'm limber.

Luke must sense I'm spiraling because he shakes his head and brings us back down to earth. He's the responsible one. "Right. I'm not hiring Alexia. I spoke to her for all of five minutes and knew immediately that I would never want her around my daughter for more than a brief encounter. I feel bad for Peyton."

"Don't worry, it doesn't sound like she'll be with her family for much longer."

He nods, taking that in.

"So if that's all…"

"I should vacate your bedroom?" I joke, trying for some levity.

Ha ha ha. SEX. I'm thinking about sex and surely you are too.

We do more of the staring, the charged eye contact. The moment passes where he should escort me out, but we stay where we are, neither of us heading toward his bedroom door.

"Luke…"

His name is a question.

It says, *Am I crazy here? Is this all just me? Surely, these feelings aren't completely unrequited?*

But he looks absolutely alarmed by where I might be trying to lead the conversation. No more light banter. It's like he thinks I'm about to propose marriage. He's hearing the looming chime of wedding bells off in the distance.

Every neuron in my brain slams on the brakes. Warning sirens blare.

REROUTE, BROTHERS!

"Oliver asked me out."

He did, in fact. Last night he sent me a text message asking if I wanted to join him and his friends for another dinner. Only this time, he wants to swing by and pick me up for a drink first, just the two of us. I wasn't sure how eager I was to take him up on it until this very moment.

I guess I'm going then. I should probably let Oliver know that.

Luke's expressions are all over the place. The alarm I thought I just saw in his eyes is eviscerated in an instant. Now, it's nothing, a blank space behind his brown gaze. His smile is now just a flat, unfeeling line.

"Okay. When?"

"Day after next."

His shrug says, *I'm not even sure why you're bothering to tell me this.*

"I'll take Harper out to dinner then."

"Okay."

"Okay."

Then he walks to the door, opens it, and holds it for me so I can get back to work.

SEVENTEEN

CHLOE

TUESDAY NIGHT, I'm in bed, dead asleep when I jolt awake. There's a presence looming at the edge of my bed, a hazy figure most likely born from the fires of hell. I choke back a scream just as Harper leans forward into the faint light from the moon peeking through the drapes. There are tear tracks on her round cheeks and her bottom lip is quivering.

I sit up immediately, whipping off my blankets.

"Harper? Are you okay?"

My heart's racing like I'm being chased by death, and it's my natural instinct to pull her close and hug her, to try to calm her as much as myself.

"I had a bad dream," she cries against me, wrapping her arms around my neck and squeezing so that even if I were going to try to pry her off me, I wouldn't succeed.

I shush her soothingly and run a hand down her hair. "It's okay."

I start to rock her forward and backward as I ask her if she wants to tell me about it. She curls up on my lap even more, trying to burrow into me.

"*Okay, okay.* We won't talk about it, but bad dreams are

only dreams. All you have to do is tell your brain no. Say, *No, brain. We aren't going to think about that silly stuff anymore.*"

I start to stand to carry her back to her room, but she whimpers and starts crying harder.

"Can't I just stay with you?"

I don't even hesitate before I reply, "Of course. Yes."

I reach over to fix my pillows so there's a spot for her to lie down beside me. I'll let her stay in here until she's calmed down and fallen back asleep. Then I'll carry her back to her room.

I had bad dreams every so often when I was a child. I still do, sometimes, and I hate that feeling of being alone in a dark room right afterward. All I want is to be tucked safely beside someone. Harper's request is so innocent I could never deny her.

I lay her down and tuck her underneath my blanket. Then I lie down beside her and rub her back, up and down, over and over again, trying to get her racing heart to slow.

She flinches and scoots closer to me.

"Whenever I close my eyes, I think about it!" she whispers worriedly.

My heart breaks for her.

"Well then we'll have to give you something better to think about. Close your eyes and I want you to think of a little butterfly in a garden. What color should she be?"

"Purple."

"Oh purple, yes. And she has white polka dots on her wings."

"And glitter too," Harper adds.

I smile in the dark. "Yes, a lot of glitter. All that glitter makes her shimmer in the sunlight. I want you to think of that little butterfly twirling around in the air then landing on a flower. She opens her wings and closes them again, nice and slow. She's enjoying the flower's sweet nectar as she takes a rest on the soft petal."

Harper's breathing starts to even out. Her face relaxes as I close my eyes and continue.

"Beside her, there's another butterfly. It's one of her friends. She has pink wings the color of cotton candy. She's smaller than the purple butterfly, but she's just as nice. They both stay on their petals, drinking nectar and watching the wind blow the petals of the flowers surrounding them. The sun is so warm, and the butterflies are so happy."

For another few minutes, I keep describing the made-up scene, trying to think of anything that might calm her. Then, I let my voice fade away when I'm certain she's fallen asleep.

In the morning, I wake up to my alarm, but Harper doesn't stir beside me. She's tucked in the blankets, her lips slightly parted, her hair scattered all over her pillow. She's so cute I can barely stand it.

I'm careful as I tiptoe quietly over to my closet to grab clothes for the day. I don't want to wake her up. I'm sure she needs to catch up on some sleep after last night. I pad down to the kitchen and home in on the coffeepot, my mouth already salivating at the thought of a freshly brewed cup. *Be still my heart.*

I have the bag of coffee open and am scooping beans into the grinder when Luke comes rushing into the kitchen. "Have you seen Harper?"

I add another heaping scoop. "Oh, yeah, she's asleep in my room."

He was already heading back out into the hall, but when he hears my answer, he jerks to a stop and turns back around. "What are you talking about? She's in your room?"

There's a frenzy to his words that makes my hands shake with nerves. I set down the bag of coffee beans before facing him again.

"She came into my room last night after she had a bad dream," I start to explain.

"Okay." He motions for me to get on with it. "So then why

didn't you put her back in her bed? Or come get me?"

I shake my head. "I guess I wasn't thinking. I mean…I *was* going to put her back in her bed, but she fell asleep. And then I fell asleep…"

He rubs his forehead like he's trying to ease a tension headache.

The whole thing seems innocent enough to me, but now I feel like I'm missing something.

"She was just so upset, I felt bad. I didn't want to force her to go back to her room while she was crying."

But to him, that's beside the point.

"Don't you see that it's a little strange for my daughter to be sleeping with you in your room?" I flinch, trying hard to not take his tone personally. "You're still a relative stranger to us. And besides that, you're the chef here, Chloe. You get that, right? You're not her nanny. What happens when she gets attached to you and then it's time for us to move back to the city and you're not there? What do I tell her then?"

I fumble over my words, hating that there are tears looming in the corners of my eyes. "I didn't…I'm sorry, I didn't think that far ahead. It was late and I guess I wasn't thinking."

"It's been like this from the beginning. I can't figure out how to make this work. You and Harper…" He shakes his head as he lets his sentence die away. Then he leaves the kitchen, already heading for the stairs.

The exchange leaves me trembling. My gaze falls to the bag of coffee, but now it just seems strange to resume my task as if everything is normal.

Is it really that big of a deal that I let her sleep with me?

Now, in the light of day, I guess I see that I could have calmed her down and then carried her down to Luke's room. That probably would have been the right choice, but she woke me up when I was dead asleep. It's not like I had all my wits about me.

And okay, even if I didn't make the exact right choice, I don't understand why he's so mad. I mean, I'm not a crazy person! I'm nice! And he knows that. I'm not a *relative stranger* anymore. Not at all. I've been here working, spending every single day with Harper and him since the start of summer.

It feels like a lifetime, but then I'm not a parent. I don't know what it feels like to have to put your trust in another human where it concerns your child. I don't know what it must have been like for Luke to wake up and go to Harper's room only to find her bed empty. My stomach drops just thinking of his panic.

Shit.

I want to rush up the stairs after him and apologize, assure him that I understand why this is all strange and complicated. I could make it clear to him that I'll try harder with Harper, no matter how cute and persuasive she is; I won't continue to cross the boundaries he set for me. But then, I'm pretty sure I'm the last person he wants to see right now, so I finish making coffee, whip up a quick breakfast, and grab my grocery bags off the counter. My plan is to make myself scarce the rest of the day.

Luke must be attempting to avoid me too because when I get back from the store, I see a note in the kitchen, centered right on the island so I can't miss it.

At the beach, no need to make lunch.
Also, I'm taking Harper out for dinner tonight like we discussed.

Right. My date with Oliver is tonight. Oh goodie.

I flip the note over just to ensure there's nothing else written on the back. I don't have anything too specific in mind, just something like:

Dear Chloe,
I long to see you so we can set things to rights. To me, you're the

sun and the moon. My passions got the better of me, but I hope you
can forgive me at once.
Yours eternally,
Luke

As you can tell, I was reading a historical romance novel before bed last night.

Anyway, the back of the note is blank. Fine. My day is suddenly free—wonderful. I take full advantage. I make some cinnamon rolls so I can let them prove overnight. Then I change into my bathing suit, grab a spare bike from where it's parked near the shed, throw a wave to Ned, and head down to the beach. Don't worry, I make sure to find a spot that's all but deserted. I don't want to accidentally bump into Luke and Harper out here.

I have my romance book, and joke's on Luke because the duke is about to rail his duchess, so I'm actually happy to have the day off, thank you very much. If reading regency porn on the beach is wrong, throw me in handcuffs and haul me off to jail.

My sunburn from when I fell asleep by the pool is long gone. My summer tan has come out to play, and after I tear through a few chapters of my book, I go out into the water and swim until every muscle in my body screams at me to stop. Then I sit in the shallow surf and let the tide wash up and over me. I love it. I can see why rich people spend so much money to buy property here. We're barely two hours from New York City, but I feel like I'm in another world. No taxis or trains or sirens or… I was about to say worries, but ha ha, I have plenty of those.

Whenever there's a swell of tension in my stomach over the idea of facing Luke again, I pick up my book or go back out into the water. I packed myself a nice little picnic lunch too. I've got cubes of aged cheddar cheese, a ripe peach, Lays potato chips, and a wine spritzer in a can. La *de* da.

I make sure to stay out at the beach until it's absolutely crunch time for me to rush home and get ready for my date. It works perfectly because the house is empty when I get back. Luke and Harper are already out at dinner, I guess.

I shower and wash the salt water out of my hair. It's usually dark brown, but in the summer, the sun gives me natural highlights, especially the strands that frame my face. I rub on moisturizer until my body is thoroughly quenched, and then I rifle through my closet. I feel beautiful. Well, on the outside at least. Inside, I'm a pit of despair, which should make me a lovely dinner companion for Oliver. The point is, I want to show off a little bit. I settle on a long maxi skirt and matching crop top. It's not exactly the safest option. I won't be covered up very well, but I can't seem to care. I like the bit of my stomach that shows between the top and the skirt. My bare shoulders and arms look toned and sun-kissed. I layer two gold necklaces around my neck and add on a pair of light brown sandals with thin straps that wind up and tie around my ankles. Aunt Amara brought them back from Italy the last time she and my uncle went for a visit with Nonna.

I toss my hair up into a glossy ponytail just as Oliver texts to let me know he's here to pick me up. His reaction to my outfit is satisfaction enough, but he also peppers in a few compliments on our way to the bar.

"Seriously, where have you been hiding all my life?"

I flush and look away, wishing I could settle more into the moment and appreciate his words. I still feel anxious about everything with Luke. Maybe it was a mistake to stay away from the house all day. If I'd hung around and run into him at some point, we could have just had it out, talked and settled things, *or* he could have fired me and I'd be crying in an aisle seat on the Jitney, heading back to the city at this very moment. Either way, this lingering anxiety would be gone.

Once we have our drinks in hand, Oliver leads me to a table he's reserved on the patio out front.

"They normally don't do this sort of thing. Tables out here are first come, first served, but I know one of the bartenders pretty well. He did me a favor. You like it?"

"I love it."

The table, yes, but the patio too. The pergola perched overhead has been overtaken by jasmine and purple vining flowers. The music playing in the background is acoustic and quiet, accompanied by the soft hum of chatter from neighboring tables. Candles burn low. Most importantly, the weather couldn't be better. A perfect summer night.

I hold up my gin martini the moment we take our seats across from each other.

"To summer," I say.

He grins and picks up his glass to clink it against mine. "To summer."

Oliver looks spiffy in jeans and a black polo. His black glasses remind me of the pair Stanley Tucci wears—who, by the way, can get into my panties any ol' time he wants. Unlike Stan, Oliver's rocking a whole head of hair. It's blond and trimmed short and sits on his head as neat as a pin. He's not at all my type, which is fine because my type has not served me well in the past. Maybe a fancy-pants sommelier is just what I need to reinvigorate my love life.

Oliver grabs a few cocktail nuts out of the bowl on our table. "So tell me how your week has been."

"My week?"

For some reason the question seems like it came out of nowhere. What does my week have to do with anything?

"Yeah, you know, work, social life, and so on," he teases.

I reach for my martini and down a heavy sip. "Good, good. Nothing really to report. My life is pretty boring at the moment. Just been cooking nonstop."

His eyes glitter with excitement. "Ah, tell me the highlights. What's the best thing you've made this week?"

Oh, now we're talking. I could do this all day.

"You know that fresh pesto I grabbed when I saw you at the market the other day?"

He nods eagerly.

"I made a pesto shrimp and artichoke linguine that made me want to weep."

"Oh my god. Tell me more."

"Sweet potato fries alongside bison burgers, cooked out on the grill, of course."

He legitimately looks turned on, and I can't help but tease him about it.

"Don't tell me you have a food fetish."

He rears back. "What?" Then he shakes his head vehemently. "I don't even know what that is." He sounds seriously offended.

I can't help but laugh, which makes him double down in his offense.

He adjusts his glasses as he insists, "I just like good food. Is that so weird?"

"Hey, I'm sorry. I was just trying to be funny, which I see now is not my forte. I'll stick to bison burgers."

The conversation is awkwardly stilted after this, as if we've lost our trust in each other. I can no longer count on him to take a joke, and he can no longer assume I won't bring up weird fetishes. Though, *come on*, the lady doth protest too much, am I right? Someone search this guy's computer, stat.

It's a while before we recover from my gaffe, but we do. We bond over our shared desire to take a trip out to California to eat at The French Laundry.

"I would give my right lung for a meal with Thomas Keller."

Oliver nods. "I completely agree."

I reach for a few nuts, trying to strategically get as many cashews as possible without being obvious about it. Seems rude to pick out the best ones, no? When I glance up again,

Oliver's attention is across the street. His head is cocked to the side, studying something.

"I recognize that guy over there. He's that baseball player who just retired. God, what's his name. I see him at the market sometimes."

I follow his gaze as he snaps his fingers, trying to jog his memory.

Behind me, on the other side of the street, Luke and Harper stand just outside an ice cream shop with a few middle school-aged boys gathered around them. The boys are jumping up and down, excitedly waving their phones in the air.

"Luke Allen." He laughs then thunks his head with his hand. "His name was rattling around in there among all the wine. Knew I'd remember it eventually."

I watch as Luke bends down to take a picture with the first boy, ensuring Harper is tucked away safely behind him, not in view of the camera.

Not that it matters. She pokes her head around the side of him and smiles really big, ensuring she's in frame as much as her famous dad. I chuckle to myself.

"How obnoxious."

Oliver's words take me aback.

"Parading around town with his kid like that…"

"He's probably just out to dinner," I say, trying to rein in my annoyance over Oliver's assessment.

He snorts like I'm being totally clueless. "There are a million places he could go and he chooses the busiest street in Bridgehampton? The guy clearly loves attention."

I could toss my drink on Oliver, get up, and storm away. That's how visceral my reaction is to him talking badly about Luke and Harper. But seeing as how that's borderline insane, or at the very least unreasonable, I'm forced to just shrug it off.

I'm proud of how calm my tone is when I respond. "You

think? He doesn't seem the type."

"To love attention? What celebrity doesn't?"

"Is he a celebrity?"

"He's a famous baseball player—same thing."

I can't sit idly by as he continues. "Have you interacted with him before? You seem like you have a personal vendetta or something."

He shakes his head, oblivious to the rising heat in my voice. Then he picks up his wine glass and swirls it around. Okay, you know what? If you want to talk about obnoxious, *that's* obnoxious. I get that wine is his passion, but the guy has been swirling, sniffing, swishing, anything *but* drinking it. *Just tip it back and call it a day.* I'd ask him what he's doing, but I don't feel like getting a lecture on how long wine needs to breathe before I'm allowed to drink it.

"I would just hate dealing with a guy like that," he goes on.

I can't help myself. I let my gaze trail back toward Luke and Harper. They're inside the ice cream shop now. I can see them through the large glass storefront. They're perusing the flavors, sampling as they go. Harper makes Luke try an ice cream that's colored bright pink, and after he tastes it, he wrinkles his nose and pulls a face. His over-the-top reaction makes her crack up laughing.

"Yeah, seems like a real monster…"

My sarcasm is utterly lost on Oliver.

I'd give anything to snap my fingers and swap places. I'd stick some other girl in my spot and dash across the street, whip open that ice cream shop door, and grab a scoop with Harper and Luke. I'd even let Harper poison me with the pink flavor.

I want it so bad.

You're the chef here, Chloe. You get that, right?

Luke's words from earlier make me wince. My insides clench tight, and I reach for my martini.

Dinner with Oliver and his friends that evening would have been okay if only I were in a better mood. I can't quite seem to care about their conversation. They're fine, nice, maybe even people I could be friends with if I were willing to try harder.

Oliver eventually catches on that the night isn't panning out well for me. There's only so long someone can sit in sullen silence before people take notice.

He calls it before we order dessert and offers to drive me home. I thank him for the offer but take an Uber instead so I don't pull him away from his friends for no good reason.

I'm tempted to give my parents a call on the way home, but they know me too well. They'd detect my mood too quickly, and I don't feel like having to explain myself. They'd be disappointed to learn that though I've switched jobs and moved cities, I'm still right back where I left off: overstepping my boundaries at work, getting myself into hot water.

They would surely be on Luke's side.

That's his daughter, Chloe. He's going to be fiercely protective of her, just like how we would be with you.

I don't want to hear their advice about minding my own business and keeping my head down at work. They don't have to remind me how good this job is. It's an absolute breeze compared to restaurant work. The pay is obscenely excellent, and beyond that, I'm enjoying it. I'd be an idiot to mess it up. The way I see it, there are two hurdles I need to get over: my infatuation with Luke and my attachment to Harper.

Sounds like I just have a big heart! Sue me!

No, *wrong*. I'm going to have to take a different approach moving forward. Platonic kindness, friendship from afar, boundaries.

Say it with me: *booounnnndarieeees*.

"Huh?" the Uber driver asks from the front seat. "Did you say something?"

EIGHTEEN

LUKE

HARPER AND I stay out later than I anticipated, and she's asleep in the back seat by the time I pull into the driveway. I carry her to her room, tuck her in bed, and make sure she's still sound asleep. I watch her for a minute. Her soft rhythmic breathing is a reassuring balm to my frayed nerves. It hurts to love someone so much, to have your exposed heart walking around on two legs all day.

I close the door slowly and head into the kitchen. Movement outside draws my attention, and I spot Chloe sitting on the edge of the pool with her skirt tucked up around her hips. Her feet dangle down into the water, bobbing back and forth. She's got a beer beside her, and every now and then, she reaches down and grasps the neck of it so she can take a swig.

So I'm not alone then; we're both wallowing. Ever since this morning, after our argument in the kitchen, I've been trying to endure gnawing guilt. I was worked up first thing when I went to Harper's room and found her bed empty. The things that run through a parent's mind in moments like that —they're not always logical or sound. I panicked, and I'm not proud of how I handled myself.

So I kick off my shoes, grab another beer from the fridge,

slide the back door open, and pad across the porch to join Chloe by the pool.

She doesn't stir as I take a seat beside her. I dangle my feet in the water too and make sure my shorts are tugged up enough that they don't get wet on the pool's edge.

Neither of us says a word, each sipping beer in silence. I peer over at her from the corner of my eyes and see she's really put a lot of effort into her appearance for tonight. A little bit of makeup, silky hair, cute outfit. So she went on that date.

I want to ask her about it. God, I could listen to every detail. *Did he pick you up? Did he open your door? Did he make you laugh at dinner?*

It's painful to sit with unrequited feelings. That's what this is now; there's no point in denying it anymore. I want Chloe, and yet, I have to sit here and look at her like it's not a searing kind of torture. The reflected pool lights dance across her face. She's bathed in pale blue. I want her to look at me, but maybe it's good that she doesn't. I'd kiss her, and we'd really be in a shitstorm then.

"I owe you an apology," she says, finally, her attention down on her thighs.

"*No.*" I'm heartbroken by the thought that she might have been beating herself up all day about what happened with Harper. "It's the other way around. I didn't mean to be hard on you like that."

"You were acting on instinct, and you were worried about Harper," she argues. "It probably scared you half to death to find her bed empty like that. I wasn't thinking."

I release a long exhale. "It's so goddamn complicated. All of it. I'm not upset Harper has taken such a liking to you. I'm upset that I can't seem to control this situation like I want to. I'm upset that life seems intent on throwing me curveball after curveball. Still, I shouldn't have taken my anger out on you like that."

Her brows shoot up, but she doesn't say anything. How can she resist looking my way?

I give her another moment, then I can't help but ask, "A lot on your mind?"

She smiles ruefully. "Like you wouldn't believe."

"That's why you're being quiet? Or you're still upset with me?"

Her brown eyes finally drift over to me, and there's sadness lurking there. "I was never upset with you. And for the record, I'm not sure I ever *could* be, but that's beside the point..." She takes another long sip of her beer. "I'm quiet because I'm not supposed to be talking to you right now."

Now that makes me laugh. It's so out of left field.

"Why's that?"

I swear to god, I'm on tenterhooks waiting to hear what she's about to say.

"I'm setting boundaries. Keeping my private life private, my work life...work."

"Oh, just like what I've been trying to do? Let me know how that works out for you."

I take a drink and stare out at the pool as we sit in companionable silence. Two coworkers. I smile at the thought.

"Is this how it always is for you? With the nannies and stuff?"

She doesn't have to explain what she means. I know exactly what she's asking.

"No."

She sighs in defeat, like she was hoping for a different answer.

"Maria's been with us forever, and she's in and out, not one for small talk. She's good with Harper, but otherwise she's focused on her own life. She has grandkids."

Chloe nods, mulling this over.

"That could be my problem. I don't have enough going on. I need grandkids."

I burst out laughing. "I don't think that's your problem."

"Well then, enlighten me."

I tip back the rest of my beer, draining it down and wishing I had another to follow it up with.

She shifts on her butt, adjusts her skirt. She's not trying to tease me. Hell, she probably doesn't even realize what she's doing is sexy as hell. To her, it's just about practicality. She's wearing a long skirt and doesn't want it in the water, but now nearly all of her legs are showing, her calves, her knees, that shadowed smooth skin between her thighs…

I keep both of my hands wrapped tightly around my beer bottle, trying to remember why we've found ourselves here in the first place.

I guess after this morning, Chloe deserves some answers.

"You might have wondered why it's just Harper and me. She doesn't talk about her mom much, at least not to me, but—"

I clear my throat, annoyed to find that I'm having a hard time getting the story out. Chloe's looking at me, but she doesn't say a word, doesn't so much as move as she waits patiently for me to continue.

I narrow my eyes and focus on forcing out one word at a time. "Harper's mom, Nadine, passed away from acute myeloid leukemia when Harper was almost two. We weren't together at the time. We never married, actually. Dated for a stint and yeah, we were lucky enough to end up with Harper. Nadine was a good friend though. I miss her like hell, and more than that, I hate that Harper barely remembers her."

I'm spinning that beer bottle around and around. A nervous tic, I guess.

I heave a heavy sigh, feeling sorry that I'm having to unload all this on Chloe. In fact, I'm about to retreat and save it for another time, or better yet, never. Then Chloe puts her hand on the concrete between us and leans closer to me. It's nothing really, but I somehow feel reassured enough to keep going.

"Anyway, after Nadine passed, my parents really stepped up and helped with Harper. They would stay in the city when I had to travel during the season, but they're getting older and my dad had a little health scare last year that forced them back to Texas so he could get treatment."

Chloe shakes her head. "*God*, Luke…"

I can't look at her if I'm going to finish getting this all out.

"He's doing okay now, but it's just not possible for them to be with Harper like before, and there's only so much my sister can do. The nanny thing is hard. Maria is great, but she's only one woman, and during baseball season, I had to have backup. There were three different nannies helping with Harper at one point. Managing their schedules and trusting them to take good care of my daughter was no easy feat.

"Last season, while I was on the road, one of them flaked and forgot to pick up Harper from school. My sister was out of town, and Maria had a sick granddaughter she needed to stay with. I was across the country and my kid needed me and I couldn't be there. In the end, it worked out. It was fine. Harper's teacher stayed with her until I could get ahold of the nanny who was originally supposed to pick her up, but that sort of shit happened *all* the time. That feeling of failure, it never gets easier. That worry that you're somehow ruining your kid…" I shake my head, more resolute now than ever. "It's not worth it. Harper is young for such a short time, and it just finally got to the point where it became impossible for me to maintain both worlds. I couldn't be a professional baseball player and a single dad without feeling like I was doing Harper a disservice."

Chloe reaches for her beer and passes it to me, offering me the last half. I take it and drink.

She lets me settle for a second, and then she asks, "Do you miss baseball?"

"Like you wouldn't believe."

Just thinking about it makes my chest ache.

"I'm sorry. I can't imagine being put in that position. I understand where you're coming from, I do. Harper is too important. I just hate that you had to give up baseball entirely."

I'm usually so quick to turn away people's sympathy, but with Chloe, I relish it. The feeling of being able to lean on another person isn't a privilege I've had in recent years. I'm so careful with my parents. I never want to worry them; they have enough on their plate. Tate as well. My sister would drop everything to help with Harper if I asked her to, but I won't. That's not her responsibility.

"I mean, it's small potatoes compared to other people's problems. I won't pretend otherwise."

"Hey," Chloe says, trying to get me to look at her.

It takes me a second, but I manage to work up the courage.

Her brows are knit together in frustration, her eyes earnest and searing. She's dead serious. "What you just told me would turn anyone's world upside down. You lost your friend and Harper's mom in one fell swoop. You're worried about your parents. You have so few people you can turn to, and I think you're doing a really damn good job of raising Harper on your own."

I don't have the capacity to do anything beyond a small nod.

She motions for me to pass her back the beer. She takes a sip then hands it back to me. We share it like that, back and forth, until it's gone.

Eventually she speaks up. "Can I ask why you shared all that with me? Don't get me wrong, I appreciate knowing more about your situation, especially with Harper. I just can't help but feel like there's more to it. Like you've left off the second half of the story."

I swallow hard and narrow my eyes out on the pond in the distance. At night, from here, I like to watch the moon's reflection on the water.

The truth tumbles out of me while I'm looking away. It's easier to do it if I pretend she's not beside me listening.

"I want you to know why, even though it's completely obvious that I've got a big ol' embarrassing crush on you, I haven't acted on it."

The silence becomes heavier than ever. I peer over, and Chloe's frozen. Her innocent eyes are round with shock. Is she surprised to hear I've got a crush on her or surprised I had the guts to lay it all out there like that?

Then she makes a little noise, an intrigued *huh*.

"So the feeling's mutual." She shakes her head like she can't believe it. "That makes me feel better, I guess."

Oh fuck. Under normal circumstances, her confession would help. Now, though, it is absolutely *not* easier to hear she's equally into me. I would have almost preferred it if she'd laughed in my face. Unrequited interest is one thing, but mutual longing? That's destined to be trouble.

I wish I had another beer. I take the bottle from her hands and tip it back, ensuring I've cleared every last drop.

"So to recap…" Chloe starts. "You've got a hell of a lot on your plate, and you're focused on Harper. Meanwhile, I just got out of a relationship with my *last* boss, and you're my *new* boss, *and* I'm living here, so things could get really complicated really fast." She shoots me a teasing glare. "Did I leave anything out?"

I pick at the label on the beer bottle. "Nope. That just about covers it."

She leans over and lowers her voice just a little. "Can I ask, though…if I were any other woman, in any other situation—"

"We wouldn't be sitting here merely talking right now."

I know that for damn certain.

"Oh wow."

I think I've managed to fluster her even more. "You're blushing."

"Uh, *yeah*." She fans her face, trying to cool off her cheeks. "It's just a lot. You're really direct."

"Cocky's another way of putting it."

"Sure, yeah, there's some of that too. I can't believe it. You think I'm *hot* hot?"

I grip the edge of the pool and shake my head. "Chloe, don't make me spell it out. It's hard enough as it is."

"Okay, but what if you just told me one time and then—" She slices her hand through the air, cleaving off the end of her sentence. "Never again. I'll pretend I have amnesia, I swear."

I give her the same reproachful glare I give Harper when she's pushing her luck.

Chloe doesn't give in. Her gaze turns pleading, and that bottom lip juts out as she tacks on a "Please."

Fine. I look up and meet her eyes, wanting to be sure she hears me the first time so I won't have to repeat it.

"I am insanely, annoyingly, couldn't-stop-if-I-tried attracted to you. I have thought about kissing you a hundred times in a hundred ways."

I watch Chloe swallow hard. My words are more than she bargained for, I guess.

"Oh shit. I think I'm about to have a heart attack."

She reaches over and takes my hand so she can press it to her chest as proof. Her heart is racing. Yeah, I'm aware of it, but I'm also acutely aware of the intimacy of the moment. Pressing my hand over her heart makes it feel like I'm branding her as mine somehow. Her smooth warm skin under my palm momentarily hijacks my thoughts.

Touching isn't a good idea. Staving this off is only possible if we're keeping our hands to ourselves, but now I can't seem to pull away.

I turn toward her slowly as my hand slides up her chest and around her neck, up underneath her ponytail. I feel her shiver when my fingers touch the tip of her spine. My pulse is pounding. *Her* pulse is pounding.

She doesn't pull away. On the contrary, Chloe turns and arches into my hand, throwing kerosene on this fire. She's so close now that when she wets her bottom lip, I swear I can almost feel it too. Does she realize what she's doing? Is she aware she's staring at my mouth like she has a wolf's hunger?

"Luke?" she asks, breathless. "What if we kissed? Just once…"

"Amnesia?" I ask, wondering if we're still playing this game, as ridiculous as it might be.

Her eyes spark with desire. "*Yes*. I'm so good at forgetting. The *best* at forgetting. I promise."

She's already leaning in toward me, and whether I meet her halfway or I'm the one to impatiently close that gap between us, it doesn't matter. Our lips finally touch. Our kiss is gentle and unsteady. Nerves get the better of us at first. I pull back and gauge her reaction. Her eyes are wide and dilated, her lips parted, and just as I lean in to kiss her again, she tips forward eagerly to meet me. Desire takes over. I kiss her hard and she whimpers. My hand wraps around the back of her neck, twining up into her hair. Her hand touches my knee then, more boldly, it clutches my thigh as she creeps even closer.

Her lips are soft and tentative, but she warms up quickly and starts to kiss me back with equal fervor. She tastes so sweet, and when I tilt her head to the side and slip my tongue past her lips, she digs the tip of her fingers into my thigh, showing me how much she likes it. Blood thunders through my veins. My restraint ebbs with the thought of her hand sliding higher up my leg, her fingers working on my zipper, touching me how we both want.

It's insane to want her this badly. We know no bounds. We've called it a kiss, but we're well past that point. She has me completely exposed. The knowledge that this moment is fleeting only further ignites us. It's painful even now to realize this is the only taste of her I'll ever get, so I'm greedy about it. Her soft moans egg me on. I scrape my teeth across her bottom lip.

The longer the kiss goes on, the faster my restraint crumbles.

I'm tipping us, about to press her down onto the pool deck when she suddenly pulls back to give me a glimpse of her fiery eyes. I can see how close she was to losing control. We're still entwined together, our chests rising and falling so rapidly.

I'm still looking at her mouth, trying to come down from our *innocent* kiss when a smile begins to spread across her face.

"Okay, new plan," she quips. "I'll quit and make this easier on us."

The suggestion sends a fissure of panic through me. "*No.*"

"You could fire me?"

"I'm not firing you."

She sighs lightly. "Oh, all right. Amnesia it is."

NINETEEN
CHLOE

I SHOULD BE GETTING a letter in the mail from the Nobel Prize committee *any* day now regarding my genius idea. You see, what you do is this: behave badly and then pretend like you didn't. It's really that simple. I don't know why someone hasn't thought of this earlier.

Made out with my boss poolside?

Uh? No I didn't. I have no idea what you're talking about.

Luke stuck his tongue down my throat? Never happened, sweetie. Get your eyes checked.

I don't even need one of those *Men in Black* memory sticks. I wake up the next morning completely and utterly prepared to tackle the day as if yesterday was same ol' same ol'. My lips remember *nothing*.

I put on a Florence and the Machine playlist while I make classic French omelets for breakfast alongside oatmeal topped with nuts and berries for Luke and bananas and Nutella for Harper.

When they stroll into the kitchen to eat, I shoo them over to the breakfast table. Then I serve them with a big smile aimed at the cute little family.

If I'm unable to meet Luke's eyes, it's only because the sun is shining too brightly in that direction.

"Looks yummy, Chloe. Thank you."

"Harper, you're absolutely welcome!"

"Thanks," Luke adds.

"Uh-huh," I say, scurrying away before we accidentally have any more contact with each other. If we *had* made out last night and it *had* been surface-of-the-sun levels of hot, I'd worry about betraying my emotions in front of Harper. Good thing that's not the case.

"I'm going on a run after I clean up breakfast, but there are freshly made granola bars cooling on the counter over here and a fruit tray in the fridge if either of you get hungry. Okay, bye!"

I break records on that run. It's my best time ever. A perk of (literally) running from your problems.

In the afternoon, I'm out in the garden with a basket over-flowing with green beans and red peppers. My head is in the clouds as I imagine all the dishes I could prepare for dinner. Then I spot Luke. He's just finished working out. How can I tell? His gray shirt is drenched in sweat. His hair is slick with it too. He looks sticky and hot, and my hands clench around my gardening shears. I watch him skirt around the garden, completely ignoring me as he heads straight for the pool. In what can only be described as a slow-motion striptease, he tugs off his shirt and tosses it onto a lounge chair, making the muscles along his back ripple and bulge. He toes off his tennis shoes and socks then dives into the water to cool off.

I am slack-jawed among the cucumbers.

The tomatoes are shaking their heads at me like, *Girl, you're in trouble.*

I take pruning shears to them and get on with my day.

"*Knock-knock.*"

Luke finds me the next morning when I'm reading in bed.

I am *this* close to finishing my historical romance. Luke sees it lying cover side up on my bed, and the most interesting thing happens: he doesn't feel the need to comment on it. He doesn't give me a salacious slow-motion wink. He doesn't so much as bat an eye at the Fabio-inspired cover. There's no *Oh ho ho! What do you have there, little lady?*

Are you kidding me, sir? Are you *trying* to make me fall in love with you even harder?

"I know you're on break, but I was just letting you know I'm going to cook lunch if that's okay with you."

I sit up. "Yes, of course. I was planning a summer pasta, but everything will keep until dinner. Are you sure you want to cook though? If you're craving something in particular just let me know and I'm happy to make it for you."

He clears his throat and looks away pointedly, staring at my window.

Alarmed, I look down, but it's all good. I'm just in a tank top and shorts. I'm not lying around in a half-gaping robe exposing my heaving breasts or something (unlike my book's heroine).

Still, I get it. If I walked in on Luke lying on his bed, I'd probably start sweating on the spot.

He crosses his arms and leans against my doorframe. "I want to grill burgers."

"Oh! I can do it."

"Contrary to what Harper has led you to believe, I can cook a few things. Burgers on the grill happens to be one of them."

I grin. "She's a tough critic. You know how often she tells me the story about the salmon you burned that one time? Every day."

He throws his hands up. "I swear I'll never hear the end of it. So our kitchen smelled like a fish market for a few weeks? *Big deal!*"

I laugh. "Well, all right. You've got the burgers. Why don't I stick to sides and toppings?"

"Deal." He holds out his hand for me to shake.

I don't. I truly can't.

He realizes that right away, curling his fingers into a fist and then tacking on a little thumbs-up.

I don't know why it makes me burst out laughing.

"Should we talk about—"

"AMNESIA," I shout, killing whatever the hell he was about to say. "Now go. *Git*."

Later that morning, the doorbell rings. Luke's out getting the grill ready, so I answer it.

It's Alexia and Peyton.

Peyton's wearing a one-piece bathing suit covered with rainbows. A coordinating towel is slung over her shoulder. Her goggles are already on, covering her eyes and making her hair stand up. For her job as a nanny, Alexia has chosen to wear sky-high platform espadrilles and a string bikini that covers so little of her skin I'm surprised she's bothering with it at all. Just let 'em fly at that point.

"Hi!" Peyton says with a big wave. "We're here to play with Harper!"

"Peyton!" Harper squeals before running past me to greet her friend. She's already in her bathing suit too, and the two of them waste no time rushing out to the pool, which leaves me with the fun task of welcoming Alexia.

"Please, come in," I say, stepping back to open the door wider.

"Oh hey."

She takes off the pool bag she had slung over her shoulder and holds it out for me.

"Oh-*kay*," I say as I'm forced to take it or let it spill out onto the floor.

She's not even looking at me. She's a shrewd hunter, her eyes surveying the house.

"Where's Luke?"

It pains me to tell her the truth. "He's out back."

She unveils a devious grin and leaves me in the dust. As she walks away, I'm treated to a view of her perky butt in her thong bikini bottom. Now there's something that truly baffles me. A thong bikini bottom? I just don't trust bathing suit technology that much, you know?

She cuts through the foyer and heads to the kitchen. I hear her bubbly "Hiii, Luke!" and then the patio door slides closed behind her.

I don't even bother taking her bag out. If she needs something from it, she can march her thonged butt in here and get it herself.

I decide I won't let Alexia get to me. She's mostly harmless, I think. I go back to pulling out burger supplies from the fridge, and I've only finished grabbing the ketchup and mustard by the time the patio door slides open again and an annoyed Alexia huffs back inside.

"Forget something?" I ask, pointing toward her bag on the table.

"No," she snaps rudely. "Luke apparently talked to Peyton's mom. He's fine with me just dropping her off this afternoon. Oh, and he'll give Peyton a ride home later. What the hell."

She picks up her bag.

Then she looks at me, waiting for me to say something.

"I...god, yeah, that's annoying?" I try to match her energy, but she can see right through me.

She rolls her eyes. "Whatever, have fun with the brats. I'm going to the beach."

"Okay! Bye!" I say with a chipper tone, turning around to get back to work before she's even started to leave.

The rest of my morning is shaping up pretty well. I whip up a garlic aioli and a dipping sauce for the French fries that I know the girls will love. I have the cheese ready to go along with the lettuce and pickles. I'm working on slicing the tomatoes when I hear Luke laughing outside.

He's standing at the edge of the pool in his bathing suit holding a water gun almost as big as his arm. Harper and Peyton stand on the other side of the pool with aquatic armaments of their own. Luke has his aimed at the girls and vice versa. It appears to be a real stand-off.

"Admit defeat and we can all join forces. There's no need to go to war," Luke taunts.

The girls look at each other as if considering his offer, and then in tandem, they shout "NEVER!" and start spraying him with a deluge of water.

Luke pretends to be mortally wounded, slowly letting his gun slip from his fingers, and then he tips sideways into the pool like a defeated villain. The girls whoop and holler as Luke dramatically slips under the surface. He's really putting his heart and soul into his performance. With baseball out of the way, he might try turning his sights on the stage.

I'm so into watching them play, when I go back to slicing my tomatoes…I accidentally include my finger.

Time slows to a halt. My eyes widen. Blood drains from my face. I look down and almost lose it.

"*Ahhhhhhhhhh…*" I let the word drag as I flutter around the kitchen, trying to figure out what I'm supposed to do.

I absolutely hate blood. *Hate it.* When we were growing up, one time Gio flew over the handlebars on his bike and wound up with a gnarly cut on his forehead. I saw it, passed out, hit my head on the sidewalk, and out of the two of us, *I* was the one who wound up having to get a CT scan at the hospital.

I recognize that I cleaned up David's blood in this very kitchen and managed to handle that well, but this is MY blood. MY BLOOD. OKAY?!

I'm still flailing around in circles. My common sense left the kitchen the moment my eyes saw the first drop of blood on my finger. I'm just repeating "Oh god, oh god, oh god" under my breath like the big man himself might actually appear and patch me up.

The pain hasn't even set in. I don't know how bad the cut is because I'm too scared to look.

I've been trained for this. I know proper kitchen protocols. There are step-by-step instructions we're meant to follow if we injure ourselves on the job, so tell me why I'm standing in front of the freezer, fanning myself with the swinging door.

"What's going on?"

I whirl around.

Luke's just on the outside of the open porch door with a towel slung low around his hips. Water drips down onto the wood at his feet. It also slides across his broad chest and wide shoulders, but now's not the time to get lightheaded, so I peel my eyes away fast.

"Nothing!"

I tuck my injured hand behind my back like a child concealing a stolen cookie from the cookie jar.

He's immediately suspicious. Those dark eyebrows lower over his eyes. "Whyyyy are you acting weird?"

I sputter out a loud laugh. "I'm not!" I step away from the freezer and let the door slam shut behind me. "Now, did you need something?"

I'm gesticulating a lot with my right hand—the uninjured one—as a way to throw him off my scent.

"Condiments? Salt? Pepper? Oh, I bet you need something to flip the burgers!"

I'm flitting around the kitchen, grabbing as much as I can with one hand. I've got a spatula, ketchup bottle, and salt and pepper shakers tucked precariously in the crook of my right elbow when I go over to him.

"Here you go. I'll bring out the rest in a second."

I'm already stepping back when he reaches out and takes my left bicep in his hand.

"Show me what you have."

"It's nothing!"

He tightens his grip just a smidge, enough to let me know he's serious.

"*Chloe.*"

"Luke!" I laugh. "You're going to ruin the surprise!"

Oh, look at me, thinking on my feet! I guess all my blood hasn't rushed to and out of my finger like I assumed.

His tone is not the least bit believing as he asks, "What surprise?"

"Uhhh…" I look around the kitchen. Then my eyes land on the early birthday card Maria mailed to Harper yesterday. I make sure to whisper when I say, "It's a little birthday surprise for Harper."

So what if I have to construct an extravagant three-tier birthday cake this afternoon to cover my ass? I'll do it.

"You have a birthday surprise for Harper tucked behind your back?"

He can barely keep the amusement out of his voice.

Okay, listen, I don't enjoy lying. Quite frankly, I didn't think he'd press me this hard. *Hello, unhand me already, good sir!*

I sound less than convinced as I reply with a slow, unsteady "Yes."

Then his mouth tips up in a smirk, and like my bones are merely molded out of Play-Doh, he tugs my arm—even as I fight against him—and lifts it up to reveal my mangled, bloody finger.

Now, from this point on, it's hazy. I think I black out for a second or two because the next thing I know I'm sitting in one of the kitchen chairs and Luke is crouched down in front of me, barking orders to Harper.

"Go get me the first-aid kit from the cabinet inside my bathroom."

Harper hops to it, dashing through the house in her wet bathing suit.

I blink and try to figure out why my heart is fluttering so fast. It feels like I just took ten shots of espresso and chased them with a couple of energy drinks.

"Am I dying?"

Luke doesn't laugh.

"OH MY GOD. AM I DYING?"

Now, he laughs.

"Relax, will you? I've got you. Just sit tight for a second."

He's on the floor in front of me, propped up on one knee like how he would propose to me if that were what was happening right now. His arms keep me secure on the chair and he already has a paper towel wrapped around my finger, applying pressure.

Peyton—*oh right, Peyton's here*—steps slowly into the kitchen, giving us a wide berth. Those damn goggles are still suction-cupped to her face, though she's no longer smiling like when she first arrived. Now, her mouth is gaping in horror.

"Why…why is there so much blood on the floor?"

Her question is delivered so perfectly—shaky voice and all—it's like she's been cast in a thriller.

I follow her line of sight, down to the floor, and I see it. The red. So much red. When I was flitting around the kitchen, unsure of what to do earlier…I guess I was also dripping—

That thought ends as my vision tunnels and my head lolls back.

Luke gently pats my cheeks. "Hey, you're okay. Come on. Sit up."

At this point, my body says, *Actually, we give up trying to handle this well. Let's just give it all we've got. Every hormone? Yeah, go ahead and release 'em. Adrenaline? Max thrusters on that.*

There's no proper coping. I'm sweating, shaking, nauseous.

Harper darts back into the kitchen, rushing with the first-aid kit, and then she SLIPS ON MY—

"Oh god, I'm going to be sick."

"HARPER, GET ME THE TRASH CAN!" Luke shouts.

No need. It's too late.

TWENTY
CHLOE

MY RATING: 0 out of 10, would not recommend looking away from the cutting board while you're using a very sharp kitchen knife. You would think after half a decade in commercial kitchens, I would be well aware of that. I've even given myself a few nicks here or there—it's a rite of passage in culinary school—but nothing, *nothing* compared to this.

I don't remember getting cleaned up before leaving Luke's house. I don't really remember the ride from Luke's house to Bridgehampton Urgent Care. I vaguely recall Luke swinging by to drop off a confused Peyton, and I know Harper was in the back seat, sweetly reassuring me that everything was going to be okay.

"When something bad happens to me, Dad gets me a toy or something to make me feel better. Maybe he can do that for you. Maybe we can buy you something to make you feel better."

"I don't want a Barbie, I just want my finger" is the response I gave to that, so as you can see, I'm handling myself very well.

Luke parks and insists on helping me get out of the car even though I've injured my finger and not my legs.

I tell him that, and he levels me with an impatient glare. "I don't want a repeat of what just happened in my kitchen."

With that, he keeps a sturdy arm around my waist and ensures Harper's right beside us as we go inside.

The lady behind the counter instructs us to sign in and take a seat. "It'll be a while."

We look up and survey the waiting room. It's crowded with all the usual suspects. There are your standard coughing, sniffly adults, of course. There's the extremely sunburned guy in the corner whose face is pinched like he's in serious pain. He probably can't laugh about it now, but the sunglasses outline around his eyes, demarcating the red skin from the milky white skin, is seriously funny. Then there's a toddler who's totally unbothered by being here. He's running around, playing. At first, I suspect he's just a tagalong like Harper, but then he complains about his nose hurting and his mom snaps, "I'm sure it does! That's why you don't shove four M&Ms up your nostril!"

Harper looks at me, and we both suppress a smile.

I get called to go back to an exam room relatively soon, just after M&M boy. I stand, and for a second, I expect to have to go back alone—something I've been secretly dreading this entire time—but then Luke and Harper stand too.

"I'm sorry, are you two with her?" the medical assistant asks.

Luke steps up beside me. "I'm her boyfriend."

Harper gasps but otherwise recovers quickly. "Yeah, and I'm her daughter!"

The medical assistant props her hand on her hips and stares between us with pursed lips. She knows something's up. "*Sure*. Well, right this way for the happy family."

Harper hurries forward and takes my right hand, squeezing it. When I look down, she smiles timidly, her big brown eyes gleaming. "You don't have to be scared. We'll stay with you the whole time."

After checking my vitals, the medical assistant waves me toward the exam table in the room. "Take a seat up there for me."

Before I can, Luke steps forward and gestures to one of the chairs in the corner of the room. "Could she sit there for now? She's almost fainted twice, and I'm worried she'll fall off the table."

"Sit wherever you're most comfortable," the medical assistant says, her voice an audible eye roll. She's either not paid enough to mask her snark, or her long career has stripped her of her empathy. "The doctor will be in soon with the sutures."

Luke doesn't miss the fact that my eyes widen on her last word.

We settle in place. Harper sits in the chair beside mine. Luke stands on the other side of me, his heavy hand resting on my shoulder.

He looks over at his daughter. She's currently taking in the room, her eyes wide with curiosity and maybe a good bit of worry too. "Harper, are you sure you want to be in here? You could wait just outside. I could give you my phone to play with."

She looks absolutely offended that he would suggest such a thing. "I'm not leaving Chloe! She needs me!"

She looks to me for backup, and I smile. "It's true, kiddo. You're so brave. Braver than me, that's for sure."

She raises her chin. "See?" Then she holds out her hand. "But, I will take your phone so I don't have to watch the blood and guts part."

Luke chuckles and slides it out of his pocket so he can hand it over.

Once Harper's ensconced in the Disney Plus app, I look at Luke. "Boyfriend, huh?"

He damn near blushes. "I didn't think they'd let me back otherwise."

"I'm sure she would have been okay with it if you'd just said you're my friend."

He shrugs and looks away. "I didn't want to take any chances. Also, it's *my* fictional scenario—why should I be friend-zoned?"

I can't help but laugh. I try to think of the situation if it were reversed. Would I want to be here if Luke was hurt? Or if, god forbid, something happened to Harper? Absolutely. I would have lied just the same.

I sigh at the heavy thought, and Luke responds with a squeeze on my shoulder just before there's a light tap on the door. A moment later, a female doctor walks in. Her intimidating white coat is offset by a short pixie cut and a big smile.

"Hi, I'm Dr. Davis. And since you've got the wrapped finger, I'll assume you're Ms. Ricci?" she says, already stepping toward me.

After I introduce myself, I launch into the short story of slicing my finger. The doctor interrupts a few times to nail down specifics, like what kind of food I was preparing ("No raw chicken, I hope?"), when the injury happened, and if I washed the wound thoroughly. Luke answers several of the questions with an almost paternal protectiveness. Normally, I might be annoyed to be spoken for, but after the whirlwind afternoon I've had, I just feel grateful.

The doctor nods and turns her attention to me. "Well, hop up on the exam table so I can take a look. Are you feeling lightheaded now?"

I shake my head.

"Good. As a precaution, I'll have you lie all the way back, and if you're willing to help"—she turns her attention to Luke —"I'll ask you to stand on that side of the table and keep a steady hand on her. Now, is it okay if I unwrap this bandage and take a look?"

I nod and immediately turn my attention up to Luke. He's gripping my right hand tightly as his thumb rubs softly back and forth. I focus on the warmth emanating from his touch. It's a comfort, especially compared to the cold saline Dr. Davis uses to moisten the inner layers of my bandage before removing it.

"Hi," Luke mouths.

"Hi," I mouth back.

"You okay?"

I nod, even though there's a tear slipping down my cheek.

"Am I hurting you?" Dr. Davis asks.

"No," I reply, sounding like there's a frog in my throat. I'm just a big baby.

"Good. Deep breaths." I feel her shifting my hand right and left, inspecting my finger with gloved hands. "Can you flex it inward?"

I bend the finger in a cheeky *Come hither* motion to Luke before the pain makes me stop.

"So do you think you can, like...glue it?" I croak expectantly.

Her face twists with remorse. "I wish I could, but due to the location, this wound needs stitches. The good news is it'll just be a few, and there shouldn't be any noticeable scarring.

"All things considered, you're lucky. If you'd nicked a tendon, it would've been straight to the E.R. for a hand surgeon referral. Those guys make the big bucks. Now, let's get started."

When we get home from the urgent care, I slip off my shoes and aim for the kitchen, intending to clean up the mess I made earlier both from prepping for lunch and from my injury, but Luke grips my shoulders and redirects me toward the couch in the family room.

"I can't leave the kitchen like that!" I protest.

"Sit down."

I sit.

"Lean back. Prop your feet up."

I do both.

Then he gives Harper clear drill sergeant orders. "She's not allowed to move. You're on watch. Can I trust you?"

Harper salutes him. "On it, sir."

"What if I need to use the restroom?" I tease as he heads for the kitchen.

"Harper will get you a cup."

Harper and I burst out laughing. She grabs the remote and nestles down next to me, arranging a blanket over the two of us, careful to place it gently around my bandaged finger. "What should we watch?"

We settle on *The Princess and the Frog* since I've somehow never seen it.

Harper can barely believe it. "Her dress is beautiful! My favorite of all the Disney princesses!"

It doesn't take long for Luke to clean. I keep peering over my shoulder to see how he's getting on. In no time, the floors and counters are all wiped down, the dishes are loaded, and the kitchen looks good as new. After, he showers and puts on sweatpants and a t-shirt, returning just in time to catch the end of the movie.

He plops down in the seat on the other side of Harper and stretches his arm across the back of the couch so that if I leaned my head back, his fingers could stroke my hair.

I don't do this, of course; I only think about it.

"Anything salvageable from earlier? For the burgers?"

It's not quite dinner time yet, but with all of us having skipped lunch, I'm sure we'll want to eat early.

He frowns and shakes his head. "I accidentally let the meat burn on the grill when I came in to check on you earlier, so that's not an option. The cheese and everything out on the counter didn't look great either. I wasn't thinking before we left. I could have put it all in the fridge."

"It's no big deal. I could make that summer salad?"

"Let's order takeout!" Harper suggests.

"You read my mind," Luke tells her, already reaching for his phone.

"Chinese food?" they both say at the same time.

Luke smiles and Harper laughs, burrowing against her dad so he can wrap his arm around her.

Harper looks to me, explaining, "It's our favorite. We usually eat it once a week, but you've been cooking such good food we haven't had it in a while."

I smile.

Harper relaxes against her dad, and they start scrolling down the restaurant's menu. The intimacy of the moment suddenly hits me, and I realize this might be one step too far. After what happened the other night and this afternoon, I'm beginning to wonder if it's even possible to delineate between work and real life while I'm living here with them. I try not to let the ease of the moment muddle my brain. I'm only sitting on the couch with Harper and Luke because I have an injured finger. I'm not part of their little family. I shouldn't be sitting here with them at all, really.

I stand suddenly, my part of the blanket slipping down to the ground. "You know what? You two order in. I'll fix myself a sandwich."

Harper looks stricken. "You don't like Chinese food? We can order something else then!"

I make the mistake of looking at her crestfallen face.

"Um…" I squeeze my eyes closed, trying to come up with an adequate excuse that won't confuse her. "It's just been a long day" is what I settle on.

"But we were going to watch *Frozen II*, remember? And I don't want to spoil anything, but Anna and Elsa get all new outfits. And the songs are *really* good!"

I open my eyes and glance at Luke. He's wearing a look of concern, studying me as if unsure how to proceed. He must understand why I'm wavering like this, how uncomfortable it feels to wonder if you're an invited guest or merely a weird interloper. Two days ago, I was getting told to stay in my lane; now suddenly I'm allowed to be the third wheel? I can't keep up.

"Stay," he says firmly. "And come on this side so you can see the menu on my phone."

He shifts the throw pillow beside him so I can take a seat, and maybe I should resist more, walk away, lock myself in my room, but I do exactly as he says.

I sit down on the other side of him, too far at first to see the menu. I have to crane my neck, and he notices, giving me a taunting glance. I scoot a tiny bit closer, and then I'm engulfed by his scent and warmth and comfort. It's so nice it's almost painful.

"Now, what do we want for appetizers?" he asks.

We end up ordering enough food to feed us for weeks. Our mistake was looking over the menu with grumbling stomachs, but everything is delicious and we eat on the couch while we watch *Frozen II*.

After dinner, Luke brings us each a bowl of ice cream with sprinkles while the movie still plays.

"How's your finger?" he asks.

I have my hand propped up on a little pillow on my lap, just to keep it out of the way.

"Good. Really, it's not hurting at all."

"You did good with the stitches."

His hand comes over to touch mine, not near my bandage; he's careful to avoid it as the pads of his fingers rub gently along the back of my hand, up to my wrist, then back down.

My stomach is squeezed into a tight ball as I hold my breath, wondering what he's doing.

Harper's right there. More than that, I thought we'd agreed on a plan.

What was it again?

I can't think when he touches me. He's looking down, watching his fingers stroke my skin like it's the most interesting thing he's ever done. It's only my hand, but it feels like there's a direct line from there to every nerve ending in my body. Little sparks fan out from where he makes contact, up along my arms, down my chest, tightening my stomach.

This is wrong.

It *feels* wrong because I like it too much.

"Luke?"

His name isn't a question so much as a plea.

Then Harper—her eyes still glued to the screen—shushes us. "This is the good part!"

Like we've just been scolded by a teacher, Luke quickly takes his hand away from mine and we go back to watching the movie. It's hard to not feel utterly robbed now that he's not touching me. I go back to eating my slightly melted ice cream, trying not to sulk. On screen, there's a whole damn plot playing out—Olaf's apparently dead?!—but I'm fully focused on Luke out of the corner of my eyes. Every single movement, mundane as it might be, is intriguing and hot. The way he picks up his water cup, his hand so large it nearly engulfs it—yeah, hot. The way he scoops up a bite of ice cream with his spoon and brings it to his lips—unbelievably sexy. He's aware of me too. He ensures I have a blanket after I shiver. I don't have the heart to tell him I'm not shivering because I'm cold.

I take the blanket and drape it across my lap, and I spend the rest of the movie wishing Luke would slide his hand underneath it. *Oh my god! I'm depraved!*

Once the movie ends, Harper takes our ice cream bowls into the kitchen, and Luke tells her to go take a shower and get changed for bed.

There's some resistance. "I went swimming earlier, doesn't that count as a shower?!"

But she ends up doing as he asks and then, like magic, we're alone together on the couch. It's not lost on me that forty-eight hours ago, we were outside by the pool, kissing each other like our lives depended on it.

Is he thinking about it now? Remembering what it felt like?

It was supposed to be a one-time thing, but why? Why can't I just have him when I want him so desperately?

He shifts to face me, and my body blooms with anticipation. Blood rushes through me. Warmth settles low in my stomach. It's blatant desire, hot and heavy.

Luke's gaze roves over my face, and I subconsciously lean toward him, so desperate for whatever he's about to give me.

Then he speaks, and it's like I've just had the wind knocked out of me.

"I'm heading to Texas tomorrow with Harper so she can visit my parents. It's been planned for a while. Nadine's dad, Harper's other grandfather, is in Texas too. I don't know if I mentioned that. He's only about an hour from my parents, so it'll be nice for them all to get to spend time with her."

"Really?"

"Yeah. My parents have a little bit of land. Not a ranch or anything. People always assume every Texan owns a ranch, but it's just a few acres out in the hill country. We'll celebrate her birthday there." He points to my bandaged finger. "And it works out well, timing-wise. You don't need to worry about cooking for us while you let your finger heal."

Someone explain to me the crushing agony of hearing that Luke and Harper are leaving for a week. Why am I sitting here feeling left out as if *I* should be getting invited on their intimate family vacation too? Like…I enjoy traveling, and I've never been to Texas, and grandparents?! I *love* grandparents! Oh my god, the breads and desserts I could make for Luke's parents. They would immediately love me. I'd hit 'em with some New York-style bagels, flaky croissants, fancy French macarons. I would make them my Nonna's spaghetti and really seal the deal.

Luke looks at me expectantly, and I realize I'm not meant to be wallowing right now. I'm supposed to be offering some kind of response. Generally, that's how conversations work.

"Oh, that sounds really fun." My tone is all but dead, so I quickly tack on something a bit more lively. "Harper's going to love that."

Luke nods, studying me. "You don't have to stay here, by the way. You could go into the city and actually attend Sunday dinner with your family. I know they'd enjoy seeing you."

I smile, but there's no jolly feeling behind it. "Yeah, definitely."

"And I'd still pay you your normal salary, of course."

Is that what he thinks I'm worried about?

"No need, truly. You pay me well enough as it is, and I haven't been spending money on rent or food or anything since I've been here. I'm saving a ton. Pretty soon I'll be hiring my *own* private chef."

He unfurls a smile that's sexy as hell, and I just have to take it. I have to boldly look into the warm sultry eyes of a man who could have my heart served to him on a silver platter (if only he wanted it!) and pretend I'm not falling…all the time, little by little.

"Dad!" Harper's voice calls from down the hall. "I need help getting the shower started. The knob won't turn!"

"Duty calls," I say, standing before he can. It feels vital that he doesn't see my face before I head upstairs. These tears would be a dead giveaway for my true feelings.

Pretend amnesia? Yeah, kids, turns out it doesn't work.

TWENTY-ONE

CHLOE

I DECIDE NOT to tell my parents I'm coming home to visit for the week, which turns out to be a mistake. I should have known they wouldn't be able to control themselves. When they open their apartment door and see me standing on the welcome mat with my overnight bag at my feet, they scream so loudly one of their neighbors calls 911, having assumed there's a madman loose in the building.

My mom scoops me inside and fawns all over me. She takes my bag and gives me another tight hug, and it makes me think of Harper's spindly arms squeezing the life out of me before she and Luke left for the airport this morning.

"I'm going to miss you so much. Are you going to miss us?"

I couldn't even make eye contact with her as I nodded for fear that I was going to tear up.

I squeezed her right back though, hard. "Take a lot of pictures while you're there, okay? I can't wait to hear all about your adventures."

"Harper, c'mon. We're going to be late."

Then she ran outside and Luke stood in the doorway facing me. Neither one of us moved to bridge the gap. He looked as sexy as I'd ever seen him in jeans, a white button-down, and boots. He'd just showered, and his hair was still damp, a darker brown than usual, combed and neatly styled, whereas most days he leaves it a little tousled. I couldn't decide which I prefer.

"How are you getting back to the city?"

My bag was already resting by the door. He must have put two and two together.

"I have a spot on the Jitney that leaves at 11:00 AM."

He frowned. "Harper and I are flying out from a private airstrip nearby. Why don't you come with us and then take my car into the city instead?"

That's the thing with Luke. He's without a doubt the nicest, most generous man I've ever met. One day, if I ever meet his parents, I'll have to compliment them on raising a man as good as he is.

"I appreciate it, but I sort of like the Jitney if you can believe it. Sitting next to strangers aside, I get to zone out with my book, and then I don't have to worry about driving in the city."

He nodded. "Good point."

"Think Ned will be able to hold down the fort while I'm gone?" I teased.

"He'll manage." Then he checked the time on his watch and sighed, peering back up at me from beneath furrowed brows. "So I'll see you when I get back?"

I don't know why he sounded so unsure.

I smiled. "Of course."

Now, my mom spins me around and around, making me rethink that greasy breakfast sandwich I bought in the bus terminal as it tries to reemerge.

"Our baby is home! Our baby!"

I don't even fight it. I let them pull me into their arms and squeeze me tight. Of course when they see my bandaged hand, they freak out.

"Who did this to you?" my dad asks, sounding like he's about to exact revenge, Liam Neeson style. If he had a gun in his hand, he'd cock it.

"I did it to myself, Dad. Knife injury in the kitchen."

"Is that why you're home?" my mom asks worriedly as she leads me toward the couch so I can sit. In mere moments, I'm covered by a blanket with an ice pack propped up underneath my hand. I have a cup of tea cooling on the coffee table in front of me and a plate overflowing with Italian sprinkle cookies resting beside it.

My mom tries to stick a thermometer in my mouth, and I bat her hand away.

"Mom, I'm fine."

"How bad is it? Oh god—can you still use the finger?!"

"Yes. Would you knock it off? I'm *fine*. I'm only home because my boss"—they both inhale dramatically at the mere mention of Luke—"is out of town this week so he said I could take some vacation days of my own."

"So generous of him," my mom says with an approving nod.

Clearly their infatuation with him hasn't died down since his impromptu FaceTime session. My uncles, cousins, aunts—they've all lost their minds over the fact that I'm working for Luke Allen. It got so bad I had to mute my family group text. These people are relentless. Imagine what they'd do if they knew we made out!

"I know a good man when I see one," my mom goes on, nodding enthusiastically.

"Yeah? So why didn't you warn me away from Miles?"

She whips her head in my direction so fast I'm surprised she doesn't pull a muscle. "*I did*. Several times. I told you in the beginning that I thought he wasn't right for you and there was something off, but you didn't listen."

Oh…

I guess there was a conversation or two at the start of my

relationship with Miles, but that was such a whirlwind time in my life because I was getting my footing at Fig & Olive and spending nearly every waking hour up at the restaurant. I most likely assumed she was being overprotective, but now that I think about it, my mom isn't usually one to warn me away from men. A traditional Italian mom through and through, her greatest hope is that I'll find an eligible man, settle down, and pop out a litter of children *pronto*. So if she did warn me away from Miles, it was for good reason. Maybe I should have listened.

She's watched me process all of this, and she's already gloating. There's no need for me to even make the statement, but she cups her hand behind her ear and waves for me to get on with it.

"You were right."

"Ahh. Music to my ears." She nods to my dad. "You hear that? I was right. *Me.*" Then she's walking away, rattling off rapid-fire Italian strung together so fast I can't even make out what she's saying.

Nonna walks out of her room wearing her favorite two-tone pink and aqua windbreaker set we bought for her one Christmas in the early '00s. She beams when she sees me.

"Hi, Nonna."

"Hi, bella." She comes over so she can give me big wet kisses on each of my cheeks. Then she steals my tea and takes the seat beside me on the couch, and that's where I spend the better part of my afternoon, catching up with my dad and Nonna while my mom starts to prep for our big family dinner. Around 4:00 PM, my aunts and uncles start trickling in with provisions. Nonna starts cursing and elbows her way into the kitchen when she thinks my mom is over-salting the sauce. I offer to help, but everyone shoos me away.

At some point, my dad disappears. I assume he was sent on an errand for dinner. That's usually the case. Someone always forgets something—wine, cheese, bread, olives—but when he returns an hour later, he's laden with two huge shopping bags from Champion Sports filled to the brim with merchandise.

"What in the world? What is all that?"

I look to Gio, but he's not the least bit surprised by our dad's purchases.

"You get me a jersey like I asked?" Gio asks him.

"Yeah, but they only had extra-large."

"That won't fit!" Gio exclaims.

"Well what the hell was I gonna do? Snap my fingers and make an XXL appear?"

Gio grumbles to himself as my little cousin Tatiana runs up and asks if my dad got her a baseball.

"I did, but listen, you're gonna have to share it with your little brother 'cause we already have too much stuff, okay?"

He drops the bags at my feet, and even though everything's crammed in haphazardly, I can still see one of the jerseys. Only part of the last name is showing, but it's enough.

—LLEN.

"Oh hell."

My dad holds up his hands. "Now listen, Chloe—"

"He's my boss! I can't ask him to sign all this stuff!"

I start digging around in the bag. There are enough shirts and jerseys and baseballs for my entire family! There are even a few gloves, a bat, a tiny Luke Allen bobblehead. Jesus.

"So you tell him it's for your grandma. There's a t-shirt in there for Nonna. Don't you think your Nonna deserves a nice t-shirt signed by the great Luke Allen?"

"He doesn't even play baseball anymore!" is my lame excuse to get him off my back.

My dad unfurls a knowing smile like he's got some great plan in the works and it's only *now* starting to come to fruition.

"Oh he'll be back. Absolutely. Just read this week that he got a new agent after his last one quit the business."

"He did?!"

This is news to me.

"Yeah, now he's being represented by Rory McNealson. Best in the biz, if you ask me. He's in good hands." He crouches down to pat the side of one of the bags. "So all I need from you is to get a *few* things signed for your family. That's all. A baseball, a t-shirt. Give your old dad something to live for."

"Surely your children are worth living for."

"Eh…"

"DAD."

———

IT FEELS weird to be forced out of the kitchen. Even though my mom and Nonna enjoy cooking, I still usually help prepare meals. Since starting to work for Luke, I can't remember the last time I didn't have something proving, baking, or cooling on the kitchen counter, ready to be enjoyed. I feel like a ship without a rudder.

Monday is nice. I relax and stay in with Nonna. We watch her Italian soap operas and then take a walk around the neighborhood, but by the evening, I'm restless. I've had to hustle and grind nonstop since finishing school. I'm still programmed for it, it seems.

On Tuesday, I meet a friend for coffee. Katie was in my graduating class at culinary school. Her dream job has always been to work at Eleven Madison Park, and she's finally landed there.

"Who cares if I'm the assistant to the assistant's assistant. I'm *in the building*."

"Is it everything you imagined it would be?"

She inhales a deep satisfied sigh as if she still can't quite believe it herself. "It's better, somehow. God, just working in the same kitchen as Daniel Humm is enough for me." She picks up her latte and takes a small sip, testing to see if it's cooled off enough to drink. "What about you? Have you landed on your feet? I heard you left Fig & Olive."

I'm not surprised she already knows. The restaurant world in Manhattan is *small*.

"Yeah, I just needed a change."

"And Miles?"

"We're done."

Her brows shoot up in surprise. "Wow. *Really?* He seemed obsessed with you. I thought maybe you two would be walking down the aisle soon."

I shrug off her remark with a smile, and it's not even forced. There are no hard feelings where Miles is concerned. Working for him and dating him seems like parts of my life that took place years ago. If anything, it just makes me feel sad to think about him and Angie. In a weird way, I hope they managed to work it out after going through all the trouble of keeping their affair a secret. "It just wasn't meant to be."

"So where are you working now? Or are you taking time off?"

"I'm actually doing the private chef thing."

Her jaw drops. "No way. That's my nightmare. Dealing with uppity entitled clients barking orders at me, feeling like I'm their personal servant?" She shivers just thinking about it. "Tell me that's not the case with your setup."

I look down at my cappuccino, surprised that the mere thought of my situation with Luke makes my cheeks feel hot.

"Not *quite*. I mean, I'm sure some people are working for tyrants, but I'm not. It's relatively easy. I set the menus most of the time, and I try to go above and beyond...desserts, bakes, that kind of thing. You know I'll always be a pastry chef at heart."

She chuckles. "Do you see yourself doing that long-term? I bet the pay is great."

My stomach tightens at the thought of what the future holds.

"I hadn't really thought about it...the family I'm working for will probably head back to the city when school starts back up."

Harper's private school is here in Manhattan, and I'm sure they'll come back permanently sometime in early August. That's only a few weeks away. I feel suddenly depressed with the realization that my life will soon be in flux all over again.

There's a chance, of course, that Luke will offer to let me stay on at the house as the caretaker as it was my original position, but I won't take him up on it. Being out of the kitchen even briefly because of this stupid finger injury has made it abundantly clear that I want to be cooking in some capacity full-time. Licking my wounds as a caretaker in the Hamptons sounded nice at the start of summer, but things have changed.

"Well if you find yourself looking for a position, I can put in a good word with my boss. The pastry department at Eleven Madison Park is completely *insane*, but you know that. You'd probably fit right in. You've always loved the frenzy."

I mull it over, trying to picture myself in their kitchen, working under Laura Cronin. She could teach me a lot, but stepping back into a restaurant—one with *three* Michelin stars to uphold—doesn't feel quite right. It's a hard life and, quite frankly, unsustainable if I want to achieve a work-life balance that suits me.

"I'll think on it," I tell her, not wanting to eschew her offer completely, just in case. "There are a million directions I could go in, you know. Actually, I was thinking the other day that the Hamptons is seriously lacking in the bread department. There is tons of summer produce, fresh seafood, you name it. I could list five farm-to-table restaurants off the top of my head, but where are the real bakeries? And not the ones filled with overpriced cupcakes and crap. I'm talking about fresh baguettes, sourdough loaves, bagels, cinnamon rolls, *done the right way."*

She's smiling as she listens to me going on and on. "Sounds like someone should fix that…"

By Wednesday, I'm missing Harper and Luke in a manner that doesn't seem all that healthy.

It's Harper's birthday today. She's down in Texas, getting showered with affection. I'm sure she has more presents than she knows what to do with, but I would have loved to make her a birthday cake, sing to her, watch her blow out her candles. I pass a jewelry store and come to a sudden halt when I look through the windows. The jewelry brand has done a collaboration with Barbie. It's meant to be! I go inside and fawn over a little bracelet filled with teeny tiny Barbie charms: a pink high heel, Barbie's iconic profile silhouette, a sparkly tube of lipstick.

A savvy sales associate comes over to let me know they're running a sale today. 30% off anything marked with a red label. And would you look at that? The charm bracelet is included in the sale. It still rings up close to $70 after tax which is probably more than I should have spent, but Harper will love it. She's right on the cusp of becoming a young lady rather than a little girl, and something like this, a sophisticated bracelet that's still pink and sweet, is the perfect gift. The store wraps it up for me in a delicate box with a bow. I'll keep it safe until Sunday, when Luke and Harper get back.

I realize after I walk out of the store with her gift that I'm not that far from Fig & Olive. The restaurant's only a few blocks south. I have nowhere I need to be until 6:00 PM when I'm supposed to meet my family for dinner, so on a whim, I turn and start walking.

I'm more than a little interested in seeing the restaurant. Like scrolling through an ex-boyfriend's Instagram feed, the temptation is just too great. Does a small part of me hope the place is shuttered and desolate purely from the lack of my presence? Sure. Mostly though, I just want a quick peek.

I'm turning the corner toward Fig & Olive when my phone starts to vibrate in my pocket. I expect it to be my mom with an errand she needs me to run, something for Nonna most likely, but an unknown number appears on my screen. For some reason, instead of letting it go to voicemail like I usually would, I answer.

"Hi! This is Chloe Ricci speaking."

There's a soft chuckle on the other end of the line and then an equally formal reply. "Hello. This is Luke Allen."

I stutter to a stop. "Luke."

"Hey."

My entire body buzzes with nervous energy. I peel off from the center of the sidewalk and huddle against the building as I press my phone closer to my ear.

"*Hi*. Is everything okay? Is Harper having a good birthday?"

"Yeah, she's actually with my mom in the kitchen. They're making a birthday cake."

Jealousy lances through me.

"That's so fun. You'll have to text me a picture after."

"She's been complaining some about the fact that it won't turn out as good as if you'd helped her with it. I told her maybe you could make her one when we get back on Sunday."

"Yes!" I cringe then modulate my tone, trying to sound a bit more normal when I repeat, "Yes. I can. Of course. I actually just picked up a little gift for her too."

I look down at the present.

"You didn't need to do that."

"No, I know. It's not like huge or anything. Don't worry, I didn't splurge and get her the Barbie Dreamhouse." I laugh. "Wait, did you?"

"Nah. I thought about it, but I want her to earn it. Settled

on a bright pink Barbie convertible instead. Ken's been spinning out in it all morning."

I smile just thinking about her opening his gift. "I bet she
loves it."

There's a short pause and then we both speak at once.

"Is that why you were—"

"Harper wanted me to—"

We laugh and he continues, "I was saying, Harper wanted
me to call and check up on you."

"Harper?"

I deflate a little at the thought. I guess a part of me was
hoping he was missing me as much as I'm missing him, but
maybe it's just Harper.

"Yeah, she's been worried about your finger."

"Oh! It's better, actually. I haven't even been needing to
take anything for pain. Tell Harper I'll be more than ready to
make that cake with her by the time she gets back."

"Good."

"And is she enjoying Texas?" I ask, continuing this weird
game we're playing where we speak through his daughter
and act as if our feelings don't factor in at all.

"Yeah, she's been out on the four-wheeler all morning.
Yesterday she rode a horse."

"*Horse?* I thought you said they don't live on a ranch…"

"We don't, but my parents have a few horses on their
property."

"You see how that kind of sounds like a *ranch*?"

I can hear the smile in his voice when he replies, "That just
goes to show how little you know about working ranches. We
don't breed any animals here."

"But you have horses—"

"Chloe?"

My name doesn't come through the phone. I recognize the
male voice behind me before I even turn around.

Miles is frozen on the sidewalk a few feet away from me

clutching a to-go cup of coffee from the cafe he likes down the street. He looks like he's headed to the restaurant; he's already wearing his chef's coat. He blinks, then blinks again, staring at me like he's seeing a ghost.

"*God, Chloe.*" He rushes forward and engulfs me in a hug before I even have the wherewithal to step away from him. "I missed you," he sighs. "Holy shit, I missed you so much."

I'm half a second delayed. I can't keep up as he steps back to hold me at arm's length.

"You're as beautiful as ever. Tell me you're coming to the restaurant. We can talk. *Please*, let's talk."

He already has a hand wrapped possessively around my forearm so he can lead me down the sidewalk.

I shake my head and look down at my phone, but just as I do, the call ends.

Luke must have heard Miles, or at the very least, our muffled conversation. I feel sick wondering what he must be thinking.

Miles starts tugging me toward the restaurant, taking advantage of the fact that my head is slightly scattered. Should I call Luke back? *Text him?*

"No."

The word bursts out of me.

I shake off Miles' grip and step aside. "No. I'm not going to Fig & Olive."

He looks wounded by my harsh tone, but I can't seem to find the will to soften it.

"Isn't that why you're here, though? You were right by the restaurant."

I hold up Harper's present. "It was pure coincidence."

"No." His eyes take on a desperate sheen and he steps toward me again. "Please. Don't you want to talk?"

Talk?

How do I put this mildly? That would be *hell* no.

In fact, it sounds like the absolute last thing I want to do.

Sitting down and having to hear all the reasons he's come up with to justify the fact that he cheated on me? I can think of a thousand sufferings I would rather endure, including *re*-slicing my finger.

"There's really nothing we need to talk about. I got my last paycheck, thank you for that. When I need a letter of recommendation, I'll reach out to Leslie."

"Angie and I aren't a thing," he blurts out, clearly having ignored everything I just said. "She means nothing to me —*less than nothing*. She's not who I want. *You're* who I want."

And to think, I wasn't sure I could feel any more disgusted by him.

"You think that makes it better, Miles? God, it's somehow a million times worse to hear you speak so cavalierly about a woman you were *having sex with in your restaurant*."

He rears back and looks around, aware now that we're out on the sidewalk in broad daylight, mere feet from Fig & Olive, but he started this conversation, so he'll listen while I finish it.

"Angie seemed pretty into you, and whether or not I agree with how you two started seeing each other, it's pretty shitty of you to lead her on."

He takes a forceful step toward me. "Who the hell cares about Angie?!" he spits, his voice filled with rage.

I realize then I'm talking to a wall. Miles won't change from this conversation. Continuing down this road is only a waste of my time.

"*You*," I respond desolately. "*You* should care about Angie."

Then I walk away, for good this time.

And I won't even lie, it feels really satisfying. End the movie, cut to credits satisfying.

TWENTY-TWO

LUKE

"DAD. CHILL."

"I'm chill."

"You're like banging your knee up and down nonstop. It's annoying me."

Does my daughter have a point? Yes. Should she mind her business because one day she'll find herself in my exact shoes and wish she'd been a little more lenient with me? Also yes.

I wipe my palms on my jeans and try to relax. I make it two minutes (I know because I count the 120 seconds in my head) before I tug the in-flight emergency protocol leaflet out of the seat-back pocket in front of me. I study the diagrams on each page like the pilot is about to come around with pencils and a pop quiz. This isn't even bragging; it's just being honest —I think I could draw the flotation raft to scale *from memory* if I had to.

Harper shoots daggers at me, and I realize I'm doing the leg thing again. See? This is why I should have sprung for a private flight like I did on the way down to Texas. Then, I could pace in the cabin like a crazy person and no air marshal would try to tackle and tase me.

"Do you have to pee? Is that why you can't sit still?"

Oh, to have the naive mind of a freshly minted seven-year-old.

"No, I'm good."

A flight attendant walks by, and I lean over Harper to flag her down. Rather than acting annoyed that I've clearly caught her en route to do something, she looks absolutely delighted when I indicate that I need help with a wave of my hand.

"Mr. Allen!" Her eyes are practically sparkling. "How can I be of service?"

"Could you tell me how much longer we'll be in the air?" I point to the screen mounted in the seat in front of me. "My TV seems to be on the fritz."

"Because you wouldn't stop messing with it," Harper whispers under her breath.

The nice flight attendant is good enough at her job to know she should pretend she didn't hear my daughter say that. "We're about an hour from touching down on the tarmac. Would you like me to get you another drink?" Her smile is ear to ear, and maybe it's friendly or maybe it's flirty. I can't be bothered to find out at the moment.

"No. I'm all right. Thanks."

When I first boarded, I ordered a Jack and Coke. It wouldn't be smart to have another, not only because I'll be behind the wheel soon but because I'd also be liable to act stupider than I already am.

The flight attendant's shoulders sag with disappointment. "It's absolutely my pleasure. If you need anything at all, I won't be far."

"She likes you," Harper hisses while the flight attendant is definitely still in earshot.

"Harper."

I say her name with my molars clenched and my voice extra low and gravelly. She should cower in fear, but my daughter doesn't bat an eyelash.

"What? It's true. I have a fifth cents about these things."

I massage the sides of my head, feeling an impending headache coming on. "Sixth *sense*," I correct.

"Huh?"

I go back to pressing buttons on my TV, trying to get it to wake up.

Harper continues, "But it doesn't matter if she likes you, because *you* like *Chloe*."

My finger stalls on the black screen—yeah, I for sure broke it—as I turn to face Harper with what I hope is a shocked expression. I've never been the best at acting. "What?"

"Yup. I heard you at the doctor's office when you said you were her *boyfriend*, remember?"

She says boyfriend in that singsong taunting way I haven't heard since elementary school.

"That was a lie." She opens her mouth, but I cut her off. "WHICH we shouldn't do, so don't even start. We don't lie, but that was a special circumstance. They weren't going to let us go back to the exam room with Chloe if I didn't say that."

She looks genuinely surprised by this, maybe even disappointed. "Oh. I thought we were playing a game. That's why I said I was her daughter…"

God, with everything else going on, I didn't even catch her say that. Now, I feel like I dropped the ball a little.

Harper looks down at her coloring sheet, but she doesn't pick up her marker.

I bump her shoulder, but she still won't look at me.

"Want to tell me what's on your mind?"

"Yes…only…" She looks up at me with a worried wince. "I don't want to hurt your feelings."

"Nothing you say can hurt my feelings." I tap my closed fist against my chest. "I'm impenetrable. Now spill."

She sighs and shifts to face me, then she just comes out with it. "Sometimes I wish I had a mom."

Whoa. Okay. Out of left field but not something I haven't

rehearsed an answer to a million times before. I knew this was coming one day.

"You *do* have a mom, Harper, and she was wonderful. Every good quality you have came straight from her, I swear it."

She frowns like I don't quite get it. "No, I know that. She was great, probably—I don't really remember. But what I'm trying to tell you is that sometimes I think about having a *new* mom. You don't think that would make my old mom feel sad, would it?"

My throat tightens, and all I can manage is a shake of my head.

She likes this answer. She was hoping for it. In fact, she leans in with a small smile, not the least bit sad about this macabre subject. Kids, man. Anyone who says they aren't resilient hasn't met my seven-year-old.

"So here's the thing. *I* was thinking maybe...my new mom could be Chloe." She holds up her hands to stop me before I can interrupt. "Or if not Chloe, maybe it could be someone *like* Chloe."

She sounds so conspiratorial I can't help but smile.

"Chloe, huh?"

"Yeah, you think she's pretty, don't you?"

"Beautiful."

Harper grins. "*Same.* And she's really nice and she makes the house smell so good when she bakes for us."

"But that's not how this works. You can't just pluck a new mom out of a crowd. And besides, Chloe's not my girlfriend. She's the chef."

Harper rolls her eyes. "You keep saying that, but it doesn't make sense. You're my dad *and* a baseball player. Why can't Chloe be a chef *and* your girlfriend? Nana says hearts want what they want."

"You talked about this with Nana?"

"Yeah. She said I'm supposed to tell you how I'm feeling,

said you aren't able to guess my emotions and boys are really dumb at this sort of thing."

I can't help but laugh. *Uh, thanks, Mom?*

"I talked to her about it too, actually."

Her face lights up. "Really?"

I nod. "She gave me some good advice."

She sits up straighter. "Okay. So what are you going to do?"

"For now? Survive this flight." I lean over to tap the screen in the seat in front of her. "Is your TV still working?"

I talk to Harper more on the drive home, trying to explain that every woman who comes in and out of our lives isn't necessarily someone who will be there for the long haul. I remind her of brief relationships I've had in the past—Fiona, the lawyer, and Erin, the design assistant—but Harper was too young to really remember them, and my mention of the women doesn't deter her in the least. She has her sights set on Chloe, and I hate the thought that it won't just be me who winds up heartbroken if this doesn't work out.

It's dinner time when we finally pull up to the house in Bridgehampton. The lights are on inside, which is a relief. Chloe and I haven't talked since that phone call on Wednesday, so while I was pretty sure she'd be here, I wasn't absolutely certain.

I catch Ned walking through the side yard from the main house. He has a heaping plate full of food balanced on his hand that he apparently couldn't wait to get started on. Noodles dangle down from his mouth as he throws me a wave then continues on his way back to the guest house.

"Chloe cooked!" Harper unbuckles her seatbelt and throws her door open just as I finish parking. She leaves the bags to me and races up the front porch steps, shouting for Chloe as she tugs the door open.

I feel jealous of my own kid getting to see Chloe first.

I grab our bags and head up to the front door. Just inside

the foyer, Chloe's crouched down, giving Harper a big hug. Her eyes are squeezed closed like she's relishing the moment, and when she opens them and our gazes meet, a new awareness trickles down my spine, a heavy want that's getting harder and harder to ignore. It's there, in her too. Her subtle intake of breath, the slight way her lips part before she gathers herself and gives me a gentle smile.

"I missed you," Harper tells her.

Chloe's gaze is still on me when she replies. "I missed you too." Then she peels herself away from Harper and steps back. "I can't believe you're *seven* now. Here, stand back and let me look at you. I bet I can see a big difference."

Harper does it, holding her arms out and straightening up as tall as she can with her chin raised.

Chloe's eyes widen like she can barely believe what she's seeing. "Oh, *definitely*. Wow. What'd you do, grow a whole foot while you were gone?"

Harper laughs and rushes forward to give Chloe another hug. I use the opportunity to study her. She's barefoot in jeans and a blue button-down blouse that cinches tight around her waist. Her hair is down and a little wavy. Her finger is still wrapped in a small Band-Aid, but nothing like the hulking thing she was sporting before we left for Texas.

She sees me looking at her hand and holds it up. "Had the stitches taken out today. They said it's healing great."

"You were able to cook?"

She shrugs a shoulder. "Some. My family actually sent me back from the city with *a lot* of food to give you. It's full Sunday dinner, so I hope you're hungry. I think it was their way of buttering you up for a favor…"

My brow arches. "Favor?"

What could Chloe's family possibly need from me?

Her gaze falls on a duffle bag resting against the foyer wall.

"I think my dad cleared out an entire sporting goods store. Bought up anything that had your name on it…"

I walk over and unzip it. Sure enough, I recognize my Pinstripes jersey and t-shirts, baseballs, gloves—you name it, it's crammed in the bag.

"I warned them that you probably wouldn't do it. I don't know how this all works. Maybe you don't want to flood the market with too many signed items, though they *swore* to me they weren't going to resell things and they just want it for themselves."

I turn back to see she has her hands tucked in the back pockets of her jeans. She's slightly embarrassed. I can tell because of the rosy pink color on the apples of her cheeks.

"Of course I'll sign them. And you know what? Back in the city, I have boxes of stuff in storage. I need to go through it, I'm sure there are some jerseys and shirts in there I could sign and give them too."

Her face tips forward as her jaw drops. "You're kidding."

I can't help but laugh.

"You don't understand," she continues hurriedly. "That'll blow their minds. Oh, I can just see their faces now. It's going to be so good."

Harper butts in here. "I want to see their faces too."

Chloe beams down at her. "Yes, of course. I'll take pictures."

Harper frowns. "No. I want to see them in person. I want to help give the gifts. I'm good at wrapping stuff—ask my dad."

Chloe blinks, and her smile fades slightly. I know she's trying to come up with some way to placate Harper without hurting her feelings.

I push off my knees and get back up to my feet. "Why don't we figure out the logistics later? I'm starving, and it smells amazing in here. I don't think I can resist any longer."

Just as Chloe promised, there's a veritable buffet laid out

on the counter in the kitchen in tin casserole containers. Chloe ushers us over and proudly presents it all.

"That's my mom's baked ziti. Nonna's stuffed artichokes. There's garlic bread courtesy of *moi*. Some fresh parmesan straight from Parma—my uncle gets it shipped to the States special order and everything. You don't put it on your pasta, just slice a piece off and eat it plain like this."

I watch her take a bite and stand arrested by her reaction —her soft moan, her head tipping back in ecstasy, eyes fluttering closed. I grip my damn plate hard enough to crack it down the middle.

We eat, and *we eat*. One thing's for certain: Chloe has forever ruined Harper and me. We'll be desolate if she ever leaves us. My sad burned dinners are too misery-inducing to even consider now.

Chloe eats with us—I insist on it—and Harper fills every possible moment with chatter. She tells Chloe everything about Texas, from the color of my parents' horses to the fact that she was allowed to stay up a little past her bedtime so she could finish watching a movie with Nana and Papa.

"Dad was a little sad toward the end of the trip, though."

Oh Lordy, here we go.

"Was he?" Chloe asks, peering over at me curiously.

I shake my head, indicating I have absolutely no idea what's about to come out of my child's mouth. In fact, I try to get Harper's attention with a not-so-subtle kick under the table, but my aim's off. I end up kicking the table leg and shaking everyone's water glasses.

"Yeah, he missed you," she goes on. "I could tell. In the morning, he'd take his coffee out on the front porch and stare off, moping."

"I wasn't *moping*," I insist. "I was just enjoying the peace and quiet."

"*And* he told Nana all about the meals you make us and

how you helped me with my lemonade stand even though you didn't have to."

I stand up from the table. "I'm going to open some wine. Does anyone want wine?"

"Me!"

I ignore Harper and look to Chloe. She nods. "Would love some. Thanks."

"Yeah, so anyway…did you miss my dad?"

Chloe laughs good-naturedly. Meanwhile, I cut to the chase, bypassing the wine rack and grabbing the Jack Daniel's from the liquor cabinet instead. I pour a finger's worth and down it in one go just as Chloe tactfully replies, "Of course."

Her answer is light and fluffy, and it doesn't appease Harper in the least.

"*No*, like did you miss him how a girlfriend misses her boyfriend?"

"Harper, go get ready for bed," I snap.

She whips around to face me with a look of utter disappointment. "But it's early!"

"It's not. We ate dinner a little later than usual."

This is a lie, of course, but I'm banking on the fact that Harper won't check the time on the oven and realize I'm, in her words, a "liar, liar, pants on fire".

She groans, and I know what's coming. Yup, another groan, louder this time, more from her chest than her throat. A stomped foot. Crossed arms. Angry eyebrows. Oh yeah, she's shooting daggers at me as she curves around the kitchen island. I am single-handedly ruining her life, and she wants me to know it.

"This isn't fair!" she shouts from down the hall.

I almost shout back "Life isn't fair!" but I bite my tongue. She's as stubborn as I am. We'll go around and around in circles if one of us doesn't put a stop to it, and since I'm the parent, it needs to be me.

I grip the edge of the counter and take a deep breath,

knowing I'm about to have a rough bedtime routine ahead of me.

Then I see Chloe stand up from the table in my periphery. "Maybe it'd be better…" She clears her throat and tries it a different way. "Would you mind if I went and helped her get to bed?"

I swing my head to look at her, *really* look. Not at the lush curves and the full lips that have filled my mind every time I've closed my eyes this week. Past that, to her eyes full of pity and her hands wringing together in front of her waist, the slow nervous swallow as she waits for my reply. Everything Chloe is sits right there on the surface. Her heart of gold is worn on her sleeve for anyone to see…and anyone to hurt.

"If you're willing…"

She's already on the move, eager to be helpful. "Yeah. Let me do it. She'll cool down with me."

I push off the counter and drag my hands through my hair. "If she keeps going on about the stuff she was just talking about…"

"It's fine. I know kids say silly stuff," she assures me. "Why don't you open that wine you promised me while I'm gone? It won't take me long."

TWENTY-THREE

CHLOE

I DECIDE to go the gentle route with Harper, letting her work out her annoyance without much input from me. I lay out pajamas for her to put on while I prepare her toothbrush in the bathroom. She changes, but with a grumpy attitude. While she brushes her teeth, I start perusing the books on her shelf, pretending I don't even realize she's watching me while I do it.

"Oh, I love *Amelia Bedelia*. I read those books when I was a kid."

Harper doesn't take the bait.

"*Pinkalicious*—that's my little cousin's favorite book character. I haven't read this one though. *Pinkalicious and the Pink Drink*...huh, sounds cute."

I tug it off the shelf. On the cover, a cartoon Pinkalicious stands in front of her homemade lemonade stand, pouring from a pink pitcher. I smile, wondering if that's how Harper got her idea to start a lemonade stand of her own.

I take the book and carry it over to Harper's bed while she finishes up in the bathroom. When she comes to stand on the threshold, her arms are still crossed. Her anger must feel so hard to let go of, and I don't say a word about it. At that age, every emotion is a big emotion.

I lean back against a soft pillow, open the book, and start reading.

She doesn't budge from her spot for the first few pages. Not an inch. But I keep going.

"Oh, wow, that lemonade looks so good."

I hold the book closer to my face as if trying to get a really good look, and Harper hurries over so she can see the picture too. I angle the book so it's in front of both of us.

"Yeah, it does look good," she says in a soft voice, like she's wondering if she's allowed to be happy again, or if she's going to be forced to apologize for the way she just acted.

I choose to let it go.

In my opinion, it's not that easy being a kid. Being told what to do all the time, following directions, sitting still, minding your manners—it all gets to be too much sometimes. If Harper can't express her feelings here, at home where she feels safe, where can she?

"Want me to start from the beginning?" I ask, no hint of judgment in my tone.

She nods, grabs her stuffed unicorn, and cuddles up beside me. I read her that book and one more *Pinkalicious* story after I'm done. Then I stand up and make sure she has everything she needs to go to bed.

"Lamp off?"

"Yes please. My dad leaves the closet light on though. Yeah, like that. Then he turns on my white noise machine and gives me a hug."

I do just as she asks, squeezing her so tight she giggles.

"Your hair smells good," she tells me before letting go.

"It's my shampoo."

"I like it."

"Maybe you can use it the next time you wash your hair.

Oh, you know what I just realized? I forgot to give you your birthday present."

Harper squirms with excitement. "Really?"

"Yes, I'll give it to you first thing in the morning with breakfast. That'll give you something to look forward to." I lean back, assessing my handiwork. "All right, are you good?"

She nods, the only things visible above her pink blanket are her hands and her face. Her soft brown hair fans out sweetly across her pillow.

"Ready to get my kisses at the door?" I ask her.

"What?" Her little nose wrinkles in confusion.

I smile. "I'll show you what I'm talking about. It's what my mom did for me growing up. She'd tuck me in just like I did for you. Then she'd walk to the door and blow me three kisses, like this." Once I'm on the threshold, I do just that. "Now you catch them and pat them on your cheek."

"Got 'em!" Harper says, following my directions.

"Now you blow me three kisses and I'll catch them too. Kisses are really fast sometimes, though, so I'll have to be quick about it."

Harper giddily blows me three kisses, and then she sits up a little and anxiously asks, "Did you get them!?"

I reach out fast and grab for the air out in front of me before clamping my hand shut. "*Phew*, got them." I pat her kisses to my cheek, and she beams. Then I reach for the door handle. "Want me to send your dad in?"

She lies back down and shakes her head on her pillow, already burrowing deeper beneath her blanket. "No, you gave me enough kisses. Can you just tell him I love him and I'll give him a hug and kiss in the morning? Just like that, okay? '*I love him and I'll give him a hug and kiss in the morning.*'"

"Got it," I say, sounding deeply serious about fulfilling my important task. "Good night, Harper. I'll see you in the morning."

"Night, Chloe!"

I close her door quietly and turn to find Luke down the hall with a glass of wine in his hand. He was listening to our exchange, and I don't know why that makes me feel suddenly exposed. Maybe it's the way he's looking at me now, not like I'm his employee. Not even close. His eyes have the power to eviscerate me, and a shiver of fear—or is it *anticipation*—racks through me as I drop my gaze and start walking toward him.

"For me?" I ask, pointing to the wine.

He passes it over, his fingers brushing mine. I pretend the ensuing sparks don't exist before I dig deep for the courage to look up at him again. The hallway is dark compared to the kitchen. Shadows conceal parts of his face, but they do nothing to dull his rugged handsomeness.

"Apparently I'll get my hug and kiss in the morning," he says, the edge of his lips rising into a smile. His voice is hushed, slightly husky—he's aware we'll be easily heard through Harper's door if he's not quiet.

"She was very clear about that," I tease.

He points over my shoulder. "That was cute, what you did with her at the door."

I fidget and shake my head. "I can't take credit. My mom came up with it."

He nods, mulling over my words, staring down at me all the while.

I bring the wine glass to my lips and gulp a greedy sip. It's really good, some kind of red blend I haven't tried before. "Guess I should go clean up in the kitchen."

"I already took care of it." He tilts his head back down the hallway. "Want to come help me sign that stuff?"

A task! *Yes.* I'm good with tasks. I wasn't sure what was about to happen. Opening a bottle of wine together isn't exactly something we've done in the past. Ever since he got home tonight, there's been a marked difference between us. The charged energy that has always existed on a low thrum is now positively *electric*. I'm on edge, nervous. His every move, every *breath* seems to bring with it the hope of something just on the horizon.

Or…maybe I just need more wine.

I've downed half my glass by the time we make it back to the kitchen. "Mind if I top this off?"

He points to the bottle on the counter. "Be my guest."

He heads over to the junk drawer to dig around for something. A second later, he pulls out a Sharpie and a scratch piece of paper. Once he confirms the marker still has ink, he takes it over to the table where he's placed the bulging duffle bag.

"You're a trooper for going through with this."

I top off my glass and watch him start to pull items out of the bag, sign them, then set them aside. I catch on to his system quick enough and come to stand beside him so I can make his task slightly more efficient. We work diligently through a few t-shirts then he pauses to take a sip of wine, and I do the same.

We're close in a way we've had very few chances to be since I first took this job working for him. There've been so few reasons to linger next to each other like this—short of his heroic efforts the day I sliced my finger, that is, though even that was more out of duty than anything else.

Does he realize how intimate this feels? My shoulder accidentally bumping his as I reach for a hat…his aftershave so distinct in the air I catch a whiff of it with every inhale…

Maybe the wine is starting to go to my head a little bit because I can't help but meet the challenge when his brown eyes come to rest on me. Is he aware of how diligently I've been watching him? Is he annoyed by it? Or…

"You like it?" he asks, referring to the wine.

"Love it."

"Yeah, me too."

"I bet it's staining my lips burgundy."

Luke's Adam's apple bobs as he looks down at my mouth and swallows hard.

Real subtle, Chloe.

I set down my glass and reach for another shirt, busying myself with folding it neatly so Luke knows right where to sign it. "So it sounds like the end of your trip went well…"

He takes the shirt from me and scrawls his signature. The first letters of his first and last name are distinct and iconic, but the rest is almost illegible. I'm sure he's done it on purpose. He probably doesn't have time to sit there and pen a perfect name when all his rabid fans are demanding attention.

"Mm, yeah, I'm glad we went down there. We were able to spend a lot of time with my parents, and Nadine's dad came over a few times. He's getting up there in years, but I know he enjoyed seeing Harper. What about your trip?"

"Oh, you know…you've met my family over FaceTime. It was a lot. A week is about all I can handle."

"Did you go out? See friends?"

"I met a girl for coffee, Katie. She and I graduated culinary school together before we branched off for our specialties."

He hums, almost like he's slightly annoyed.

Then he takes another shirt out of my hand and says, point-blank, "Sounds like maybe you're back with Miles?"

I sputter trying to rush out my reply as quickly as possible. "*No*—the opposite." Is that what he thinks? "I would be okay if I never had to see him again as long as I live. I did run into him. You probably heard that—we were on the phone when I saw him on the street."

His jaw tightens, like he's grinding his molars to keep from saying something.

"I didn't seek him out or anything. The jewelry store where I found Harper's gift was right around the corner from my old job. I was mildly curious about the state of the restaurant so for a second, I thought it might be fun to walk by it. Miles happened to be arriving for work." I turn to face him, too curious to squelch my next question even though it's slightly more direct than I usually am. "Is that why you hung up? You thought I got back together with my ex-boyfriend?"

He takes his time answering. He licks his bottom lip, caps his Sharpie, then leans his fisted hands down on the table and lets his head hang for a minute. He's studying some indeterminable spot on the wood as he says, "No. I didn't answer, and I didn't call you back…" He straightens back to standing and turns to face me fully. We're almost chest to chest now because neither one of us is stepping back. I crane my neck to look up at him just as he finishes, "Because I told myself I couldn't."

Thanks to that red blend, I have the courage to boldly ask, "Why?"

"Because my reaction to hearing your ex-boyfriend call you beautiful was enough to make me want to bash his face in. And I say that as a man who's never actually gotten into a real physical fight outside of what happened with David."

His self-deprecating smile could melt my panties on the spot.

"Never? Not even during a game?"

He looks alarmed by the mere suggestion. "*Definitely* not during a game."

"Okay…so—"

"So it didn't seem right to call you back until I'd sorted some things out."

"What things?"

He shakes his head and makes to turn like he's going to pick up his Sharpie again and continue on just like we have been. *No.* Me and my two glasses of wine want answers.

I grab his forearm, or at least as much of it as my hand can hold (which is only like halfway around), and I tug so he'll stay facing me. No turning away now. No shying away from the truth.

"What…things?"

His nostrils flare as our gazes clash. I'm pushing, and he doesn't like that. Or maybe he likes it *too much*.

"Oh okay, for starters, I'm so attracted to you I can barely restrain myself when you're in my presence. I'm a fool for you, constantly, wanting you every damn minute of the day."

I swallow past that confession then reach up to feel my pulse. Yeah, I'm still kicking.

If only I'd had the forethought to press record on my phone before this conversation. I'd have him repeat that again right into the mic. *Yes, again...'barely restrain myself when you're in my presence'...mhmm, good.*

He watches my fingers slip away from my neck and shakes his head like he doesn't know what to do with me.

"I'm dead serious."

"*Okay.*" I draw the word out like I'm a bit slow on the uptake.

"*But* if I'm going to pursue something with you, I'm not hiding this from Harper. I'm not sneaking around, stealing you into shadowed corners and taking advantage of the situation."

"Yes, we wouldn't want that," I say lamely.

I feel woozy.

He notices.

But instead of pushing me back to sit down in a chair, he turns me so I'm angled back against the table.

"You good?"

"Not in the least."

A brief smile and then his hands wrap around my waist. He hoists me up until I'm sitting on the edge of the table, feet dangling in midair. There's an obvious change in him. In this moment, he's in command. His hold on me is firm.

"So we do things by the book," he continues.

His hand reaches up, and he strokes my neck with the back of his finger, up just over where my rapid pulse pushes back against him. He turns his hand and grips me there, holding me steady. I've never had a man look at me like this, full of barely restrained need.

"By the book..." I reply just as his attention falls on my mouth.

Blood rushes through me as he lowers his lips to mine and claims me with the sweetest, most tender kiss.

All those promises of his fly out the window. He might not be stealing me away into a shadowed corner, but he's spreading my legs on his kitchen table, pressing himself between them, and taking full advantage of how compliant my desire has made me. I'm goop in his hands.

You want to kiss?

Let's kiss.

Suddenly, a change moves through him, like he's gained ground and refuses to retreat now. His firm hold on me elicits a shiver of delight as one of his hands slides up into my hair to cradle the back of my head. He invites me to open my mouth, and he takes charge, dipping his tongue in to stroke against mine in a way that makes my bones disappear from my body altogether.

My hands reach up to cup his face, answering his urgency in equal measure. He scoots me to the edge of the table, and our bodies align so well. I feel him through the layers of clothes—that hard ridge rubbing up against the center of me makes my breath come in shallow, clipped bursts. He's as turned on as I am, as rabid as me.

All common sense has left the building. Should we be in a safer spot? Behind a locked door? Yes, but we don't always get what we want. I've got a baseball hat digging into my left butt cheek, but you don't hear me complaining about it.

He tries with my blouse, gathering the fabric and pushing it up, but it's too tight and he's too impatient. *To hell with it.* He presses his hand up underneath it instead, roaming over my quivering stomach to my lace-covered bra. He peels one side away like it was never meant to be there at all, and then he's cupping my breast, kneading and toying with it until I'm a shivering achy mess.

I thread my fingers through his hair as he tears his lips away from mine and bends down to capture the tip of my breast through the fabric of my blouse. With my bra pushed down, it's just that silky material separating his lips from my skin. Everything feels overly sensitive. As he closes his mouth and sucks, I fist my hand in his hair and slam my eyes shut. His tongue swirls over the peak and I shiver, arching my back as hot pleasure courses through me.

Is this what it's supposed to feel like?

Is this pure unadulterated lust?

It's heady and hard to wrap my head around. He pays my breasts equal attention, and then with unabashed urgency, his mouth collides with mine again. I'm as much supported by him as I am by the table. My legs wrap around his hips and his hands come around my thighs to hoist me up.

Oh god.

Every ounce of feminism leaves my body in a great big *poof*.

The height difference is divine. The way he can pick me up like this, like I'm just a barnacle along for the ride...it should not turn me on this much, but it *does*. His hands are dangerously close to the apex of my thighs. His fingers dig into my jeans.

Let's do it. Let's tear each other's clothes off and get on with it. I need to know what it feels like to have him press inside me, to stretch and fill and sate this need—

The sound of footsteps suddenly stops us in our tracks.

We're flying apart, breathing hard, avoiding eye contact, all in three seconds flat. I press the back of my hand to my lips to further conceal the evidence then watch in horror as Luke's attention shifts toward the back porch.

The noise was outside, I realize, just as I turn to see Ned and his cat standing together on the other side of the glass door. His eyes are as round as saucers and his mouth bobs open and closed like a guppy's. His hand belatedly flies up to cover his eyes, but it's too little too late.

He waves his dinner plate in the air. "Was just coming back for seconds! Forget I was even here." He hurries off the porch, calling his cat after him.

I would laugh if not for the fact that I'm holding my breath, waiting to see Luke's reaction.

We just lost ourselves in a way that could have been extremely dangerous. Had that been Harper instead of Ned, this would be an entirely different situation.

Luke's back is to me as he brings his hand up to rub his neck. It's red there, from where my nails were biting into his skin. His hair is tousled and in a state of disarray that would have completely given us away even if Ned hadn't had a front-row view of our foreplay session.

Slowly, Luke turns to face me.

I'm relieved there's no anger there, or worse…remorse. He looks slightly confused, a little amused, and still—I look down at his pants—*turned on*.

My cheeks flood with color just as he speaks.

"So that was a good example of what I'm *trying to avoid*," he quips.

I clear my throat and prop my hands on my hips. Never mind that my bra is totally askew underneath my blouse or that my lips are bee-stung. I can only imagine what my hair is doing, and I have no doubt my pupils are totally blown out. I'm trudging forward as if everything is hunky-dory.

I have the voice of a staunch academic when I reply, "I *see*. That was a very good demonstration of what *not to do*. I was slightly confused before, but now you've really cleared it up for me. Avoid kitchen table make-outs." I make a little check mark in the air. "Noted."

He sighs and walks over, dropping his hand to my waist and turning me toward the stairs.

"Come on, I'll walk you home."

"You don't have to. It's a long way," I say, picking up the thread of the bit.

"What kind of gentleman would I be if I didn't ensure your safety on a dark night like this?"

"No gentleman at all."

We make it to the stairs, and he motions for me to go first.

"Think I can swing a second date?" he asks.

"Was that a first date?"

"Oh, did I not make that clear?"

"I tell you what—you give me a call tomorrow, and I'll see what my calendar looks like. I'm very busy this time of year, but I might be able to squeeze you in." I throw a wink over my shoulder as we reach the second-floor landing.

We make it to my room, and I open the door and stroll in. Luke, however, stays put out in the hallway.

"What are you, a vampire? Can't take a step past the threshold unless I explicitly invite you in?"

He smiles like it pains him. "I don't think it's a good idea if I come in."

He says this while eyeing my bed.

"Oh."

"Yeah, not sure if you could tell from the way I just attacked you downstairs, but I'm pretty interested in fucking you."

The air whooshes out of me.

I was wholly unprepared for his blunt confession.

Holy smokes, warn a girl next time.

"Among other things," he says, looking far too devious and far too tempting.

I walk over to my dresser to grab my pajamas, if only to conceal how much I liked what he just said. No need to show him *all* my cards. "Do we have a plan in place moving forward? Clearly the amnesia method didn't work. Maybe we need to go back to the drawing board."

I grab a camisole and some soft sleeping shorts out of the top drawer.

"Like I said...I don't want to sneak around."

I nod then motion for him to turn around so I can get changed. His eyes darken as he shakes his head. In fact, instead of turning around, he tucks his hands into his pockets and leans his shoulder against the doorframe, making himself nice and comfortable.

Fine.

I turn my back to him and accept the challenge.

I grab the bottom of my blouse and tug it off over my head in one smooth motion. Then I let it dangle on my finger for a fleeting second before it falls to the ground. I slip my hand behind my back and unclasp my bra, letting that fall away too.

I know even though I haven't turned on any lights, the moonlight pouring in through the window is enough to illuminate the slope of my naked back, and if he catches sight of my perky breasts as I turn to get my camisole, well...*oops*.

I hear his sharp intake of breath, and my ego grows three sizes.

I feel his heated gaze on me as I slip the camisole over my head and tug it down. My jeans get unbuttoned, and then I push them to the ground and step out of them. I happen to be wearing that pink thong I accidentally left behind in his bathroom the first night we met. If that's not kismet, I don't know what is.

I reach over to grab my sleeping shorts. My fingers brush the material just as Luke's warmth suddenly engulfs me from behind.

"Do you realize how unbelievably sexy you are?" he asks as his chest presses against my back.

His hands come around to circle my waist. His palms are so big, calloused and rough as they splay across my lower belly, making butterflies take flight and my stomach squeeze tight in anticipation. It's a slow, torturous descent as his fingers toy with the top of the silky satin that barely covers me. His left hand curves around me, acting as a steel bar across my belly, ensuring I'll stay put as his right hand leisurely dips inside my panties. I look down, watching as his fingers trace the most intimate part of me. It's the exact spot that's been begging for attention all evening. Suddenly, I'm overheated and needy.

"Oh god," I groan, tilting my head back against his chest and arching my back, trying to contend with the sudden and intense onslaught of pleasure.

His warm lips touch the side of my neck as he bends down to kiss me just below my chin. His seductive kiss matches the intense, almost unrestrained way he touches me. All the urgency we've felt all evening seems to only be magnified here in my dark room.

The pad of his finger rubs circles over me and sparks skitter across my skin. Back and forth, his fingers rub between my legs, taking me to new heights.

"He could have had you..." Luke sounds incensed over the idea, like it nearly enrages him. Then, on his downward stroke, he presses his middle finger inside me.

My mouth falls open with a soundless cry.

"He could have worshiped you. *Like this.*"

I rise up onto my toes at the deep intrusion. A loud moan tears through him as his fingers pulse inside me.

"But now you're mine, Chloe." His voice drops as he repeats it again against the shell of my ear. *Mine.*

I squeeze my eyes shut tighter in a futile attempt to conquer the electricity surging through me.

His hand that was gripping my stomach now slides up to peel down the top of my camisole. I'm so utterly exposed to him as he teases me, switching from one breast to the other as his fingers continue to pump inside me. It's so hot.

He grazes the perfect spot, and it makes me gasp.

He knows. He watches me shattering before him. I'd be on the ground if not for him holding me up, keeping me steady as ecstasy starts to build. It crackles across my skin, down my spine—delicious tingles overtake me as I come with a racking cry.

All the times before this, orgasms I've given myself, orgasms I've had at the hands of past lovers—they pale in comparison. This bliss is blinding. *Petrifying.*

I go limp in his arms as the realization dawns that this isn't so simple, not by a long shot. Luke is not the love 'em and leave 'em type of guy, and I want him in ways I've never felt before.

I'm utterly drained, and yet my heart still races. Luke turns me and cups my face, tilting it up so I'm forced to meet his eyes in the moonlight. He doesn't ask me if I'm okay; he checks every inch of me, looking for himself.

He straightens my camisole and opens my drawer so he can pick out a new pair of panties for me to change into. After, he helps me into my shorts, going down on his knees in the process, and once they're sitting up on my hips, and I'm fully dressed, he looks up at me.

I swallow as he rises to his feet and bends to kiss my cheek. "This is just the beginning."

TWENTY-FOUR

CHLOE

IN THE MORNING, I go for the longest run I've managed all summer: 4.79 miles and not a step more. Had I pushed it to 4.80, I'd be crawling around this kitchen right now. The run was a necessity. It helped me clear my head and burn off some of my nervous energy, but it doesn't last for long.

Turns out, I'm not the only one who needed to exercise this morning. I'm tossing together ingredients for a green smoothie I'll share with Harper when the porch door slides open and Luke appears, hot as hell in his workout clothes. His baseball hat is turned backward, and I watch a drop of sweat roll down his neck. The fact that I want to find out what it tastes like tells me all I need to know concerning where my head's at.

My dirty mind goes there before I can tell it not to. I get distracted by the thought of Luke sidling up behind me and grabbing ahold of my hips. He'd tug me back against him then peel my clothes off just like last night. We'd go at it without caring that we're both sticky with sweat.

That's...that's when I flip the switch on the blender and realize I never put the lid on. Green smoothie splashes onto the counter, the backsplash, and the floor at my feet. Oh, and me.

"*Shit.*"

The curse word flies before I can help it. Yet another offense to add to the list this morning.

"I'll help!" Harper says, shooting to her feet. "But first, let me take my bracelet off. I don't want it to get dirty."

I presented her with her birthday present as soon as she emerged from her room this morning. She tore off the wrapping paper and bow with eager abandonment and audibly gasped when she saw the delicate charm bracelet nestled inside the box. She loved it as much as I hoped she would.

"No, it's okay, Harper. You keep playing. This is my mess."

Luke's already at my side, grabbing a towel to help out.

"Between your finger and this, maybe we should say the grill is off limits until further notice," he teases.

From this distance, I know better than to look at him.

"I was distracted both times..." I say, unable to meet his eyes.

In truth, things like this are going to keep happening until Luke and I can spend a week alone together locked in a padded room. I can imagine it now. We'd go at it like crazed animals, surfacing only for air, water, and the occasional protein bar.

"Have a good run?"

"Yeah. Felt great. What about your workout?"

"Not nearly as satisfying as I'd hoped." His words drip with innuendo.

Luke, Luke, Luke. You're killing me here!

We finish cleaning up, and I replenish the ingredients in the blender just as the front door opens and a woman's voice sounds from the foyer.

"Yoohoo! *Anyone home?!* I brought presents!"

Harper screams so loud my ears start ringing. She flies off

her barstool where she had her Barbie convertible set up and rushes out of the kitchen as fast as her legs can take her.

Meanwhile, my brain has a hard time catching up. That was a female voice, so a woman just let herself into Luke's house? She feels comfortable enough here to not bother with knocking or ringing the doorbell, and Harper clearly knows and loves her. So who is she? A nanny? Friend? Ex-girlfriend?

I'm so hung up on the last possibility—no matter how preposterous it is—that when a pretty brunette walks into the kitchen, my heart sinks.

She's petite with shoulder-length brown hair and big hazel eyes. Her dimpled smile is infectious, and there's an endearing spray of freckles dotted across her nose and the apples of her cheeks. She's the spitting image of Harper, all grown up.

"Chloe! This is Tate!"

Harper thrusts her toward me, and before I know it, I'm shaking her hand.

"Pleased to meet you," I say, sounding nervous. "I'm Chloe, the chef."

"*THE CHEF!*" She squeezes my hand tighter so there's no chance of me getting out of this overzealous handshake. "We met on the phone, remember? You're freaking gorgeous! Oh, this is just so hilarious. My brother thought he'd hide that fact from me? Nice try." She keeps her hand on mine and turns me to face her brother. "She's gorgeous, Luke. And don't bother denying it. I have EYES."

"No, it's okay, Aunt Tate. My dad told me just yesterday he thinks Chloe is 'be-yuuu-teee-ful'!"

Luke acts like he's not happy about this turn of events, but it's just that, an act. He's clearly pleased about Tate's arrival. Even now he's fighting back his smile.

Still holding my hand, Tate turns to face me again. "Oh, hello, duh. Let me formally introduce myself. I'm Luke's charming, funny, *cooler* younger sister. You can call me Tate."

"What else would she call you? That's your name."

She ignores her big brother and edges in closer. "You know my mom called me about you. We were just talking, actually."

Luke sighs and shakes his head. "That's really good, sis. You're doing a good job of playing it cool."

Tate rolls her eyes. "Fine, I'll settle down. It's just been a helluva drive from the city. Traffic was a bi—"

"*Tate.*"

"A witch!" she amends, for Harper's sake. "And I could use something to drink."

"It's barely 9:00 AM," Luke chides.

"So?"

I laugh. "There's some red wine. We opened it last night, but I think there should still be at least a glass' worth left in there."

This piques her interest. "A little vino for two, huh? Romantic evening in?"

She looks between us like a shrewd detective, and though I tell myself explicitly *not* to, I can't help but peer over toward the dining table—the scene of the crime, if you will—and I just know my face says it all. I've incriminated myself.

"Nothing like that," I rush, my voice high-pitched and telling. "Last night was just a chill night. Super chill."

I sound like I'm seventy years old trying out slang for the first time. Our night? Yeah, it was hippity-dippity.

"Riiight." She smiles a knowing little smile and I think she's going to press for more, but instead, she points to the blender. "As much as I would kill for that leftover wine, I think I might be better off starting with that. Is there enough to share?"

I pour us each a smoothie, knowing how much Luke appreciates when I make these in the morning. I tuck in all sorts of fruits and vegetables, and Harper's none the wiser because it ends up tasting mostly like banana and almond milk.

Tate's eyes widen on her first sip. "Oh god, this is good." She holds the cup up to inspect it. *"Why is this good?* It shouldn't be. It's the color of celery, and I hate celery."

"You shouldn't say hate. That's a very strong word," Harper declares. "You should *hate* bad guys and bullies. Not *celery."*

"When did you become so wise?" Then she turns to me, and I smile.

"The smoothie has a lot of good stuff jam-packed into it, but no celery, so you're in the clear."

We're all quiet for a moment as we drink it down. Then slowly, one by one, we take note of Harper fidgeting in place, her eyes jumping back and forth between the kitchen and the front foyer.

"I was just wondering…I heard that you brought presents…"

Tate gets it right away. "Yes! Those are yours! Bring them in here and you can open them."

Wasting no time, Harper dashes into the foyer, but then not long after, it sounds like every single present she was trying to carry crashes to the ground. Then Harper's faint voice follows. *"Uhh…guys?"*

"Coming!" Tate sets down her smoothie and hurries to help her niece.

Awareness trickles down my spine. Being alone with Luke feels perilous. He turns to meet my gaze over the kitchen island.

"Morning," he says, unfurling a private smile that makes my toes curl.

"Morning."

"Sleep okay?"

"Oh…can't complain. You?"

He stayed in my room last night while I got cleaned up. I

brushed my teeth as he sat on the edge of my bed watching me, an indeterminable expression on his face. It was like my very existence completely puzzled him. Then he stayed with me while I slipped my legs under the blankets and laid down. I wanted him to take the spot beside me. The bed is plenty big enough for two, but I knew he'd want to be downstairs with Harper in case she woke up in the middle of the night and went looking for him.

He picked up a framed picture off my nightstand and asked me about it. It was a photo of my family I brought with me from New York at the start of summer.

"That was taken at my cousin Tatiana's 5th birthday."

"Must have been some party."

In the photograph, my entire extended family—all 8 million of us—is crammed together on the dance floor of a banquet hall. A disco ball glimmers overhead. Tatiana is front and center with her hands on her hips in a full diva pose, but everyone else is acting like a damn fool. Nonna has her cane raised in the air, about to thunk Luca with it because he stole a sip of her champagne. My dad is laying a big kiss on my mom's cheek, and she's laughing and batting him away. Two of my little cousins wrestle on the floor at Tatiana's feet. If memory serves me correctly, they bowled her over exactly two seconds after the photo was taken. Meanwhile, way in the back, Gio has his hands hooked up underneath my armpits so he can hoist me up. Otherwise, I wouldn't have been seen. I have my hands raised in the air and a big smile on my face.

"Haven't you figured it out yet? My family does *not* do things in half-measures."

He chuckled and set the picture back on my nightstand. "Oh believe me, I know. I have no doubt my hand will be cramping by the time I finish with all that gear downstairs."

"You don't have to do it tonight. There's no rush." Concern laced my voice. "In fact, I forbid it."

He shook his head. "It's fine. I want to, and it'll give me time to think. I doubt I'd be able to fall asleep right now even if I tried."

"Really? I feel like I'm half-asleep already."

To prove my point, I let my eyelids flutter closed and hummed a happy little sigh as I nestled deeper into my bed.

He laughed and reached up to brush my hair off my forehead while I kept my eyes closed.

"What am I going to do with you?" he asked, more to himself than to me.

I stayed quiet as he traced the back of his finger along my cheek. It felt so deeply intimate, almost more so than everything we'd just done. There was emotion behind his touch, feelings we weren't yet comfortable voicing aloud coming to surface in the gentle way he slid his finger down along my jaw to my chin. Then he leaned down and kissed me good night.

I was nearly asleep by the time he reached the door.

I'm thinking of that kiss now when I hear Harper's voice drift back into the kitchen.

"Chloe got me this." Harper holds the bracelet out for Tate.

Tate drops the stack of birthday presents on the counter and leans in close, thoughtfully taking the time to inspect every charm on Harper's new bracelet.

"It's beautiful. You'll take good care of it?"

Harper cradles the bracelet against her chest. "Of course."

It's fun watching Harper tear into the gifts her aunt gave her. You can tell she spoils her. There are a lot of Barbie accessories, some sparkly gel pens, even a set of play makeup that makes Luke groan.

"You got it!" Harper screams. "I knew you would!"

"You think I'd let you down, kid? Now, be sure to ask your dad to let you practice on him with that eyeshadow palette."

Tate winks at Luke, and I find myself smiling along with them as if I'm part of the crew. Their relationships seem effortless in the same way mine are with my family. It says a lot about Luke that he's managed to stay close with his sister and his parents even through all the fame.

Sometimes, I have a hard time remembering that side of him exists. It's hard to reconcile that inside Luke—the sexy casual guy drinking the smoothie I made him—lies an intimidating professional athlete. In normal circumstances, we would have probably never met. He exists in one world, and I exist in another; they aren't even in the same universe. Maybe there were a few times where our paths crossed in the city. A fleeting moment when his Range Rover swept past me as I walked home on the sidewalk. A night when he was a patron in one of the fancy restaurants while I worked in the kitchens. But maybe not even then.

This everyday, downright-humble version of Luke isn't the version so many know: the man in his Pinstripes uniform, walking to take the mound in a stadium full of bright lights and thousands of adoring fans shouting his name in awestruck unison. I feel a little sad I missed that era of his life.

Or did I?

A little later in the morning, I'm cleaning up the kitchen and unloading the dishwasher while Harper gives herself a face-full of makeup in the guest bathroom down the hall. Luke and Tate took their second cup of coffee out onto the porch. The weather's nice, and they've left the door open. I'm not going out of my way to eavesdrop on their conversation, but it's hard not to pay attention when they're talking about such an intriguing subject.

Tate's the one who brings it up. "I heard about the new agent."

"It was time."

That's all Luke says about it. I'm grateful he doesn't seem eager to share details about what transpired between David and me. I get the sense if she knew the story, Tate would cheer on her brother for defending me like that, no questions asked, but still—I'd rather not get into all of it again.

"Thinking about going back for one more season? There's been speculation."

I can hear the annoyance in his voice when he replies, "You know I try to avoid all that. I can't be bothered to keep up."

"Easy enough to do out here, but in the city? I can't walk past a newsstand without seeing your face splashed across the front of a sports magazine or newspaper. The Pinstripes want their golden boy back, and they haven't been shy about letting the world know."

He grunts. "It doesn't matter."

"I can step up more—"

"I'm not doing this. I'm not having this discussion. She's too important. End of story."

"You don't have to tell me that. I *know* how important she is." Tate sounds angry and defensive as she goes on. "She's my niece, and I want to protect her more than anyone."

I'm glad Harper's in the bathroom, out of earshot. I checked on her a little bit ago and she was very focused on her task at hand: humming *Love Story* by Taylor Swift while digging her new makeup brush into a vibrant shade of blue eyeshadow. She then streaked the vivid pigment across her closed eyelid, continuing confidently out to her hairline because why not?

"I just think, maybe, you stepped away too soon. There's a way to make it work," Tate continues.

Luke laughs sadly. "What'd they have to pay you to come and talk to me? Did Josh put you up to this?"

"That's not even funny, Luke. I obviously have your best interests at heart. I want what you want, *and* I know it just so happens to be what they want too. I'm the biggest Pinstripes fan there ever was, and I can't help but feel like there's unfinished business between you and the organization. You were one season shy of breaking all the records. *One championship.*" She tacks on a soft chuckle. "And you can't sit there and tell me that's not eating away at you. I know you've been training out here. How many hours do you spend pitching every morning?"

"Enough. You've made you're point."

Tate doesn't heed his warning; she doesn't back down. "Have I? Because in truth, I was pretty nervous to come out here and tell you what everybody else seems too chickenshit to say. I think you were wrong to leave the sport altogether. There's a way to make it work with Harper. You need a better support system, I understand that. I can step up and be that for you, and there are other people who want to help too." She turns slightly back toward the kitchen, and I immediately jump back into working. "So I'd think about it if I were you. It'd be a shame if you woke up ten, twenty years from now wondering what could have been."

Luke doesn't argue with that. In fact, they both go radio silent. I finally look over, something I was too scared to do before in case they caught on that I could hear them. They're sitting side by side, facing the pool and the pond as they sip their coffee. With their backs to me and their attention focused so far in the distance, I have the chance to see all the similarities between them, which are visible even while they face away from me. Tate has Luke's same shade of hair: a light chestnut brown that picks up color so easily in the summer sun. They lean back in their chairs at the same angle, lift their mugs to their mouths with the same hands. She's smaller, obviously—a bull would be smaller than Luke—but I get the feeling she makes up for it with quite a feisty personality, as evidenced by the conversation I just overheard.

Tate's the first to drain her coffee, and then she stands to come back into the kitchen. She smiles warmly when she sees me wiping down the counters.

"You make a good cup of joe, Chloe," she compliments as she walks over to put her cup in the dishwasher even though I attempt to get it from her and do it myself. It's interesting to have her here. This morning, I haven't felt like the help so much as a dutiful host. Maybe it's just the way she is; she seems as down to earth as her brother.

"Harper, hey," Tate calls down the hall, and Harper pokes her head out of the bathroom. Tate's eyebrows shoot up when she catches sight of her niece. "*Wow...that...that* is some cool makeup, girl. You look fierce. Want to come shopping with me in town? I saw a little shop that sells t-shirts and swimsuits just up the road. I can't believe I forgot to pack mine." Then, she turns to me. "Chloe, you want to come?"

Her offer seems genuine rather than born out of pity. She's roughly my age, I think, maybe a year or two younger. Even from what little time we've spent together, I get the sense that we could be friends outside of these circumstances, so I don't overthink it. Luke's still outside, cradling his coffee. Clearly, he has a lot on his mind, and maybe some alone time is just what he needs.

"Yeah, okay. Let me grab my sandals."

TWENTY-FIVE

CHLOE

TATE TELLS me she plans to spend the week with us out in the Hamptons. She took time off work to relax, she says, though Tate's definition of relaxing is wildly different than mine. Within the first few hours of her arrival, I come to realize she's one of those people naturally gifted with an endless font of energy. We go into town to shop, and she quickly picks out a bathing suit, a cover-up, glasses, and a new pair of jean shorts—all within five minutes. After, she suggests we swing by a deli for lunch. Then off to a candy store, then bookstore. Once we get home, she throws on her running shoes and she's off. An hour later, she's back from a nine-mile run. *Nine.* Then, THEN, she asks if anyone's up for a swim.

I'm fatigued just keeping track of her activities.

That night, we make pizzas in the outdoor oven and play Monopoly Junior with Harper while the sun sets. I expect Tate to crash early, and okay, sure, maybe I'm *hoping* she'll crash early so Luke and I will get a tiny bit of alone time, but nope. By the time I'm about to drop dead—we're talking one yawn feeding directly into another—she suggests we switch to Scattergories. Jesus Christ.

The next morning, I come to find out she's also an early riser. While Luke trains and Harper sleeps on, Tate strolls into the kitchen wearing an oversized t-shirt and sleep shorts. Her hair is a bit disheveled, but she's still somehow gorgeous. The Allens are blessed that way.

She heads for the coffeepot.

"Morning," I tell her.

"Morning!"

"Sleep well?"

"Like a baby."

She sighs blissfully as she takes her first sip of coffee then asks if I need help with anything. Rather than shoo her out of the kitchen, I explain that I'm whipping up some items for Harper's lemonade stand. Last night, as I put Harper to sleep (she requested my "kisses at the door" again), she asked me if we could set up Sugar Stand today. When Harper wakes up, I'll have her help me with the cookies and lemonade, but separately, I thought it could be fun to set out some breads and see if they sell. It's silly, probably. No one comes to a kid's lemonade stand wanting focaccia, but I figure it can't hurt.

Tate grins. "I'm on it. You just tell me what to do because I'm absolutely hopeless in the kitchen."

I get her set up with the ingredients for a brioche, and we fall into easy conversation. I ask her about her life. I learn she has two roommates in the city, Daphne and Sophia; she's a pediatric ICU nurse back in New York; and her love life is seriously lacking because every guy she meets inevitably ends up pursuing her for the sole purpose of meeting her brother. *"Like does Michael Jordan have a sister because I bet she has a hell of a time in the dating pool!"*

One of her roommates is dating a guy who plays on the Pinstripes. I ask her why she isn't. She's beautiful and athletic, charming and outgoing. Seems like a match made in heaven to me.

"Don't even get me started." She laughs like the idea is

completely ludicrous just as Luke comes in from the back porch.

Like always, the mere sight of him post-workout takes my breath away. I'm Pavlov's dog at this point, salivating at the thought of having him.

He looks annoyed today, maybe even frustrated. His dark brows are tugged together, and his mouth is curved downward. I'd say that's a full-on scowl.

"Chloe, can I talk to you for a second?"

Uh-oh.

He sounds serious, so I don't even hesitate. Who cares if my apron is covered in flour and my hands are a sticky mess? I still rush to follow after him. Worry takes over as I round the corner out of the kitchen and follow him into a side hallway. I'm wondering if this is something to do with Harper. She had a bad dream the other night, but I did not let her stay in my bed again! Instead...I carried her back to her room and stayed with her until she fell asleep in there. If I snoozed beside her for a few hours too, well, he doesn't need to know that.

I'm barely there, barely around the corner at all, when his hands come up to capture my face and he kisses me.

Oh. *OH.*

His lips are soft, oh so soft, and then he's gently parting my lips with them, sliding his tongue inside my mouth as he backs us up against the wall. Maybe we're not being very quiet, but I can't be bothered with that at the moment. Luke's kissing me with unrestrained hunger, and it's so hot I lose track of everything beyond it. When our tongues meet, I moan softly into his mouth. The sensation is too perfect.

His movements turn possessive, his body hard against mine.

He's sweaty from his workout. I'm sticky from baking. We're quite a pair.

It's just a kiss and yet I'm melting into him, opening my

mouth wider, welcoming him in. Deeper, harder—whatever he wants.

Then suddenly, he breaks off, panting hard, looking down at me like I'm the problem, like I'm the reason there's a scowl on his face.

"Is…is that what you wanted to talk to me about?"

He doesn't even answer. He just studies me with his surly expression.

I have to press my lips together to keep from smiling.

"OH *HARPER*, GOOD MORNING!" Tate shouts from the kitchen with an exaggerated, emphatic voice. It's clearly her way of warning us we're not being nearly as subtle or quiet as we think we are.

Luke lets his head fall as he laughs. "I've lost my damn mind."

"If it helps…so have I."

He looks up at me, and his harsh expression has finally broken. I'd kiss him again, but at that inconvenient moment, my timer goes off in the kitchen and Harper comes bounding around the corner to give her dad a good morning hug.

I spend the late morning and early afternoon manning the lemonade stand with Harper while Luke and Tate go into town to have lunch together. I bet it's pretty rare that the two of them get any kind of alone time, so I don't mind hanging back with the kiddo.

We go a whole hour without anyone coming around to purchase anything, even with our signs posted out on the main road. Harper doesn't let that bring her down though. She has a tracing pad set up with markers and pencils, and when she needs a break from that, she makes me watch her loop around in a circle, doing cartwheels in the grass.

Eventually though, an older woman drives up in her sleek Bentley. She has coifed white hair and a navy blazer and scarf.

"I heard there's some lemonade for sale," she says with a twinkle in her eye.

She buys two cups of lemonade, a few cookies, and three loaves of my bread (one brioche, one sourdough, one focaccia). An hour later, another car pulls up, and the woman who steps out tells us her friend sent her.

"She raved about the lemonade, but she said I absolutely could not walk away without getting some of your bread."

By the time we're done, we've had two more customers and we completely sold out of bread. Harper can barely believe she finally has enough for her Barbie Dreamhouse.

"My dad's not going to believe it!"

Tuesday evening, Tate invites me to join her on a run because I mentioned to her that morning while we were baking that I had recently gotten back into exercising.

It does not go well.

I should have known if she barely broke a sweat while running nine miles, we'd maybe not be the best running partners. We make it one mile in, side by side, but it's like she's merely *strolling* along compared to my max-effort, haul-ass sprint. She's carrying on a full conversation, meanwhile I'm over here fighting for my life.

"Why don't you go on ahead," I tell her, mid-pant. "I've got a little cramp in my side."

"Yeah! Okay! I'll loop back and catch you!"

The moment she turns the corner, I bend forward, grip my knees, and gasp for air like I'm taking my dying breaths.

So clearly, she's athletic. I suppose it runs in the family.

Wednesday, we decide to head to the beach. Originally, I was going to stay back, but the three of them insisted I join, and it just got to the point where I was resisting for resistance's sake. Obviously, the work-life separation is now utterly obliterated. I'm not just Luke's chef. I mean, sure, I'm still on his payroll, and yes, I'm still working and cooking in his home, but more often than not, there's a second pair of hands helping me with prep and with cleanup at the end of the day. And quite frankly, the man cannot keep his hands off me. He corners me again as we're getting everything loaded up to head to the beach. I'm in my room, changing into my bathing suit when he knocks and lets himself in, closing the door swiftly behind him.

I laugh and grab my bikini strings behind my back so my top doesn't fall off. Thankfully, I already have my bottoms on.

He's in his navy swim trunks and a white t-shirt. A little dab of sunscreen is visible on the bridge of his nose where he's forgotten to rub it in.

His jaw goes slack when he sees I'm only partially dressed. "Fuck" is growled low and menacing.

And then he's backing me up to my bed. My calves hit the edge and he keeps pushing me until I land on top of my soft blankets. His hands come up to lace through mine so I have no choice but to drop the untied strings of my bikini top and let it hang loose. If I look down to see just how much I'm on display right now, I know I'll flush with color.

"Luke…" I laugh. "You're going to get us in trouble."

He comes up on top of me and presses me down onto the bed. I take his weight, and I like it. That pressure of him on my hips is a reminder of just how out of control I am in this situation. He leans down to kiss me, but not for long. It's like he knows better, knows we can't go down this path. We only have a few minutes while Harper's helping Tate load drinks into the cooler. I've already packed our picnic food; they'll be calling our names any second now.

He sits back up, lets go of my hands. I lie still on the bed as his gaze roves over me. His eyes are heavy-lidded as if he's on the edge of restraint. I fight back the urge to squirm, knowing it's me who's made him this way.

"What did I say? What was all that bullshit about not sneaking around? What am I supposed to do, Chloe? I'm incensed. Crazed."

He reaches out to touch me then, just one finger tracing

down the center of my ribs, tugging down the material of my swim top until cool air caresses my breasts.

He groans and then leans forward, taking each breast in his mouth in quick succession, sucking and closing his lips around the tip until I'm writhing underneath him. His hand slides up my leg, up underneath the smooth fabric covering the center of my thighs. He's pulling it away, unveiling me.

"Just give me this. *Please*."

He almost sounds apologetic for it, like he knows he's acting inappropriately but just can't help himself. In response, I part my legs as much as I can. I give him access to whatever he wants because it's what I want too. I look down and see he's hard and straining against his swim trunks. My hand touches his length over the navy fabric, and he hisses.

If we're quick…

If we just…

His fingertips trace spirals up until they brush against the most intimate part of me. The moment he makes contact, I inhale fiercely, shuddering.

My hand slides up underneath the bottom of his swim trunks, gathering the material. It's more efficient this way compared to me trying to untie the knot at his waistband, and it's so easy to get him in hand, easy to grip ahold of his smooth, warm length and take as much of him as I can get. He's silk in my palm as I pump up and down. I can't even see my hand, not completely, but I close my eyes and I feel— almost too much.

It's hotter than it should be. Desire pricks my skin as I arch up off the bed. He gives me so much with his mouth. Raspy moans, hot kisses, the gentle scrape of teeth against my shoulder.

I reach new heights just as he does, wetness seeping onto my stomach as waves of pleasure rack through him.

There's no apologizing for it. He knows I like it. I'm sure

he can see in my lust-filled gaze how much I wanted him to brand me in this simple, sexy way.

I'll clean up quickly and so will he. He'll wash his hands and straighten his trunks and fix his hair. He'll rub that little bit of sunscreen in on the bridge of his nose and then we'll go to the beach and we'll keep our hands off each other because that's what we have to do. But it won't be easy.

———

AT THE BEACH, I lounge around, reading. Meanwhile, Tate swims laps in the ocean like she's hoping for a spot next to Katie Ledecky in the next Olympics. When she's done, she plops down on a lounge chair for all of five seconds before hopping up again and asking Harper if she wants to go collect seashells. I have no idea where she gets her energy. I'm exhausted just watching her.

Luke, meanwhile, isn't here. Just as we were all getting into the golf cart, he got a phone call.

"It's work," he said, staring down at it.

"Take it," Tate encouraged.

He looked up from his screen with a frown. I knew he was still undecided on whether to take it, but his phone wasn't going to ring forever, and after everything I'd heard him talking about with Tate over coffee, I thought he owed it to himself to see what they wanted.

"We'll do a girls' trip to the beach instead," I suggested. "It'll be fun. If you can, just join us later."

He nodded, swiped his finger across the screen, and answered the call as he walked back into the house. "Hey, Rory."

TWENTY-SIX

LUKE

THURSDAY NIGHT, I pull the door open at Surfs, a run-down bar not far from my house.

Chloe sits up on a barstool, leaned forward with her elbows propped up on the wood. She's absentmindedly stroking the neck of her beer bottle. The bartender smiles at her. He's trying to strike up a conversation, but her eyes are glued to the TV mounted on the wall over his head.

ESPN is on. The usual suspects are talking on screen, the four of them sitting side by side behind the *SportsCenter* desk speculating on the headline boldly printed at the bottom: LUKE ALLEN COMING OUT OF RETIREMENT.

Ah hell.

I should have known it would leak. Never mind that I haven't even fully made up my mind…

The bar's busier than I expected it to be. Old-timers and locals crowd into booths. I tilt my head down, but I still see a man nudge the guy next to him, nodding in my direction.

Everyone's pretty good about minding their own business out here. It's not like L.A. where people feel comfortable coming right up to you and asking for an autograph. Celebrity culture in the Hamptons is a little more hush-hush, and I'm glad for it. Every now and then, a group of excited kids will stop me for a picture or to get something signed, but other than that, I almost feel normal here.

I tug out the barstool beside Chloe and, at first, her brows are furrowed into an annoyed scowl at the fact that someone has the audacity to sit right beside her even though there's plenty of open seating at the bar. Then, when she realizes it's me, her expression gentles, her lips part. She blinks and takes me in as I smile and lean down to kiss her cheek.

"You're supposed to be at home with Harper and Tate," she says, sounding pleasantly surprised.

That was the plan, sure.

Tate's leaving in the morning. Chloe made an early dinner then said she was going to head over here to give us a little time to be together. Just the family, she said. None of us wanted her to go, but there was no convincing her otherwise.

"Yeah well, they pulled out all of Harper's new makeup and nail polish…"

Judging by her delighted grin, Chloe loves the sound of this.

"They painted my toenails. After that, I got the hell out of there."

The bartender comes by, and I ask him for the same beer Chloe has. If he recognizes me, he doesn't show it.

Chloe laughs and shakes her head. "What color?"

I give her a side-eye. "What do you think?"

"*Barbie pink.*"

Just in time, that bartender slides me my beer.

My non-confirmation is all the confirmation she needs. She throws her head back and laughs.

I take a long sip of my beer and glance up at the TV. It's not loud enough to be heard over the music and chatter in the bar, but they've got the subtitles on.

"Back as early as August…"

"Some news, huh?"

I shake my head. "It's not confirmed. Word leaked, I guess. That tends to happen."

"But you're considering it?"

I take a second before replying, wanting to be absolutely sure before I take us down this road. "Yeah."

She's quiet, and I peer over at her, trying to ascertain how she's feeling about all of this.

"I'm glad."

My arched brow betrays my surprise.

She shrugs. "I think it's the right call."

"Even with Harper?"

"Yes, even with Harper."

It feels good to hear her say that. Single-parenting is difficult, not just because of the day-to-day minutia, but because half the time it feels like Harper and I are on an island. Without a partner, there's no one to bounce ideas, worries, options off of. Making these important decisions all on my own is tricky and tends to come with a lot of second-guessing, so it's really nice to have her here beside me, telling me I'm doing the right thing.

"I don't get it though. How can you just go back that easily? I mean, I know next to nothing about this stuff, but didn't you retire?"

"Yes and no. I've always signed short contracts with the Pinstripes. My last contract with them lasted five years, including a player option year. That's this year. Instead of becoming a free agent, like players usually do, I stepped away from the game altogether. But I'm still under contract, *technically*. They were going to pay me out for this year whether I played or not because of how long I've been with the team, capitalize on the good press and all that. I mean, hell, maybe they were even counting on me wanting to return. So...really, I can go back at any time."

"Yeah, that's what it sounded like they were saying up on the TV. That's interesting."

I sigh and tug my hand through my hair. "I just haven't figured out how it's going to work, exactly. I want to have an iron-clad plan in place with Harper. I won't let my travel affect her. It's not worth it."

"Of course, yes. I can step up and help."

Then, as if she's embarrassed to have put herself out there in that way, she reaches for her beer and drinks a long sip.

"I've been thinking about that actually…"

She stays quiet and lets me finish.

"I want you to move back to the city with us."

She sets her beer down and studies it as she talks. "That's been my plan too. I know you might still need a caretaker for the house, but I just don't think I want to be stuck out here with Ned as my only companion through fall and winter…"

"No, I know. I'll get someone else to keep tabs on the house. That's not my main concern."

"What is?"

I turn so I'm facing her. My knee bumps her thigh, and I take hold of it, tucking my fingers up underneath her leg. "Figuring out how to make this work with the three of us. I want you to move in with Harper and me."

Her eyes widen. "Move in…as your chef? Like I've been out here?"

I clear my throat. "Not exactly. More as my girlfriend." My smile is slightly self-conscious. My heart's beating like I'm stepping onto the field.

She's about to reply when the bartender comes around.

"You two need anything?" He leans against the bar like he's planning to stay a while. "Another drink? Some nuts?"

A LITTLE BUSY HERE, BUD.

"I think we're okay," Chloe answers quickly. "Thanks."

He nods to me. "It's cool to have you in here, man."

So he *did* recognize me.

I nod, trying to skate the line between polite and unwelcoming.

"Is it true?" He points up at the TV. "What they're talking about?"

Chloe leans forward. "Actually, I'm kind of tired of this beer. Could you make me some fancy cocktail? Something with like ten steps?"

The bartender laughs, not catching on.

He surveys his station. "I don't have much back here."

Chloe gives him a warm, encouraging smile. "Oh, whatever you come up with, I'm sure I'll love it." The second he walks away to get to work, she turns to me, eyes wide with alarm. "Go on, quick. We don't have long."

I laugh and lean in. "Well...I asked you to be my girlfriend."

She nods. "Yes, I got that part."

"And if I'm being honest, I'm hoping you can be someone I can trust to stay with Harper when I'm out of town. Maria will be there to help too, of course. I'm not trying to overload you and I don't want you thinking I'm only asking you to move in because I need help with my daughter. Tate is going to be involved as much as she can be."

She takes her bottom lip between her teeth, considering everything I've just laid on her lap.

I'm worried I've overwhelmed her. "Is this all too much too soon?"

She shrugs. "Yeah, I mean, it could be. Aren't people supposed to do it in a certain order? Date casually, get more serious, talk about moving in...yada yada."

"It's a lot of pressure. I didn't mean to make it sound like I'm only interested in you because you might be able to help with Harper. That's not it at all." I tighten my hold on her leg. "We can figure something else out. You don't have to move in. You can just be my girlfriend without being involved with

Harper. That's not something that should fall on you, I realize."

This suggestion does not make her happy. In fact, she looks almost offended that I would suggest it. "Are you kidding? I'm more loyal to Harper than I am to you."

I laugh. "I just want to do this the right way, but I don't live a normal life, so my relationships can't be normal either."

Goddammit, the bartender is back.

"Here's that cocktail. Let me know if you don't like it and I can—"

"I'm sure it's going to be great!" Chloe says with an exaggerated smile. *"Thank you."*

She takes it and turns back to me, pointedly showing him we're in the middle of something. Finally, the guy gets the hint.

She sips it, pulls a disgusted face, and then sets it back down. "How do we do this?"

"I don't know. I haven't formulated a plan yet. I didn't want to get too far ahead of myself. What if you'd told me no?"

"I mean, technically, I haven't said yes. I guess you've been out of the game for a little while—you're supposed to send me a note while we're in class. 'Do you want to date for real' and the number 4 should actually be substituted for the word to convey how chill you are about all of it."

I nod, playing along and taking her instructions seriously. I wave down the bartender. "Could I grab a pen if you have one?"

"Sure thing."

Chloe laughs. "I was kidding! *Luke!*"

The bartender finds a pen behind the bar and hands it across to me. I take a cocktail napkin and do exactly as she says, adding two little boxes underneath the question, one for yes and one for no.

When I slide the note her way, I tell her she's supposed to check one.

"Do I have to check one now? I'm going to be late for gym class."

I lean in and kiss her in front of every person at that bar.

"Say yes."

"Yes." She smiles against my mouth.

I shift on the barstool, grab my wallet from my back pocket, and toss down cash.

I'm tugging Chloe out of the bar before she even realizes what's happening.

"I didn't get to finish my cocktail," she protests half-heartedly as I push the door open and we spill out into the night. It's raining now, though it was bone-dry when I went into the bar a few minutes ago. It's just a summer rain shower. It'll be done in ten minutes, but I don't want to wait it out. We make a run for it, trying to avoid the worst of the puddles on our way to my car. It's parked around the side of the bar, surrounded by mud. I swoop Chloe up into my arms so her shoes don't get ruined, and she squeals and clambers closer, wrapping her arms around my neck.

"You're insane!" she shouts.

I tug open the back door of my car and drop her down onto the bench seat. "Scoot."

Harper's booster seat is in the way, but I unbuckle it and toss it behind the second row.

"What the hell are you doing!?" Chloe asks, backing up against the door opposite me like she's trying to get away.

I close the door, locking us in. The windows are already foggy. The air in here is warm and muggy.

"What does it look like? I'm taking advantage of my girlfriend."

"*Luke.*"

"You didn't think I was just going to take us home so we

could get roped into a game of Monopoly with my sister, did you? No, Chloe."

I take her foot in my hand and start sliding her sandals off. One gets tossed to the floor, the other is…somewhere. I'm too busy to notice where it lands. She has these jean shorts on that are so goddamn short I could just slip my hand right up them. I'll bet she's already turned on. I want to feel it.

"This is absurd! You barely fit back here."

My responding smile is nothing short of sinister. "I can be resourceful."

"Have you done this before?" Her jaw drops. "*You have.* When?"

"In high school."

She rolls her eyes. "I can just see you back then, the cocky jock. Girls probably lined up outside of your car, waiting for their turn in your back seat. How long was the line, Luke? Around the parking lot? *Around the block?*" I smile, and she reaches out to playfully shove my shoulder. "You're supposed to deny it!"

I come up and over her, planting a kiss on her lips. My hands drag up her legs, from her slender calves up over her soft thighs. *Fuck me.* My hand tightens reflexively.

Teenage Luke would have given his right arm to be in the back seat of a car with Chloe, and now it's hard to believe I have her pinned underneath me, her lips on mine, her soft moans escaping before she can help it.

This is what happens when you want something, constantly. Watching her in my kitchen, seeing her take Harper under her wing, memorizing her laugh, her smile, the way she pours a spoonful of sugar in her coffee and then every morning, without fail, adds twice as much more before she's satisfied.

You're a three scoops of sugar kind of girl, Chloe.

And you're mine.

I lean down to take her lips again, and I stretch my body

over hers. She fits easily on the seat, but I don't. One leg is on the floor taking some of my weight off her as I start to unbutton her shorts and tug down the denim. Her little blue panties sit askew. I don't even have them down to her knees before my hand covers that sensitive skin between her thighs. The wetness I find nearly undoes me. My hand strokes forward and back, rubbing, teasing. I can't help but watch her. There's enough light that I can see her every expression. Her head tips back, her delicate chin quivering with every unsteady breath. I slide a finger inside her, and when I feel the unmistakable heat, my breath hitches.

I'll never get enough of being close to her like this. It will never be enough.

"More" falls from her lips like the desperate plea of a tortured woman, and I don't deny her.

She blinks her eyes open, our gazes catching. Behind the lust and longing we both share, there's something else, and my heart almost skitters to a stop at the sight of it. It's deeper, gentler, the first signs of something more.

As if she realizes I've seen it, she rises up off the back seat, captures my neck in her soft hand, and kisses me hard. Maybe she's worried I'm seeing too much too soon. She wants to retreat back into the feel of this, and I don't push for more. We'll get there, she and I. I know it with absolute certainty.

Her lips part and our tongues meet. The connection makes my pulse pound. My hand scoops behind her neck and we kiss until we're panting, until her shirt is on the floor, her bra is unclasped and slid down her arms. Her hair splays out on the seat, an alluring sight. When I have her entirely naked, I press back as much as the cramped back seat allows, and I take in every curve and dip of her body. Her skin is heated and flushed. My fingers follow my gaze, tracing a line down the center of her chest, lingering on her full breasts, that alluring dip in her navel, the freckle on her right hip.

She's beautiful and sun-kissed and so receptive to every little touch.

I bend to kiss her neck, licking and nipping and sucking— and then my fingers dip inside her, deeper, until I reach a spot that makes her writhe and push back against my hand.

She comes apart for me first like that, her loud cries echoing in the quiet car. The heat sets in. It feels like it's ten thousand degrees in here as she tears at the waistband of my jeans, pushing the zipper down, taking me in hand. Her impatience is evident in every fast stroke, every quick breath. I shudder as she rolls her palm over me, squeezing, tightening her fist until I groan—no, *growl*—and grab both of her hands. I lace my fingers through hers, hoisting them up over her head, pressing them against the door of the car.

Our bodies press together everywhere, sweaty and sticky. Every tender touch sends tiny pinpricks of arousal through me.

I kiss her briefly then peel back, assessing her face, checking in. She's soft and eager, her hips rising and bucking with impatience as I hold us like this, suspended in the moment.

Trust is what I'm searching for, consent, and she gives it to me with an infinitesimal nod as her hands break free of mine and she wraps her arms up and around my neck to drag me down on top of her.

I go slowly, aligning us, and then I inch myself inside her, ensuring she can take it, making sure she's still here with me. I know there's pleasure laced with the uncomfortable bite of pain I see in her pinched mouth, the slight wince. I stroke her as I slide in and out, fighting to keep the tenderness when everything inside me rages for more.

It's not long until her features relax, until her teeth bite into her bottom lip to quell her moans. Pleasure wins out as I start moving faster, hitting a spot inside her that makes her tremble as my thumb rubs expert circles in the center of her thighs. It's so intense, the pleasure so deep and wild.

It's terrifying.

I'm more desperate, losing my grip on sanity with each stroke. She's so utterly exposed—everything in her heart seems right there for the taking. I look down at where I'm moving in and out of her, our bodies tangled together. She tenses tighter and tighter, her body clenching around me, and then she comes on a shudder. Everything in her seems to splinter with each wave of her orgasm.

I watch her, enraptured. And then, with my knee, I nudge her legs farther apart and drive into her so deeply she cries out. I'm impatient and possessive, crushing my lips to hers as my whole body stiffens. I pour heat into her and she kisses me, her quick breaths the most beautiful sound.

We lie there, my body heavy over hers, her face buried in my neck. Her fingers run through my thick hair.

"We'll figure it out, okay? I promise we'll figure it all out."

TWENTY-SEVEN

CHLOE

THE NEXT MORNING, I wake up alone in my bed. It feels...*strange*, given the gravity of last night. I mean, not to brag or anything, but we really did a number on Luke's car. At one point my butt cheeks were stuck to the leather seat and the windows were so fogged up it felt like we were in a tropical rainforest. I think, but can't be certain, that I dug my nails in a little *too* hard and broke through the leather on his headrest too. *Guess that's coming out of my paycheck.* Maybe he should take the car in for a little scrub-down before he straps Harper's booster seat back into that second row.

We went for it not once, but *twice* before regaining our composure, which was wildly reckless of us for multiple reasons. First of all, anyone could have walked out of that bar, turned the corner, and seen Luke buck naked in that back seat. Second of all, there was absolutely no discussion about birth control prior to either wild sex session #1 *or* #2. It's like our brains completely left our bodies. I mean, I have an IUD, but he didn't know that. I told him on the way home, and he didn't seem all that relieved to hear it. It was more like I was stating a fact. *Oh look, that street name is Huckleberry Lane. I like sandwiches. And by the way, my gynecologist placed a copper device in my uterus so there will be no surprise pregnancy for us.*

It also felt important to mention I'd been screened recently given the circumstances with Miles *cough* the asshole.

"I'm sorry for not being more clearheaded," he said, taking my hand across the center console. "We should have talked about it."

"Hey, it's okay. We're equally to blame. And to be fair, that was like *really* hot. The way we just tore each other's clothes off like...dang." I exhaled an unsteady breath, still trying to regain my composure. "Had you pulled out a condom, I probably would have chucked it out the window anyway."

He laughed, but I could tell it was still bothering him. He takes his job as a protector so seriously. It comes so naturally for him. I've seen the way he is with Harper, and I know he feels like he might have put me in harm's way by skipping those important questions, but in the end, he didn't. We'll be okay.

When we got back to the house, it was late. Harper and Tate were both in bed, so we tiptoed through the house. I tried to kiss Luke good night at the stairs and send him packing, but he wasn't having it. He trailed behind me, our fingers laced together as we took turns shushing the other's too-loud footsteps then trying to quell our laughter. Up in my room, he took me into the shower and we washed off together. There was some above-the-waist fondling, of course. I don't think a guy can be around a pair of naked breasts and *not* touch them. That led to other things...like me on my knees on the tile, my mouth becoming very well acquainted with his penis. Then after, I gave myself a bubbly soap mustache and beard, which totally killed. *Take notes, ladies.*

He helped me into my pajamas and sat with me on the side of my bed.

"What's going to happen now?" I asked sleepily.

He bent down to kiss me. "We'll figure it out tomorrow."

Well guess what, it's tomorrow, and I feel like my life is spiraling out of control. It's all blowjobs in the shower one second and then MAYBE MOVING IN WITH A PROFESSIONAL BASEBALL PLAYER the next!

I've never had one, but I feel like I might be on the verge of a panic attack. What in the world is happening? My palms are sweating. My heart is going so fast it can't be healthy. Surely it'll burst. I press my hand against my chest and tell myself to calm down, but I don't calm down.

I look over at the clock. It's 9:05 AM. I've overslept.

I *never* oversleep. How embarrassing.

Luke is going to think I'm already abusing his good will. This is still a job until specified otherwise. I have to cook.

I immediately toss myself out of bed and put together an outfit from the first clean clothes my hands touch in the closet. My hair gets tossed into a bun and my teeth get brushed, sort of. Then I'm flying down the stairs, thinking of what I can make for breakfast that won't take too long. Eggs, of course. I can whip up some fluffy cheesy scrambled eggs in no time at all.

It doesn't seem odd to me that the rest of the house is eerily quiet or that the backyard is still pitch black through the kitchen windows. In fact, I'm relieved to find the kitchen empty. I assumed everyone would be down here, tapping their feet, anxious for food, but maybe they all needed a little extra sleep this morning too. It's only when I go over to get some coffee brewing that I read the time on the oven.

6:12 AM.

WHAT?

Oh god. My sleep-addled brain must have flipped the 6 to a 9 upstairs in my room. I didn't oversleep. In fact, my alarm has yet to go off.

Well hell.

I guess there's a lot of time to prepare a real breakfast now. I have pre-proved croissants in the freezer ready to be popped into the oven, but I make another batch to replace those. I work in the dim light of the kitchen, laying out each ingredient, feeling that tight ball of anxiety in my chest start to ease as I complete each step. I love rolling out the butter, creating a large rectangle that's easy to laminate into my pastry. I can remember Ms. Paulette first telling me croissants are about precision and clean lines, and I revel in that control this morning. I sprinkle some flour out onto the counter and get to work with my wooden rolling pin, layering and layering the pastry.

I sip my coffee while the croissants start their first prove, and then I start thinly slicing fruit for a breakfast tart. Luke walks into the kitchen when my fingers are sticky with sweet raspberry juice. He comes up behind me, his hands sliding around my stomach, up underneath my shirt as he tugs me back against him. The sensation of his palm dragging across my navel elicits a whole swarm of butterflies.

"No more sleeping in separate rooms." His face presses against my hair. "I missed you all night."

"Well good morning." I barely manage the words without sounding completely lovestruck. I clear my throat and try again. "*Morning.*"

He laughs and reaches out to take my wrist firmly in his hand. I'm confused for a moment as he lifts it up toward his mouth, but then he gently sucks the raspberry juice dripping down my finger.

My jaw widens so much it practically comes unhinged.

Wellllll good morning to you, sir. I need to go swap my panties now.

"Tastes good," he says, all husky and sexy.

It's barely 7:00 in the morning! *7:00* in the morning!

"Really? C'mon, can't you two like keep it contained to certain hours? Say 10:00 PM to 6:00 AM?"

Tate's taunt sounds behind me, and while I startle and make to step away from Luke, he keeps his arms clamped tightly around me. The point is clear.

Tate smiles wide. "So it's officially official. Look at you two. Is that even edible at this point?" She points to the fruit then arches her brow at us. "From the looks of this tableau... probably not."

I laugh and slide away from Luke so I can wash my hands at the sink. "It's perfectly fine. Your brother was just telling me good morning."

"By humping you in the kitchen?"

A laugh bursts out of me before I can help it.

Luke sighs deeply, like five days with his sister is officially enough days.

"When are you leaving again?"

"Driver's coming to pick me up in an hour."

"Perfect," I butt in. "This tart won't need long in the oven because I've already blind-baked the crust."

Her eyes narrow in confusion. "You did what now?"

"Never mind. Point is, I'll have food on the table in thirty minutes if"—I look pointedly at Luke—"*you* leave me alone."

He holds his hands up in mock innocence. "I won't cause any trouble."

I hurry back over to start assembling my fruit in the crust. Fruit tarts would usually take me a little longer, but I want Tate to get to eat before she leaves, so I don't worry about making the pattern too precise as I layer fruits in concentric circles: kiwis, strawberries, blackberries, raspberries. Harper's going to love it.

While I'm finishing up with breakfast, Tate sets the table and starts to clean the kitchen a bit. I tell her she doesn't need to, but she just ignores me. Harper comes in, rubbing sleep from her eyes. She walks right up to me and hugs my waist.

"You didn't do kisses at the door last night."

Oh no!

I hug her close.

"I'm sorry. You went to sleep before I got home, or I definitely would have remembered."

"Tonight?" she asks, hopeful.

I brush her tangled hair out of her face. "Tonight. Absolutely. Now, do you want to help me serve this fancy fruit tart to everyone?"

Her eyes light up when she sees it up on the counter where it's cooling. "It's *so* colorful."

We eat around the breakfast table, Luke sitting beside me with his arm slung across the back of my chair. Harper squeezes close to Tate, wanting to make the most of her last few minutes with her aunt.

After breakfast, Harper tears up a little when Tate's driver arrives.

"You'll see me soon," Tate assures her. "You'll be coming back to the city any day now."

She shakes her head. "But there are still a few weeks left of summer. We'll stay out here, won't we?"

Harper looks back to Luke, who then looks to me.

Tate chuckles and shakes her head. "Looks like you all have a lot to talk about. Let me know if I can help. I'm just a phone call away." She bends and spreads her arms out so Harper can run toward her. She squeezes her neck in a tight embrace. "Love you, kiddo. Be good for your dad and Chloe, okay?"

"I'm always good for Chloe!"

We stand out front as her car pulls away. Harper hangs on to her dad's waist, sniffling.

"Hey, why don't we head down to the beach?" Luke suggests. "I didn't get to go with you guys the other day, and we might not be staying out here in the Hamptons too much longer. We should go soak up the sun while we can."

Harper perks right up at the idea of spending her day in the sun and the sand.

She starts running back into the house. "I'll go get my mermaid Barbies!"

TWENTY-EIGHT

CHLOE

THE BEACH IS CROWDED, but we've managed to find a nice little spot away from the chaos. The sun is high overhead, beating down on me while I recline on a beach chair. There is no escaping the summer heat now. I've already been swimming twice, and I'm drying off with my head tilted toward the sky and my eyes closed. I have a forgotten paperback resting on my legs, but I can't find the energy to read it. I could fall asleep, but I've learned my lesson already this summer.

Luke is sitting beside me, his hand covering mine. He's let me just be for a while, reading and swimming, but now his fingers lace through mine and he squeezes my hand to get my attention.

I peer over at him to find he's studying me with one winked eye, trying to block out the sun as best as possible.

"Why were you up so early?"

I decide on brutal honesty. It's a little late to try to appear normal when I'm far from it. "I think I was having a little pre-dawn panic attack."

"About us?"

I think about it, and no, out of everything going on, Luke

isn't the thing that worries me. If anything, he's the one calming presence in all the madness, a safe harbor in the middle of the storm.

"More so about all the change, and the fact that there's still so much left up in the air. Like, my work, for example. Obviously, I don't feel comfortable taking a paycheck from you now that we're dating…"

He looks troubled as he sits up so he can face me, giving me his full attention. "I understand. I mean, the fact is, you do a hell of a lot and you deserve to be compensated for it, but I've never been in a situation like this. I don't know how to handle it in a way that doesn't feel like a business transaction."

"Right. Exactly."

"Do you want to go back to working in a restaurant?"

I've tossed the idea around some in recent days, and my answer has remained firm. "No, not really. But I also don't want to quit working altogether. To be honest, you've majorly overpaid me these last few months, and I've been saving every penny. I could get away with not working for a little while, especially if I move in with you guys in the city."

"I can support you in any way you need," he insists. "You know that, right?"

"I have no doubt that you can, I'm just not sure I want to lean into that setup so soon. To be clear, I'm not with you for your money or your gargantuan house or your fancy car. Though that pizza oven is pretty slick…"

He smiles.

"The whole other part of this dilemma is that I know I'm going to have to be flexible if I'm going to be able to help with Harper as much as you need me to and as much as I want to." I want to be clear about the last part. I'm not accepting this role out of pity. I've fallen in love with his daughter, and I genuinely enjoy being around her. "So even if I wanted to go back, restaurant work wouldn't really fly anyway. The hours are too erratic."

He furrows his brows in frustration, probably wondering how in the world I'm going to manage to work and take care of Harper while he travels.

"I've actually been thinking…" I'm still slightly embarrassed to voice the idea aloud, but I shouldn't be. It's something that really excites me every time I think about it, and beyond that, it's pretty low stakes. "Maybe I could try to get something going with my bakes out here in the Hamptons…sort of like what we were doing with Harper's lemonade stand, only a proper business. I don't want anything too intense. I'm thinking a once-weekly bread drop through the summer months. If word spreads, I think it could be really popular. In the meantime, I could perfect my recipes and whittle down what I want to offer on the menu."

The longer I talk, the wider his smile spreads. "I think it's great."

"Yeah? It's not silly?"

He looks frustrated that I'd even suggest that. "Silly? Chloe, have you tasted your breads? Those croissants this morning…*I ate four*. They were insane. Everything you make is amazing."

His words seem almost unbelievable, and I know why. Miles was always quick to shut down my ideas any time I'd gather the courage to voice them to him. Even though I was supposed to be in charge of the pastry department at Fig & Olive, he insisted on coming up with the menu offerings himself. My ideas were quickly dismissed, even occasionally ridiculed. In that relationship, *he* was the creative genius, and he wanted to make sure I knew it. I'm reminded once again how different Luke is compared to him.

"I can help," Luke says, point-blank. "Not with the food, obviously. You don't want me messing that up, but I can reach out to a few friends who'd maybe have some tips for branding, packaging, all of that."

I don't know why I'm tearing up, but he notices and leans over to wrap his hand around my neck. His thumb brushes up and down against my quickening pulse, and then he leans in to rest his forehead against mine. "We'll figure this all out, okay? I'm in if you are."

"I'm *so* in."

"You sure?" There's uncertainty in his gaze, maybe even worry. "It's hard, Chloe. I won't sugarcoat it. The season gets intense, and the travel can be relentless."

"We'll get through it one day at a time," I say with a small, encouraging smile.

I'm not naive. I know we have quite a hill ahead of us. Climbing it won't be easy, but the alternative? Walking away from Luke and Harper? That would be absolutely impossible. I can't even imagine going back to life as I knew it before them. Finding a sad studio apartment? Cooking for one every night? Never getting to hear Harper's laugh or feel Luke's lips brush against mine again...no. It's unthinkable. So we'll climb that hill—no matter how difficult—and hopefully, we'll be stronger for it in the end.

"We'll have to head back to the city soon," he tells me with a pinched expression. "I'm thinking by this Sunday at the latest. They want me back with the team for the second half of the season. I'll debut at a three-game series down in Miami, and I want you and Harper to come down. She doesn't start school for another few weeks, so as much as you two want to, you can join me on the road for the remainder of the summer."

"Okay."

It's simple.

But he stares at me like it shouldn't be. Like I should be asking for more, *demanding* more. What is there to demand? I know what day-to-day life with Harper looks like; I've lived it for the last two months. I know I'll have help from Maria once school starts up, and there will also be days where Luke is traveling and responsibilities will fall on me. That said, I won't be alone. My entire family is in the city. My parents, brother, aunts, uncles, cousins—they're going to go crazy for Harper. Nonna will be trying to fatten her up the minute she walks through the door. So Luke doesn't need to worry about us. We'll travel with him while we can, and then we'll settle in the city when her school starts back up again.

"It's just for one season. And not even a full one," I assure him, surprised that of the two of us, I feel like *I'm* the one doing the comforting. I realize how hard he's had it the last few years. No partner to rely on, no one by his side to share the burden of parenthood. I know this is still relatively new and we're jumping the gun a little (okay, *a lot*), but I also firmly believe in trusting your intuition, and everything inside of me is screaming that I can give this man my whole heart. In fact, I'd be an idiot not to.

"I'm actually excited about it now that things are falling into place."

He looks awestruck as his gaze roves over my face. Then, like he can't hold back for one more second, he kisses me hard. Harper's giggling draws us apart after only a brief second. She's looking up at us from where she's been digging in the sand.

"You *kissed* Chloe," she singsongs. "You *like* her!"

Luke laughs, and I push off my knees to stand. "Why don't you two talk? I've been wanting to take a little walk down the shore anyway."

He nods and I set off, grabbing my sunglasses and sunhat. I take a bucket with me too, knowing I'll need it in case I stumble upon any cool seashells during my walk. Harper likes to collect them and paint them at home, and I told her I'd help her with the craft this afternoon. I'm not really surprised by how much I enjoy doing things with her. I've always loved being around the younger kids in my family, and it's like having a little built-in buddy. Harper's something special though. She has such a zeal for life. She's so eager to be by my side, in the kitchen, in the garden, anywhere. She's hungry for female companionship, and though Luke is a wonderful dad, sometimes, it's just not the same. I braided her hair before we left the house this morning. I told her it would help keep it from getting tangled from all the sand and salt water.

"Could you maybe…could you do an Elsa braid?" She rushed out the second part of her question like she was slightly nervous to ask. "You know the one that loops down over one shoulder?"

"Of course! I did it for my cousin, Tatiana, last Halloween. I practiced for weeks to get it just right, and now it's like riding a bike. Here, tilt your head like this, and I'll see if I can do it on the first try."

When I finished, she looked in the mirror with tear-rimmed eyes. "It's perfect. It looks just like hers."

I dropped my hands to her shoulders and kissed her head. "I can braid your hair anytime you'd like. Okay?"

Her fragile brown eyes met mine and she nodded. "Okay."

Now, I walk along the beach slowly, trying to soak up as much of this summer feeling as I can. I can't believe we'll be leaving the Hamptons by the end of the weekend. In some ways, I'll be returning to the city under extremely different circumstances than how I left it at the start of summer. In other ways, some could argue I've put myself in the exact same position: shacking up with a boyfriend, putting too much faith in him, relying on him too much too soon.

What good do warnings do? What difference does it make if Luke started out as my boss or some stranger on the street? The decision to pursue a relationship with him seems so utterly out of my hands. That quickening of my pulse when he walks into a room, my awareness of him when he's near, the way I absolutely melt when he puts his hand on me, whether it's on my elbow or under my shirt...there is no fighting this. What's the point of slowing down when he's only given me every reason to push the throttle with him? Why harden my heart in an effort to protect it from the *possibility* of aches and pains in the future? If love breaks, it breaks, but I won't hold back for fear of that. I won't shy away from the feeling of falling simply because it doesn't fit someone else's standard for what's appropriate or safe or healthy. I wholeheartedly unsubscribe from the idea that anyone else gets to tell me how to live my life.

So I'll do this. I'll give Luke and Harper everything I have because I know they'll do the same for me. If we're in this, we're in it together. I'll never regret living life with my heart on my sleeve.

My only concern in all of this is Harper. I won't come into her life to simply slip back out of it again on a whim. My connection with her will have to be its own, protected and conserved outside of my relationship with her father. I already plan to talk to Luke about it tonight. Part of my terms for continuing this with him will be based on the understanding that I'm a lifer. Once I love you, you're stuck with me. If Luke and I part ways, I won't walk away from Harper. I'll stick around, support her however I can, in whichever way she wants. I'll be her big sister, her cool aunt, her second bonus mom—if that's what she wants, I'm hers.

"CHLOE! *CHLOE!*"

I hear my name screamed from down the beach and turn to see Harper booking it toward me, running like she's trying to break a world record. She stumbles in the sand, rights herself, then keeps going.

I laugh and walk toward her, catching her as she falls into me. Her little body is stronger than it looks, and I teeter on one foot, off balance for a second before we both go crashing down to the sand, a mix of jumbled limbs and laughter.

"YOU'RE GOING TO LIVE WITH US IN THE CITY!" she screams, grabbing me around my neck and hugging me as tight as she can.

I laugh and drop my hands to her shoulders, trying to get her to take it easy. "Yes, that's the plan, but only if you want me—"

"I want you to! I want you to!"

She's hugging me again, squashing her face right up against my neck. Her glee is so infectious that I'm crying before I realize. Big fat tears roll down my cheeks as I laugh and try to catch my breath.

I hold her and wrap my arm around her back, keeping her against me, knowing she needs to feel my arms around her tight and steady.

She peels back just enough to look up at me. "The first week of school, there's a Moms and Daughters Welcome Back Tea. Last year, Tate went with me, but I was thinking you could go with me this year instead. It's really special. Moms wear fancy dresses, but you don't even need a fancy dress because you're so pretty and you could just wear your jean shorts and you'd be the prettiest mom in the room. And also, I was thinking maybe you could help Dad find me a ballet class? I've been wanting to ask him about it, but he's been so busy and I don't think he really knows about that sort of stuff. Like he tried to sign me up for a *TODDLER* class the last time we looked into it! I was the only first grader there! And can you be the one who takes me back-to-school shopping? I wear a uniform, but still, *everyone* has like the coolest shoes and socks and backpacks and I feel like I don't even know where to look for that stuff!"

There's no interjecting and no way to cut in and answer one question or respond to a remark before she's rattling off another. It's as if for the last few years, she's been bottling up everything she would ask if only the right person came along. Turns out, I'm that person.

"Also, do you like getting manicures? Dad got me a gift card to get my nails done for my birthday. He said he would go with me, but I could kind of tell he *really* doesn't want to have to go, but you'll go, right? You'll get your nails done with me?

"And you don't have to be nervous about dealing with a kid because Maria tells me I'm the best kid she's ever nannied!" She nods eagerly. "Really, she said that! And you can tell me no and send me to my room and say stuff like, 'Well no dessert for you tonight, missy!'" She wags her finger for emphasis. "And I won't even be mad. I won't! I'll just be so happy you're with me."

She buries her head against my chest, and we sit there for a second.

The crushing weight of a child's love isn't crushing at all.

It's weightless. Termless. Restriction-less.

It's the most freely given love there is, and I wish more than anything that Harper's mom was here to experience it. She would be so proud to see what a wonderful young lady Harper has grown up to become. So thoughtful and energetic, savvy and sweet. I hold Harper on my lap as I promise her we will go back-to-school shopping together, we will find a pair of shoes she feels comfortable and confident in, we'll get her some fantastic socks too, and a backpack she loves. I tell her my little cousins like to put keychains on their backpacks to make them feel more personalized, and Harper immediately loves this. She has the genius idea of making some keychains out of the seashells we've collected today. We'll sort out the ballet lessons, and I'll be dressed to the nines at that mother-daughter tea. She doesn't need to worry.

Before we stand to walk back to Luke, I pause and look out at the ocean, past the white-capped waves crashing to the shore, past the rippling blue water shimmering with the reflection of the sun. I find the farthest point in the distance, on the horizon line where blue meets blue, and I make a solemn promise to Nadine to take care of her baby girl, to watch out for her, to stick up for her, to be a consistent loving force in her life, a shoulder to cry on, an ear when she needs one. She's safe with me.

Together, with our hands linked, we walk along the shore to find Luke. He's starting to pack up our beach toys, dipping one mermaid Barbie after another into a water bucket to get the sand out of their hair. He sees us coming and stops to smile.

"What were you two talking about?"

"Oh, just girl stuff." I wink at Harper, and she attempts to wink back at me.

The rest of the weekend consists of a lot of packing and logistics. I deep-clean the kitchen Saturday afternoon, and we order takeout for dinner. Luke goes over his schedule with me for the next few weeks. It's daunting but doable. He'll start practicing with the team on Monday, and Thursday we'll head to Miami. He asks me privately if I'd prefer to have Maria or another nanny accompany us down there, and for now, I'd rather keep Harper close. The two of us will get by just fine. We can hang out in the hotel and order room service and watch movies, we can stretch our legs on the beach and, of course, cheer him on from the stands during the games.

On Sunday, we load up, leave the Hamptons house, and head back to the city. We pull up to Luke's townhouse on the Upper East Side by late morning.

"I can give you a tour," Harper says, taking my hand and tugging me inside.

It's a warm and inviting house that checks all the fancy boxes. A hoity-toity person would salivate at the idea of living here. There's a whole *room* dedicated to wine, a butler's kitchen off the main kitchen that's bigger than Miles' whole apartment (not that that fills me with glee or anything...), an elevator, a gym, a garden, a terrace. What stops me in my tracks, though, are the signs of life among the amenities: the gallery wall in the hallway leading to the kitchen that's covered in framed artwork Harper's brought home from school over the years, the stack of puzzles in the living room, the *Pinkalicious* books lined up on the bookshelf near the TV where there are probably supposed to be prized antique sculptures.

Harper leads me to her room, and I hold my breath, expecting some kind of two-story bunk bed with an attached slide, a working carousel, Cher's closet from *Clueless*.

She flips on the light, and I find it's…wholesome. Down-right normal. The walls are a pale pink. Her queen bed is covered in a butterfly comforter with matching pillows. The room's not overflowing with toys either. It's neat and clean, and I can tell she's really proud of it. She shows me her treasures lined up on the shelf by her bed, the basket of stuffed animals she missed while she was gone, then the view, which is…okay, it's of Central Park. So we were pretty *close* to normal, but not quite. Still, it's great. Luke's clearly trying to keep her as grounded as possible in a world where she could easily know nothing but excess.

"And this"—she gestures to an empty corner of the room —"is where I'm going to put my Barbie Dreamhouse once I buy it!" She runs over to take my hand. "Now, c'mon. I'll show you your room."

Down the hall, past two other rooms, the door is cracked to the primary bedroom.

"This is where you and my dad will sleep! Isn't it pretty?"

It is. Beautiful. The expansive room has tall ceilings, pale blue drapes, a landscape painting hung above the four-poster bed. We walk through a door that leads to the other half of the suite with the bathroom and closets. Luke's standing in a mostly empty closet.

He looks back, sees me, and waves me in. My bags sit at

his feet. Clearly, he was making sure I had everything set to unpack in here.

"I'm surprised you don't have more stuff."

The closet is quite literally bare save for some golf clubs he tugs out and puts in the main part of the bathroom.

"Oh, there are his and hers closets. I've never put anything in this one except my clubs, so you should be good to go. Do you think you'll need more space than this?"

I level him with a stare that says, *Get real.*

The closet is huge. It has an island in the center of it! In a minute, I'll unpack every single clothing item I have to my name and it will fill exactly one rack and one drawer, *maybe* two.

"I'll manage," I tease.

He nods. "Right. Harper, did you unpack yet? I need your dirty clothes in the hamper in the laundry room. The toys you brought with you to the Hamptons need to be put back where they go too. Those throw pillows too!"

Her face falls. "Do I have to? I want to stay with Chloe. Can't I do it later?"

"You can't do it later," I say, cutting in before Luke has the chance. "Because...I was thinking, if we unpack and get settled in, there's somewhere I'd like to take you guys this afternoon."

Harper claps her hands excitedly. "Oh! Oh! Where!?" She doesn't even wait for me to answer; she's flying out the door. "I'm going to go unpack right now! Don't leave without me!"

As if we'd ever leave without her.

"Go eat a snack too!" Luke shouts. "And change into some nice clothes! There's dirt on those shorts!"

"Okay!"

Then he looks at me. I look at him. He raises an eyebrow. I tilt my head in question. He waits a beat, listening as Harper scurries to her room. Then he's on me instantly, backing me up into my dark closet, hoisting me up onto the island.

"There's no time!" I chide.

But it doesn't matter. There's no convincing him. We slept together Friday night in his room (well the sleeping part didn't really happen), but then last night we stayed up late trying to get everything settled with the house, finish packing, arrange travel plans for Miami and the weeks ahead. I went to bed close to midnight, and Luke didn't climb in beside me until well after that. In the morning, there was a heavy make-out session, but then Harper ran in and jumped on top of us, asking if someone could please cook her breakfast because she was starving, and also, she didn't know who did it but *someone* spilled milk in the kitchen while trying to pour themselves a bowl of cereal…

Now, Luke locks my closet door so fast it's like his life depends on it. Clothes quite literally go flying. My bra gets tossed and lands up on a second-story rack meant for seasonal clothing. I'll never manage to get it down without a ladder.

I laugh, but when Luke takes my mouth in a passionate kiss, it dies swiftly.

My world shrinks to him—the tender kisses he strings down my body, his hands peeling my thighs apart, his fingers finding my sensitive skin and then his lips following after. He tastes me between my thighs, and I fall back on that cold marble island, absolutely consumed by his touch.

Everything is so quick. We have to be fast—who knows how long Harper will be distracted with all her tasks—but that only heightens the intensity. It's like we're trying to get away with something bad, racing against the clock to have each other.

"God," he moans like he absolutely loves the taste of me, and I swear I've never heard a sexier sound in all my life.

I already feel the tingles building, that possessive need clawing at me.

If he kept at it for another minute, I'd come apart like this, but I want him inside me. I want to feel him there and he knows it, mostly because I'm making that very clear with explicit instructions. He swipes me off the island and we're down on the plush carpet. He lines us up, captures my mouth, and slides inside me to the hilt.

There.

Bliss.

"*Holy shit*," slips from my mouth like I'm in rapture.

"Hold on," is his warning.

He takes me on the floor like I'm his heart, body, *soul*. My arms wrap around his neck. He kisses me and builds that hard, fast rhythm. Then one of his hands snakes between us so he can caress me where I need it.

I come so quickly it surprises me. There's no possible way to hold back and regain control; he knows just how to work me up.

"Another one," he insists, the greedy bastard.

"We can't!" I laugh.

But his hand is still there, rubbing in slow, tantalizing circles. He stays inside of me, but he stops pulsing in and out. He stills and focuses on me, hitting that perfect spot even as I resist, even as I feel overly sensitive from my first orgasm. He rips a second one from me and I arch up off the ground, an animalistic cry piercing the quiet space.

Then he takes my hips in a crushing grasp as he thrusts into me over and over, sating his need. In the dark shadows, our eyes meet as he stiffens inside me. A groan tears through him and his head falls to the crook of my neck, his breath hot and heavy.

I knit my fingers through his thick hair and hold him against me.

We don't have long. Maybe not even a minute.

"Chloe…"

He sounds so vulnerable, a heart splayed open. His head

turns and his lips brush against the shell of my ear. When he speaks, it's nothing but a faint whisper.

"I love you."

I squeeze my eyes closed and let those words settle over me.

Love? Truly?

He says it again, more emphatically, and I can barely believe it.

"You aren't supposed to laugh," he teases.

"I can't help it. I'm just so…"

Happy.

I'm so unbelievably happy.

EPILOGUE

CHLOE

THE SUNDAY we move back to the city, I take Harper and Luke to my parents' house for family dinner. Only, I don't tell any of my family they're coming with me. I have a whole plan, very dramatic, very well executed. I walk in first, and everyone's surprised to see me.

"I thought you were still in the Hamptons" yada yada.

"Nope," I say, holding up the sports gear Luke signed for them. "I needed to deliver this stuff to you guys."

This was exciting enough. You would have thought it was Christmas morning in my parents' small apartment. Little cousins tore through those bags like they were looking for a winning lottery ticket. Signed shirts flew through the air, everyone slipped on the baseball hats and jerseys and thought they were hot shit. But then, *then*, I said, "Oh, you know what? I actually forgot one of the bags out in the hall."

Only…I didn't forget a bag. I went out there to grab Luke and Harper, and then I pushed them into the apartment.

My family went absolutely bananas.

I swear to god I was scared my dad was going to have a heart attack. He couldn't talk for a solid five minutes. He just stuttered, stammered, opened and closed his mouth about a million times before he laid a hand over his heart, closed his eyes, and tilted his head toward the heavens like he was thanking the good Lord for this opportunity of a lifetime.

So, anyway, I'm the family favorite. I'd like to see someone try to take my spot now. Sorry, Gio.

Later that week, Harper and I go down to Miami with Luke as promised. We buy matching bathing suits and swim in the hotel pool, we go to the zoo together, and we spend time at the beach. We lose our minds at the baseball stadium when Luke takes the field for the first time. The fans *also* lose their minds.

"That's my dad!" Harper says, bouncing up and down in the private suite.

We both end up with tears in our eyes.

Once we get home, life mostly…settles. Not in a boring way, but in a healthy structured way. I relax into my relationship with Harper. With Luke's guidance, I set boundaries and clear expectations. She knows she's supposed to load her dishes in the dishwasher after dinner and help pick up her toys in the evenings. We keep a consistent bedtime for her and make sure we're not piling too much on her plate. Once school starts, I cook her breakfast every morning and then walk her to school. I'm there early for pick-up every day too, ready right when she walks out so she never has to worry about who will be there to get her. I meet Maria and she and I become quite the team, especially when Luke's out of town. It turns out it's a pretty small world. She knows my mom really well—they used to work at the Plaza together—and we take a liking to each other immediately. I respect what a great job she's done with Harper over the last few years, and she sees that I'm clearly in it for the long haul. At the end of her shifts, I send her home with all sorts of food for her family, and not just dinners—croissants, cookies, breads, you name it—and for that, she loves me a little extra.

Maria's not needed in the same way she was before I

moved in, but we find a rhythm that works well for everyone. Luke transitions her to more of a house manager and gives her a raise, though she still helps a lot with Harper. If Luke is traveling, Maria and I will tag-team after-school duties. She'll start prepping dinner while I take Harper to ballet, or she'll sit at the kitchen table with Harper and help with homework while I pack her lunch for the next day. Once or twice a week, my mom will come over after school to hang out and cook with us too. It's a *real* party then.

A little over a year later, I'm walking on the sidewalk, heading to the grocery store, running through a mental tally of all the things I need to get done while Harper's at school. We're hosting my family for Sunday dinner. *Oh yes—everyone.* Luke insisted since we have more room than my parents. Everyone's excited about it. Me? I'm scrambling trying to make sure I have everything we need, all those last-minute items I know I'll forget. Did I get olives? I thought I saw some in the pantry, but now I'm second-guessing myself.

I have my head down, checking the notes app on my phone when I hear my name called. I look up to see a woman right in front of me on the sidewalk. In fact, had she not stopped me, we would have run directly into each other.

"*Chloe.*"

I pause, taking her in, and I can't immediately place her. I've met so many people in the last year, moms from Harper's school, wives and girlfriends of other baseball players, Tate's friends—my world has drastically expanded.

Then it sinks in.

Angie. Angie from Fig & Olive. Angie from Fig & Olive whose butt cheeks were pressed against that refrigerator door!

"Oh my god. *Hi!*"

She looks taken aback that I'm so happy to see her.

"Hi. Wow…it's been a while." She shakes her head and

continues, "I'm actually so glad I bumped into you." Her follow-up smile is uncomfortable to say the least.

I chuckle. "Yeah?"

"*Yes.*" She takes a step closer and lowers her voice. "You have no idea how much I regret my actions from last year. What I did with Miles—" Her face contorts into a mask of disgust. "Had I known what an asshole he is...what a complete and utter jerk..." She shakes her head and sighs. "But...that's no excuse. It's completely beside the point, actually. I should have never been the other woman in your relationship, and I feel so guilty about hurting you like that. I'm sorry. *I really am.*"

She reaches out to squeeze my forearm, and I see in her eyes how much pain she still carries over her actions. I don't condone what she did, but I'm also not in a position to judge her for it. I can't absolve her of her guilt, but I can certainly help her move on.

"You know what, Angie? To be quite honest...it's kind of the best thing that ever happened to me."

She looks disbelieving. "Seriously?"

Behind her, at the grocery store entrance, I spot Luke waiting for me. He's out on the sidewalk with his baseball cap tugged low and his hands tucked into the pockets of his shorts. He scans the crowd, probably hoping no one will notice him. When he sees me, he breaks into a heart-stopping smile, dimples and all. Then, as if my soul was not already always-and-forever his, he gives me a little wave, and I can't help but wave back. God, I love him.

"*Seriously.*" I sidestep her, eager to get to Luke. "Consider yourself officially off the hook. Good luck with...everything."

Then I walk away without looking back, partly because I don't owe her any more of my time and partly because I'm laying eyes on the hottest man north of the equator. Hell, *maybe the entire world.* And he doesn't even know it! He couldn't care less! He gets a trim only when his hair's a little too long. He shaves his stubble only because he knows I like it that way. His muscles serve a purpose on the field, but beyond that, he wouldn't be pumping iron in the gym for the hell of it. He is the least self-absorbed man I know, and it means he's all the more handsome because of it.

Luke is still playing in the MLB. His final season didn't go as planned. The Pinstripes narrowly missed their opportunity to make it to the World Series, and the night he got home from the stadium after the hard loss, wearing a look of utter defeat, I was waiting for him, ready with a proposition. Before Luke could broach the subject of staying with the team for another season or two, I gave him my blessing. More than that, I encouraged him to do it. He's still at the top of his game. He has so much more he wants to leave on the field. His legacy isn't complete, and we can all feel it.

No regrets, I told him. We're in this together.

At the time, his greatest concern was for Harper and for me. After all, he'd promised us it would only be one more season and he didn't want to break our trust in him, but there was no issue. We have it figured out. We're a well-oiled machine when he's away. I won't lie and say I don't miss him during the height of the season, but we prioritize each other. We talk every day when he's traveling. Sexy FaceTime sessions keep the spice alive, no problem. My phone can't even look me in the eye at this point; it's seen too much.

Harper is doing really well too. She's surrounded by people who love and care about her, and when her school schedule allows, we never miss the opportunity to travel and watch her dad play. She loves to see him pitch as much as I do.

Now, the crowd fades into a blurred background as I walk toward Luke—or, *I'm sorry*, let me try that again. The crowd fades into a blurred background as I walk toward my *fiancé*. My dazzling diamond ring distracts me and stops me dead in my tracks at least three times a day. I still can't believe it's mine.

Luke watches me approach, not even hiding the fact that he's checking me out. His gaze lingers like a soft caress on my bare legs. It's late summer in New York—absolutely sweltering—and I can't be bothered to wear anything but light sundresses. Luke *loves* this. Easy access, he tells me.

When I reach him, he holds his hand out for mine and tugs me close, then he bends down to kiss me hello, wrapping his arm around my lower back and scooping me closer until we're pressed together tightly. The kiss is hot—too hot for public. When we break apart, I give him a reproving glare, but he doesn't even have the decency to look contrite. I mean, I'm panting here. He knows he's won.

"Ready to shop?" he asks, too cocky for his own good.

"Ready."

He motions for me to go ahead of him, and then he grabs a cart and starts pushing it along as I get distracted by a fruit display near the front entrance. I'm choosing between two sets of grapes when he casually mentions, "I think Tate's finally met her match."

My hand stills and I perform a slow, dramatic spin. My mouth is agape. My eyes are wide. "What? *Who?*"

He shoots me a mischievous smile. "Where's the last place she'd ever look…"

Easy. I don't even have to think. "Professional baseball."

He raises his eyebrows, signaling I've hit the bullseye.

My hand flies to my mouth. No. *No way.* Tate would never date a baseball guy. At least, I didn't think she would. She's been around the sport her whole life. She's seen the good, the bad, and the ugly. Most of Luke's teammates are nice guys, but there are a few who fit the stereotype a bit too well: huge egos, arrogant personalities, more than a little proud of their player status *off* the field.

"*Who?*"

I'm about to grab him by the collar and shake the answer out of him.

He doesn't immediately say, but I know. I already know because there's only one guy on the Pinstripes who would make Luke look *that* troubled.

Oh, this is too good.

"Tell me everything you know…and start at the beginning."

Tate meets her match in *Blushing in the Big Leagues*.

Coming summer 2023

Made in the USA
Monee, IL
23 August 2024

64392827R00163